EVE SILVER

SINS OF THE FLESH

HQN™

Recycling programs
for this product may
not exist in your area.

ISBN-13: 978-0-373-77484-5

SINS OF THE FLESH

Copyright © 2010 by Eve Silver

This edition published by arrangement with Harlequin Books S.A.

For questions and comments about the quality of this book please contact us at Customer_eCare@Harlequin.ca.

® and TM are trademarks of the publisher. Trademarks indicated with ® are registered in the United States Patent and Trademark Office, the Canadian Trade Marks Office and in other countries.

www.HQNBooks.com

Printed in U.S.A.

Acknowledgments

Thank you to my editor, Tara Parsons, who is brilliant and patient and funny. To my agent, Karen Solem, because without her encouragement and support this idea would not have flared to life.

To everyone at Harlequin Books who had a hand in helping this book (and the other two in the trilogy) along the way.

To my writing pals who share in the ups and downs and all the moments in between: Nancy Frost, Michelle Rowen, Ann Christopher, Caroline Linden, Kristi Cook/Astor, Laura Drewry, Lori Devoti and Sally MacKenzie.

Thank you to my family. To Dylan, my light; Sheridan, my joy; and Henning, my forever love. They fill my heart and replenish my well.

And a special thank-you to my readers.

For Henning

My hero

SINS OF THE FLESH

Spawned. Spurned. I might have lamented my fate if I hadn't found a way to love it instead. Chaos. Anarchy. Ah, the tenets of my youth: Filch. Swindle. Lie. I was a lawless brat who danced one step ahead of a beating or starvation or the long arm of the law. Back then, boys like me got hung by the neck till dead. If they got caught.

Back then, boys like me thought the devil would welcome them home.

In my case, he did.

—Malthus Krayl

CHAPTER ONE

To me belongs yesterday, I know tomorrow.
    —*The Egyptian Book of the Dead*, Chapter 17

MALTHUS KRAYL CROUCHED on the balcony railing, powerful thighs flexed, forearms resting on his knees. The street was sixteen stories below him, shiny and black from the recent rain, reflecting the stars that freckled the night sky and the lights of the buildings that rose on either side like sheer canyon faces of steel and concrete. He shifted his weight onto the balls of his feet and leaned out, almost far enough to tip and fall.

He relished the thought, pictured the possibilities.

Freefall.

The cold wind in his hair, making his skin sting, billowing his shirt out behind him. Exhilaration tearing through his veins.

Tempting.

He was the first to admit that he was an adrenaline junkie. He had a liking for the razor's edge, for the thrill surging in a wave of tidal proportion.

But he didn't let himself do it. Not because he could die from the fall, but because he couldn't.

Oh, he might break a bone or two, but he would heal—his kind always healed. And he could just imagine the expression on his prey's face if he fell from the sky like a dark angel.

The thought made him laugh.

He was more devil than angel, but in strict truth he was neither. He was a soul reaper.

He killed. He harvested the hearts of his victims. And the darksouls. Those, he fed to Sutekh, luscious entrées of pure power, spiced with lust and greed and unadulterated evil.

Nice work if you could get it. A tad messy. But nice.

Sutekh. He went by many names. Seth. Seteh. Lord of the desert. Lord of evil. He was the Underworld überlord of chaos. Which Mal figured made *him* what mortals would call the devil's spawn, because he wasn't just any soul reaper; he was Sutekh's son. One of four.

No, he reminded himself, not four. Not anymore. Only three now. Lokan was dead. Skinned. Butchered.

Mal stared out at the night sky and fought the pain that twisted him in knots, focusing instead on the moment. The hunt.

Tonight's prey was special. Not only was his soul so dark it might have been dipped in toxic waste, but he was a potential source of information that Mal wanted so badly he could taste it.

Like any good predator, he waited, hunkered on the balcony rail.

If patience was a virtue, it was one of the few he possessed.

A taxi edged around the corner, water spraying up from the tires. Senses humming, he leaned out as far as balance and gravity allowed.

The cab slowed to a stop and after a few seconds the back door opened and a man climbed out. Pyotr Kuznetsov, High Reverend of the cult of Setnakht. Mal's attention sharpened and narrowed. The hunt had started to get interesting.

Kuznetsov turned back to the cab and offered his hand to the passenger still inside.

A woman stepped out. Blond hair. All curves. Human. Kuznetsov steered her away from the cab toward the lobby doors.

Mal cursed softly.

Looked like the hunt had just been postponed.

COLORED CONTACTS CHANGED Calliope Kane's eyes from their usual all-too-memorable green to dark, liquid brown. Her dark hair was slicked down and pinned and tucked up under a long auburn wig of full curls. Subtle use of highlight and shadow altered the appearance of her nose, her cheeks. She didn't look like herself. Even the clothes she was wearing—short, low-cut Lycra dress, impossibly high heels—were a far cry from her usual utilitarian choices.

But that was the whole point.

Tonight wasn't about being utilitarian. It was about freeing the part of herself that craved human contact.

No. Not true, and if she would be nothing else in the endeavor, she would be honest. Tonight was about sex. Clean, simple, *necessary* sex.

Twenty-eight months since she'd allowed herself to be touched, held, stroked to fulfillment. The longest she'd ever gone before this was seventeen.

She'd pushed it as long as she dared, held on to her rigid control and her impenetrable serenity, blunting her emotions with her usual success. But she'd lost her cool a few weeks back when confronted by four soul reapers in her own home. She'd made bad choices. And she hadn't been able to fully get it back together since then, even though three of the soul reapers were dead, and one of them was almost an ally.

Almost…but not quite.

As her former acolyte Roxy Tam was fond of saying, almost only counted in horseshoes and hand grenades.

So tonight, a fast and dirty impersonal encounter was on the menu. Just enough contact to make her feel as though the ice that ran through her veins wasn't so cold, so complete. To make her believe that the edge she perched on, so close to losing it, wasn't precipitously sharp.

The edge would be better afterward. And worse.

It always was.

But she was out of options. Her kind had two choices. Sex, or blood.

For her, blood had always been the hardest path. She closed her eyes for a second, pushing back the memories. The past had no place in her present. She would not let it free.

She left the ladies' room and made her way through the crowd, searching. She'd seen him earlier, dressed all in black, the sort of man mothers warned their daughters about.

The sort of man who lured daughters to ignore the warnings.

She found him in the crowd on the dance floor, and for a moment, she simply watched him.

He didn't dance for others. He danced for himself, for the pure joy of it. The way he moved was a thing of beauty, the flick of his hips, the sway of his shoulders. His hair moved as he moved, dark and straight, lifting to reveal the glint of metal hoops in his ears, then falling to settle in a clean line against his jaw.

The bass from the powerful speakers pounded up through her spine and into her skull as she made her way a little closer. She'd been watching him since he'd arrived about an hour past. He'd downed a double shot of whiskey, neat, as soon as he'd walked in. Then he'd gone out on the floor and been there since. A couple of women had gravitated toward him, and after that a couple of more until there was a small crowd of six or seven vying for his attention now.

If she left him to it, he would pick one and take her to his bed tonight. But Calliope had no intention of letting that happen. He was hers. She'd spotted him and stalked him, and she meant to have him. No harm, no foul. He would go on his way happy, and she would go on her way with the gnawing ache inside her tamed. For the moment.

Turning to the side, she edged through the throng of gyrating bodies and then she was there next to him, close enough to see that his lips were sculpted and full, the perfect blend of hard and soft. A scar sliced a thin, white line from his lower lip to his chin, pale against the dark stubble that shaded his jaw.

She wanted to run her tongue along that scar, to feel the rasp of his stubble on her tongue.

His gaze slid over her, impersonal, disinterested. And then it slid back.

She didn't look away. She didn't smile or flirt. She only held his gaze and moved as he moved.

One song bled into the next. The girl to his right tugged at his sleeve. He glanced down and smiled at her, white teeth flashing, then bent to hear what she offered, only to straighten and shake his head.

His reward was a pout, and then the girl turned her back and stalked off through the crush of bodies. But he didn't watch her go. His gaze had already returned to Calliope, and she knew in that instant that he was hers. For this moment and the ones that would immediately follow, he was hers, and she meant to take all she dared from him.

Catching his hand, she led him off the floor. He let her, glancing down at her with a slightly puzzled expression. The lights flashed, painting his features in colors and shadows and hollows.

This close, she could see that his eyes were a clear, pale gray, startling against dark lashes. She had a thing for dark hair and light eyes. Gray eyes in particular.

Because, once upon a time, a gray-eyed man had come to her rescue. After a fashion. But that had been forever ago.

His gaze held hers, assessing. She frowned. For such liaisons, she preferred a man who was less than observant. Perhaps even less than intelligent. This man was too sharp. She saw that now as he studied her, his gaze sliding slowly over her features, marking every detail. She almost turned and walked away.

But something stopped her. The flash of insight that told her it was *this* man she would take inside her tonight.

Calliope was a blooded Daughter of Aset. All her kind had unique abilities that played up the natural talents they had had while still mortal. Prescience was Calliope's gift. She had been intuitive as a mortal; as a supernatural, she was hyperaware of coming events. Not that she could tell the future—she couldn't. It was more of an instinct that things were going to happen and a knowledge of who might be involved in those things.

Outcomes were changeable. Her prescience didn't account for every possible choice of free will. But it did give her an edge as events unfolded. She had the ability to see what would come, not in clear, distinct panorama, but in hints and whispers.

So she knew he was the one she'd come here to find. With him, she would drop her walls, at least as much as she ever allowed herself. For a few moments she would give in to the hunger, until she went back to who she was, who she would always be.

He was smiling now, teeth flashing animal white.

Leaning close to her so his voice would carry over the music, he said, "Do I know you, darlin'? I'd swear we've met, except I'm usually good with faces and I can't seem to place yours."

"You've met me now," she said. And after tonight, they would never meet again. "Come." She reached out to lace her fingers with his as she offered him a smile that told him everything he needed to know.

For a millisecond, she felt a crackle of energy, and she froze, thinking she'd made an error, that this man whom she'd read as human, wasn't. She felt the molecules of air hum and vibrate, not quite strongly enough to be a supernatural's energy signature, but there was something…

She reached for it, tried to place it, but in the end found nothing.

It was only static electricity. She was being too cautious, too suspicious. He was human. He was mortal.

Which made him fair game.

She had never taken from a supernatural. Not sex. Not blood. She wanted no one from her world. She wanted a man, a human man. And when she was done with him, she wanted him to go away.

"Come," she said again, modulating her voice an octave lower than her usual range. Then she led him toward the back of the club, keeping hold on his hand as they wove between tables and bodies.

He appeared content to follow, staying close at her back so every few steps his thighs brushed the back of hers, or he bumped up against her buttocks. She thought those touches were no accident.

They made her uncomfortable.

This encounter was hers to control. Her terms. Her way. She would take. And she would give only as much as she wished. There was no other way that she could bear to do this.

She led him down a narrow hall then pushed open a door and led him down a flight of metal stairs to the basement. The door swung shut behind them, muting the overpowering volume of the music.

There came a soft laugh from behind her.

"You've done this before?" His voice sent a little shiver rippling up her spine.

"No." She hadn't done this before. Not here. Not in this particular club. But there had been many others over the years.

Again, that soft laugh, warmly encompassing, as

though they shared a secret. She thought he did this far more often than she. But tonight, she meant to give herself this. A brief encounter of skin against skin and the feeling of a man stretching her, filling her. She would free her rigid control—not completely, but enough—just for a handful of moments, and then she would be herself once more.

She opened a door and led him through a cluttered storage room to a second door at the far end. Then she opened that as well and led him inside.

There was a single tiny window set high in the wall. It let in just enough ambient light that she could see the stacks of chairs and folded tables and several large boxes set in the corner. She'd been here earlier and made small preparations, taking a chair off the stack and setting it apart from the clutter.

"I have a comfortable bed less than ten minutes away..." Her prey's voice trailed off in suggestion.

"No," she said softly. "Here is fine." Better than fine. Perfect. She didn't want to lie in his bed. She didn't want to be inside his home. She didn't want to see personal things like photos or a book lying on a bedside table. She didn't want to know where he lived or anything else about him.

And that wouldn't matter to him. She'd watched him tonight before she made her move. He wanted what she wanted. Sex. No strings.

She didn't know his reasons, only her own. Her kind, blooded Daughters of Aset, fed from the prana—the life force—of others. For most of her kind, that meant taking blood. In the early days, Calliope had had no choice. Despite the personal horror she experienced each time she fed, she had been forced to ingest blood in order to sip the life force of another. In the beginning, there had been no way to separate the two.

She'd never gotten used to it, never gotten past the horrific memories that act stirred.

But her instinct for self-preservation had trumped her repugnance, and so she had done what she must.

Now, she was old enough and adept enough that she could sip the life force without the blood.

A choice.

With a price.

Because she fed on pure prana without a physical conduit, she craved a release for the power she took. Sexual release.

Sex or blood. She needed to take one or the other, and she'd pushed herself about as long and as far as she could without taking either one.

So tonight she would deal with the problem the most logical way she could. With sex. With a man who would feel neither remorse nor regret.

She tried to draw her hand from his then, but he tightened his grip. She turned her head to look at him over her shoulder, and he spun her the rest of the way, backing her up against the wall.

His mouth shaped a close-lipped smile.

Awareness uncoiled in the pit of her belly, petals in

the sun, and she shivered, hungering for him and the pleasure he promised.

Then he let go of her hand and skimmed the backs of his fingers up her arm, along the curve of her collarbone and finally the swell of her breast above the neckline of her dress. Her pulse edged up. Her breathing became faster, shallower. Just from that small touch.

She'd chosen well.

He traced the tip of his index finger up her neck, pausing for an instant at her pulse, then along her jaw, her cheek, her brow. His smile widened, wolfish.

"Dark eyebrows. Dark eyelashes. Not a natural red-head?" he asked.

Her breath caught. In this light, how could he tell that her brows were dark? Then she looked at his face, really looked at it, and realized that despite the gloom, she could make out his coloring. Dark hair. Light eyes. Dark lashes and brows.

Of course he could see the same.

This was exactly why she usually chose dull men with no interest other than a quick fuck. A smart man could notice details she had no wish to reveal. But no matter. She didn't answer, neither affirming nor denying his observation. Better he know as little about her as possible.

"What's your name, darlin'?" he murmured, dipping his head so he spoke close to her ear, his breath fanning her cheek. "Mine's—"

"Don't tell me," she whispered. Because it went both

ways; she also wanted to know as little about him as possible.

"Anonymity—" he glanced at the storeroom door "—and the possibility of discovery. Aren't you an adventurous girl?"

"Complaining?"

He laughed, low and sexy. "Not in a million years. More like thanking my lucky, lucky stars."

Yes, she thought, he was a man to have exactly that reaction.

With a small smile, she pulled his shirt from his slacks and slid the buttons free. He nuzzled her neck as she pushed his shirt open and laid one palm on the swell of his chest. Hot skin. Hard man. Not an ounce of fat.

"Damn, you smell good." He pressed his lips to the hollow where her neck met her shoulder, and he inhaled. She felt his tongue on her skin, his teeth.

Letting her head fall to the side, she drank in the sensation as he dragged his lips along her jaw, toward her mouth.

She didn't want to cede even that much control, didn't want to let him lead her into a kiss.

Arching off the wall, she pressed against his naked chest. She cast him a look through her lashes and walked him backward until his thighs hit the lone chair that stood apart from the stack.

Then she pushed a little harder, and he sat.

She bent forward to trace her tongue along the swell of his pectoral, tasting salt and man.

"Let me do this my way," she said, her teeth grazing his skin. The temptation was there to reach for his life force, to drink of it and take his prana into the stream of her own.

"Go right ahead." There was a smile in his voice.

For a split second she imagined he invited her to drink of him, and then she realized he meant he was happy to let her take the lead.

She supposed he found it a titillating game, her wanting to be the aggressor.

The scent of his skin was intoxicating. She breathed him in and licked his chest again, letting her mouth open over his flesh, biting him just a little.

She dragged his shirt down his arms but didn't pull it free of his hands. Instead, she left the cuffs buttoned at his wrists and the rest of the shirt looped around the back of the chair. Not that she had a second's doubt about his ability to pull free. But, for the moment at least, he seemed accepting of—perhaps even aroused by—the illusion of his bondage.

Sinking to her knees before him, she kissed and licked and bit her way down his chest, his belly. His body was art, beautifully muscled, long lean lines and smooth, hot skin.

A thin line of dark hair led her down to his belt. She pressed her lips to his navel as she undid his buckle and then his fly. She didn't look up, but she could feel his eyes on her.

The hard ridge of his penis, erect, thick, pushed

against his black boxers. She lifted her head and watched his face as she clawed her fingers and raked her nails along the length, smiling a little as his erection jerked beneath her touch.

"No fair, darlin'." His voice was smoke and gravel now. "I want to play, too."

"Soon," she promised. Never. She would take what she needed from him and leave him sated. A fair trade. But she would not forfeit her control any more than she absolutely must.

She curled her fingers in the waistband of his slacks and edged them down his hips a little. His boxers slid down, too, baring more of his skin and the very top of the triangle of dark hair at his groin.

Her arousal unfurled a little more, warm and soft and new. She wanted him in her hand. In her mouth. Inside her body.

"Lift up."

He did, and she worked his pants and boxers down to the tops of his thighs. His erection sprang free, thick and hard.

Playing her nails down his belly, she watched his muscles twitch and jerk. Then she closed her hand around his penis and sucked in a breath at the feel of him, smooth and male.

She tore the condom wrapper with her teeth and worked it down the length of him. Not that any mortal disease could harm her. But there was something to be said for appearances. She didn't want him to remember her among the sea of women he fucked. She didn't want to be special or unique in any way.

Rising, she pulled up her skirt. She wasn't wearing any underwear.

"Damn," he murmured, then sucked in a sharp breath as she straddled him, bringing the broad head of his penis to her moist folds, rubbing herself against him, letting only the tip slide inside.

The energy she'd kept locked down for over two years burst its dam, and she felt it surge through her body, luscious and rich, pushing her to do this. To take him. To release the prana she'd held under tight rein.

Sex, or blood.

She stared at the pulse beating at his throat.

Sex. Only that.

She lowered herself a little more. So good. The stretch and burn.

The air was tinged with power, sparking wildly, and she tightened her hold, drawing it back, appalled that her restraint was so tenuous that she'd set so much free all at once.

Only, it didn't draw. It surged and grew, outside her control. Because it wasn't hers. It was…his.

She broke off. Her breath caught as she realized her error. Her head jerked up and she stared at him, his gray eyes pale and bright in the dimness, heavy lidded with lust.

"I can't—" She pulled her hands away. She surged off his thighs and stood staring at him, panting.

The air was alive and heavy. Sultry. Wet.

The fine hairs on her forearms rose, as did those at her nape. Though she was no longer touching him, she could feel him imprinted on her fingertips and there, between her thighs.

She took a step back.

She'd made a mistake. A horrifically stupid mistake.

He watched her warily, and it took all her focus to keep her own energy signature masked. Bad enough that she had made such a terrible error. Worse if she were to allow him to realize that they were like-to-like, that she, too, was supernatural.

The feeling of electricity amped up to crackle over her skin with visible sparks for a single fraught second before it disappeared once more.

But that second had been enough.

Not only was he a supernatural after all, but one powerful enough to be able to mute his signature. He was doing that now. Putting up barriers to any who might read his power. And that power was vast.

She could only pray that she was doing a better job of concealment than he was.

Tipping his head to the side, he spoke softly. "It's all good, darlin'."

He shifted on the chair, as though he meant to pull his arms free.

"Don't," she ordered, her voice cold and flat.

"It's all good," he said and then settled back in the

chair, as though he figured any sudden moves might make her go ballistic. "Whatever has you spooked, you're fine. You're safe. I'm not going to hurt you."

A bubble of laughter tickled her throat, and she choked it back.

No, I'm not safe.

And I *just might hurt* you.

CHAPTER TWO

I have brought darkness by means of my power...
I have separated Sutekh from the houses of
the Above...

—*The Egyptian Book of the Dead, Chapter 80*

ALASTOR KRAYL KEPT a tight hold on his mate, Naphré Kurata. Black smoke billowed before them as they stepped from the icy portal. Once they were through, Naphré broke away from him to lean forward at the waist, palms on her thighs, head bowed so her sleek, dark hair hid her expression.

He didn't need to see her face to know it was a perfectly lovely shade of green. He took a circumspect step to the left, just in case she hurled. No sense putting his shoes in harm's way.

"All right, then?" he asked, and shot his cuffs so a bit of white showed beyond the charcoal-gray merino wool of his jacket.

She held up one hand, palm forward, and waved him away.

"Sugar'll help," he said. He fished around in his pocket and came away with an English toffee caramel.

"It won't. Not fast enough. Just kill me now." But she took the candy. Then, "I *will* get used to that."

"You will," he said. *In about twenty years,* he didn't say. Traveling via portal between Topworld and Underworld took a bit of getting used to. Why squelch her optimism? "It's an acquired taste."

Straightening, she shot him a pained look. "Like opera."

He'd been right. She was green.

His brows rose. "I like opera."

"I know. My tenants know. The whole neighborhood knows. Morning, noon and night." She blew out a breath and glanced around.

Following her gaze, he evaluated their surroundings and realized that Naphré wasn't the only thing that was green. They stood on overgrown grass. Before them was a shack with a skewed roof and a door that hung on by a single hinge. Towering over that was a massive tree whose canopy stretched so wide it obscured the sky. What appeared to be a thin layer of fungus or moss clung to every spare inch. They stood in a monochromatic world painted the muddied color of old mashed peas.

"We in the right place?" Naphré asked, her brow furrowed as she looked around.

"Yes." Alastor had no doubt of that. He could feel the faint surge of energy that had been Lokan. Some part of his dead brother was here.

And that left him breathless.

He and Mal and Dagan had failed in every attempt to locate Lokan's remains. Now, after so many weeks of failure, at last, success.

The air around them was still and thick, humid, like a Southern swamp in the middle of July. And Alastor felt certain they weren't alone. He stepped closer to Naphré, crowding her.

With a sigh, she shot him a long-suffering look over her shoulder, but she didn't argue. They'd been over this before. She knew he needed to be in control, needed to protect and defend her, needed to know she was safe.

As safe as he could make her in a place that was neither Underworld nor Topworld, a place he had no real knowledge of.

"I'll take the shack. You poke around out here," Naphré said.

"Right. About that..." Alastor caught her wrist and held her in place. She wanted to be an equal partner in their relationship, and he was having trouble with that. He'd thought this would be an easy trip, safe, a sort of middle ground where they could each do a little learning about give-and-take. He'd been wrong. The vibe he was getting here was manky.

Her lips tightened. He recognized that look. It didn't bode well for his peace of mind. He worked hard at maintaining rigid control at all times, and Naphré Kurata shattered it like a sledgehammer on Wedgwood.

"Fine," she said. "We'll stay together."

"Bloody hell. It isn't safe," he clipped. "I'll send you back—"

"To wait for you, barefoot in the kitchen," Naphré muttered. "Are we going to have this argument every time there is the slightest whisper of danger? Because if we are, it's going to get old fa—"

She broke off and looked around warily, obviously feeling what he felt. His skin crawled with the sensation of being watched.

Tipping his head back, he stared up at the umbrella of branches and leaves that arced overhead.

A multitude of slitted amber eyes stared back at him.

"We have company, love," he murmured.

"So I see. You have any clue what they are?"

"None." Given where they were—a limbo that was technically neither Topworld nor Underworld, unclaimed as territory by any god or demigod—there should be nothing here, just as there had been nothing in Jigoku, the purgatory he and Naphré had almost been consigned to for eternity. It was that experience that had made him think of looking for other "null" pockets. In a place where time passed but did not pass, a place that was devoid of life, a soul reaper's remains would go unnoticed.

The thing was, he'd figured it was relatively safe to bring her here. When they'd been in Jigoku, the only threat had been their own perception of the passage of time. Armed with that knowledge, he'd erroneously assumed that would be true of all such null places. Obviously, a mistake.

"Best we complete our business before they decide it's polite to come and introduce themselves," he said.

The sound of claws and nails scrabbling against bark accompanied a shifting of dark bodies that emerged from the shadows then faded back just as quickly.

"Roof." Naphré dipped her chin toward the sagging hut.

He looked. What had been empty a moment past was now covered by massive creatures that bore resemblance to both a rodent and an arthropod. Their bodies were armored in a jointed, bony exoskeleton while their limbs were covered in sleek, shiny fur, like a seal's. They clung to the branches and the roof of the hut, eerily still.

Beneath his feet, the earth shifted, a subtle tremor.

Something stirred in the leaves over their heads, disturbing the sultry air. Alastor glanced up. The number of amber eyes looking down at them had increased exponentially.

And the sensation that he *felt* Lokan here had increased, as well.

He hesitated, torn. He ought to get Naphré out of here, get her somewhere safe.

"Don't waste this opportunity," she murmured, squirming from his hold and dipping to draw a knife from her boot.

She was cool and calm and competent, and he reminded himself that she had survived as a Topworld enforcer for years before he came along. But that tidbit of logic went only so far in the face of perceived threat. The emotions he kept chained howled for release.

Again, the earth shifted, enough that he was forced to correct his balance. The creatures on the lowest branches snapped and snarled, baring teeth that were arranged in rows, pointy and serrated.

The next shift was anything but subtle.

"Whoa!" Naphré grabbed at him as the earth beneath their feet gave a great, undulating roll, like the coils of a massive snake unwinding. When the ground finished its sickening lurch, the tree appeared to have grown even taller, the roots more exposed.

Trapped in the gnarled, twisted morass of roots and earth and slick, green slime was a rectangular box. It looked like a coffin sized for a small child.

He took a step forward. The rodentlike creatures surged along the branches, nails clicking, teeth bared. Slowly, he took another step forward. Again, they moved in equal degree.

Attention split between them and the box, he took yet another step.

The creatures held still, which ought to have pleased him, but instead made him strangely uneasy. The air felt as if it hummed with pent-up energy and expectation.

"Do this, before they get hungry," Naphré said.

With a flicker of regret—he'd bought these slacks less than a month ago—he got down and crawled through the tangled roots toward the box, his fingers sliding along the slime-slick surfaces. He grabbed hold, gave a tug, then tugged harder. Extricating it from the roots proved unexpectedly challenging. He tugged. He yanked. The box was well and truly stuck.

But this close, any doubt he'd harbored evaporated. He could feel Lokan here. Something inside that box had belonged to Lokan. Or was Lokan. He hated that thought, but he couldn't discount it.

The roots were thick and twisted and the more he pulled, the more they seemed to close in on the small coffin. He dug his fingers into the earth, underneath a root and, with a twist, snapped it off.

"Alastor." At Naphré's call, he rolled onto his back. "Try this."

Her knife sailed through the air toward him. She was already pulling a second knife from the sheath at her waist.

He caught the hilt and rolled back over to hack at the roots and work at freeing the box. Naphré stood nearby, knife in hand, watching his back.

With a high-pitched shriek, one of the braver creatures dropped from a low branch. The weight of the thing forced the air from his lungs as it landed on his back. Hot breath fanned his neck and saliva dripped to his skin, sizzling like acid.

With a snarl, Naphré dragged it off.

Alastor was on his feet in a blink, moving toward her, but she shot him a look so hard it'd turn a diamond to dust.

"Mine," she said, and he knew that with that single word she was saying a great deal more.

He had to trust her to watch after herself. He had to swallow the urge to coddle her to death. Or he'd lose her. He knew that.

"Bloody sodding hell." Then, "Spit's nasty," he warned.

The creature snapped and snarled and lurched for her throat. It took everything Alastor had not to leap into the fray. With a grunt and a thrust, Naphré took it out, stabbing deep to its underbelly and dragging the knife up.

The blood that sprayed them both was cold and black.

"Quickest way to get me out of harm's way is to get the damned box," she said as another creature braved the drop.

From the corner of his eye, he saw Naphré stabbing and punching at its head. He went for the box.

Others leaped from the lowest branches. Not to attack her but to attack their fallen comrade, Naphré's first kill. They fell on it, and in seconds there was nothing left but an exoskeleton shell.

Alastor hacked at the tree's roots, focusing on his task, aware that behind him, a stream of black blood flowed along the earth as the creatures began dropping down on them like rain.

TWENTY-FOUR HOURS LATER, Mal was back on the balcony railing, waiting for Kuznetsov and obsessing over the wacko chick who'd left him in the basement of the club with his dick so hard it hurt and a not-so-lovely case of blue balls.

Damn, she'd been hot. And crazy.

Not a great combination.

He had no idea what had made her bolt. Whatever it was, he figured it was a problem that ran deep and had little to do with anything he'd done or said.

Hell, she'd been the aggressor. It wasn't as if he'd dragged her down there by the hair.

So why the fuck was he left feeling like crap about the whole thing?

Maybe because he had his own deep-running issues. The thought brought a dark smile to his lips. Yeah, he did. No question about that. And one of those issues was finding his brother's killers.

Which was why he was here, to follow the lead that had led him to Kuznetsov, not to think about some girl.

He didn't have long to wait. Maybe twenty minutes later, a cab pulled up. Mal leaned forward, forearms on his thighs, weight hanging a thread away from freefall.

The High Reverend got out, followed by a woman. Her white coat was pale and bright, a fall of straight, dark hair swinging forward as she dipped her head. Her hand rested on the open passenger-side back door. She made no move to close it.

"Damn." High Reverend Kuznetsov habitually came

home alone. Damned fucking inconvenient that he'd altered his habits two nights in a row.

Kuznetsov bent and said something to the cabbie then straightened and looked at the woman. She shook her head, the movement graceful and controlled, almost languorous. No…wrong word—serene. Her bearing, her movements, everything about her was serene. Something nagged at him. Mal found himself wishing he could get a clear look at her features.

Be careful what you wish for.

She tipped her head back and unerringly turned her face toward him. As if she knew he was there. Which was impossible, because Mal couldn't be seen unless he chose to be. And at the moment, he didn't. So anyone, mortal or supernatural, looking at this balcony would see only an empty rail.

Except the woman was looking straight at him.

Seconds ticked past. Then she looked away.

Catching her hand, Kuznetsov tried to draw her close, but she resisted, holding her place at the edge of the curb. He took a step and went to her. Her body language was reserved as the High Reverend embraced her.

The angle made it hard to be certain, but it looked to Mal as if she dipped one hand inside Kuznetsov's coat and the other caressed the back of his neck. Embracing him? Something about the way she held herself made Mal think that wasn't the case. Repelling him? That didn't quite fit either.

She turned her head, avoiding the press of Kuznetsov's lips. He grazed her cheek, and then the interaction was over. The woman stepped back, gliding off the curb onto the street, her hand resting once more on the open cab door.

Something about her held Mal's attention. A supernatural? He opened his senses, reached for her and found nothing. Not even a hint of supernatural vibe. She read as mortal.

Still, Mal stared at her a moment longer, intrigued. His senses were telling him she was human. But pure instinct was telling him she wasn't. And since he himself could camouflage his energy signature, he had to assume others might be capable of the same.

With a last word, the woman turned and climbed back into the cab. Kuznetsov slammed the door shut. Guess he didn't like having his intentions thwarted. The taxi rolled away, picked up speed and, finally, disappeared around the corner.

For a long moment the High Reverend stood there, staring down the now-empty street. Mal didn't need to be able to see his features in order to read his disappointment. It dripped off him like melting snow.

Finally, Kuznetsov turned away and entered the building directly opposite Mal's perch. Alone.

The night was looking up. The cold air suddenly felt sharper, the lights of the city brighter. Kuznetsov and the knowledge he harbored were dancing almost within reach.

About fucking time. Lokan's soul was missing, his

body hacked to bits and scattered over the world. Mal and his remaining brothers needed to get Lokan's remains and his soul in one place.

And they had to find the identity of his killers.

Having Lokan back was the real prize.

But Mal knew they might be forced to settle for vengeance, served cold and raw and bloody. Unlike his brothers, he wasn't convinced they could bring Lokan back. Even if they found his remains, time was running out for his soul. If he partook of the food of the dead while he was trapped somewhere in the Underworld, he would be lost to them for eternity.

An eyewitness put Kuznetsov in the right place, right time the night Lokan was killed. Witness or participant. Either way, he had information Mal wanted.

Staring at the building across the street, Mal drummed his fingers on his thigh as he waited for the High Reverend to make it home. He imagined Kuznetsov greeting the concierge, taking the elevator, stepping off at the sub-penthouse, into the marble entryway—

A faint glow filtered through the floor-to-ceiling windows of apartment 2602.

"Honey, I'm ho-o-ome," Mal murmured. Only honey wasn't there. She'd left in a cab. Without even a kiss. For some reason, that made Mal grin.

He waited, giving his prey plenty of time to settle in. Twenty minutes later, he hopped off the rail and eased open the balcony door of the unoccupied condo. The commingled scents of dust and varnish and paint hung in the air. He'd done his homework. The previous owners had moved out weeks past, and the current owner was remodeling everything before moving in, right down to the marble sills on the windows. Which made the place perfect for surveillance.

He strode through the empty living room, made it halfway to the front door.

Then he paused, turned and looked back at the balcony and the star-flung sky. Adrenaline surged. He'd made twelve stories before without a scratch.

Sixteen just might be his lucky number.

Besides, he fucking hated elevators. He found the confines far too similar to a cell.

With a laugh, he sprinted back toward the balcony rail, vaulted it and soared.

CHAPTER THREE

...may my heart guide me
at this hour of destroying the night.
—*The Egyptian Book of the Dead, Chapter 22*

CALLIOPE GAVE THE CAB driver an address on the opposite side of town. As the car pulled away, she glanced back to see Kuznetsov standing where she'd left him, staring after her. But his gaze wasn't the one that made the fine hairs at her nape prickle and rise. Someone else watched her.

She detected no supernatural energy signature, which suggested her unseen voyeur was human. *Suggested,* not proved. And she was all about proof. Especially after the near-disastrous error she'd made last night.

No. She wouldn't think about that. It would serve no purpose to chastise herself endlessly. Learn from her mistake. Move on. But there was still the issue of the buildup inside her, bubbling and steaming and nearly ready to blow the lid off the pot. She would need to find a way to correct that.

When the cab was several blocks away, she leaned

forward and said, "I've changed my mind. I think I'll walk from here."

The driver swiveled his head to look at her over his shoulder. "From here?"

His tone suggested he only barely refrained from adding, "Are you crazy?" Which prompted her to glance around. They were in an office district in the heart of downtown, an area all but deserted at this time of night. It was as though the place locked its doors and rolled up its carpets as soon as the workday ended. To a mortal, the darkened buildings and even darker shadows must look threatening.

"I think it is not safe for you here," the driver muttered.

Lovely. Of all the cabdrivers in the city of Toronto, she'd drawn the one whose fatherly concern appeared to extend to the entire female population.

"I have a daughter your age." He shook his head. "I wouldn't want her walking here alone at night."

A daughter her age. She very much doubted that.

"Maybe I take you somewhere with more people?" he asked. The reflection of his face in the rearview mirror showed three parallel lines in his furrowed brow and dark eyes narrowed in concern.

She didn't want to go somewhere with more people. She wanted to get out and head back the way she'd come, but if she pushed, he'd remember her, and she preferred to draw the least amount of attention possible. She thought for a second then altered her plans and gave him the name of a popular restaurant several blocks to the northeast, back in the direction they'd come from.

Things changed. It was always easiest to change with them, like water flowing around rocks that emerged in its path. Eventually, it was the rocks that wore away and the water that found its true path.

As she settled back in the seat, she pulled out her phone. Until that instant, she hadn't been expecting a call. But now she was. She even knew the caller's identity.

Less than ten seconds later, the phone rang.

"You've found it?" she asked, already certain of the answer.

"You creep me out every time you do that." Roxy Tam's voice carried through the phone.

Calliope smiled a little. "After ten years, you ought to be used to it."

"Yeah, I ought to be used to you by now, but I'm not. It's still creepy that you know shit before it happens." Roxy paused. "And, yes, I've found it. I'll send it now. Just don't watch it while you're eating. Not pretty."

It was a brutal video clip that had made a brief appearance on YouTube before the powers that be yanked it because of subject matter: the skinning of a man's chest. Calliope wanted that clip, and now Roxy had found it for her.

"Thank you," Calliope said. "I appreciate the help."

Three weeks ago, Calliope wouldn't have said that.

Three weeks ago, it would have been Roxy's job and duty to get the information. But things had changed. Roxy had left the Asetian Guard, allowed to muster out only because she had been low in the hierarchy, privy to no sensitive information.

And because Calliope had bent the truth about Roxy's reasons for going. Not outright lied, but not been wholly forthcoming.

It would be Calliope who would pay the price for that when her superiors called her to the carpet.

Roxy laughed. "No need to thank me. I'll send you a bill."

"A steep one, I'm sure," Calliope replied. "Did you show the video to—" she pressed her lips together "—him?"

Dagan Krayl. Roxy's mate. A soul reaper, son of Sutekh, ancient enemy of Aset and her Daughters. Calliope's enemy.

But not Roxy's.

Which made for a convoluted, tangled mess.

"I didn't have to show it to him," Roxy said. "I got it from him."

Calliope kept her tone even, masking her surprise. "Did he know you meant to forward it to me?"

"He did." Roxy paused. "He said that another set of eyes looking at this puzzle could only be a good thing. He wants his brother's killers. If it means sharing information to enhance his chances of finding them, he'll do it."

"Even though he knows we have diametrically opposed goals?" Calliope's directive was to make certain the dead reaper stayed dead. Dagan's intent was to bring him back to life.

As long as she'd been in the Asetian Guard, Roxy's orders had been to work against him. But now….

"Are you helping him?" Calliope asked, her tone merely curious, weighed by neither judgment nor scorn.

Roxy's laugh was hard-edged. "You know, we agree on a lot of things. That isn't one of them. If Lokan Krayl is returned to life, he'll name his killers. Sutekh's forces will go after them. Allies will get dragged into battle on both sides. Blah, blah, blah… End result will be an apocalyptic war spilling over into the mortal realm. Dagan says that once we find the killers, that'll happen regardless, and if there's going to be a war anyway, he might as well get his brother back."

"It isn't that simple," Calliope said, shooting a glance at the back of the cabdriver's head and choosing her next words with care. "To accomplish his goal, there are certain things—"

"Spells," Roxy supplied.

"—that require specific ingredients—"

"Souls of the innocent."

"—and alliances—"

"Deals with demons."

Despite the weighty topic, Calliope couldn't help but be amused by Roxy's long-suffering yet faintly acerbic tone. "Yes. And that will stir up certain groups who will not be pleased."

"I get that," Roxy said. "It's about more than just finding the killer. If it was just about that then, sure, bring Lokan back to life. But it's about the sacrifices and the blood of innocents, and I can't get my head around that. And once you start with dark spells, it's going to stir up the Underworld gods and demigods... We've talked about it ad nauseum. And Dae sees my point of view..."

"...he just doesn't agree with it," Calliope finished for her.

"No." Roxy paused. "I'm helping him to a degree. I get that he needs to mourn his brother. Maybe find his remains so he can have some sort of ritual closure. I just don't know how far I can go." She sighed. "Loving Dagan doesn't change the fact that I'm a Daughter of Aset, that I was a soldier for the Asetian Guard for ten years. And I can't see my way clear to sacrificing nameless, faceless *innocent* people so he can have his brother back. I understand how bad he wants it. But I can't agree with the process." She gave a short laugh. "Who ever said relationships were easy?"

Calliope had no answer. Having never allowed herself that sort of relationship, she didn't feel qualified to comment. She rarely even allowed herself close friendships. Roxy was an exception. And Zalika, her own mentor.

But she did know that despite her friendship with Roxy, she'd step in her friend's way if it meant following the directive set by her superiors in the Asetian Guard. Lokan Krayl would stay dead if Calliope had any say in the matter.

She ended the call just as the cab pulled up in front of the restaurant. She paid, got out and moved to blend with the line that snaked out the front doors. Once the cab was gone, she hurried away, cutting through back alleys to minimize the chance of anyone noticing her unnatural speed. She stopped only once to drop her too-memorable white mohair coat in a large box that was clearly serving as someone's home. Then she peeled off the tailored hip-length jacket she'd worn to dinner, leaving her in a matte black catsuit with a healthy percentage of spandex. Ease of movement was key.

In minutes she was in the alley behind Kuznetsov's building, her pulse barely escalated, her breathing steady. It would take more than a short run to make her sweat.

Stepping behind the Dumpster, she moved several large metal cans and found the package she'd stored long before dawn in anticipation of tonight. She opened it and tucked a knife in her boot, strapped one to her thigh and slid her third blade into a sheath at the small of her back. Finally, she lifted her sword and settled it in place lying flat along her spine.

She checked her watch. Sixteen minutes had elapsed since she'd left Kuznetsov standing in the street. That left her nine minutes' leeway in her time line.

She pulled out her phone and downloaded and saved the video Roxy had sent her. Then she hit Play.

Black-gloved hands wielded blades with expert skill as they skinned a man's chest. Not a mortal man. A soul reaper. Rumor had it that a week after the video aired, the skin had been sent to Sutekh as a gift, stretched and pinned in place in a black plastic frame. It was a clear step toward war, but the killers had yet to make themselves known.

The soul reaper's skin was tattooed: an ankh with wings and horns. The dark mark. The mark of Aset. A mark no soul reaper would willingly put on his body. Someone had put the ink into his skin, an inverted mark.

But Calliope wasn't interested in any of that. It was old news.

What she wanted was a fresh clue. She wanted to know who had done the deed.

The Underworld was divided in much the same way that Topworld crime syndicates marked territory in human cities. Territories were held by Osiris, Hades, Pluto, Izanami, Sutekh—the überlord of chaos and evil—and a vast list of lesser gods, demigods and genies that populated all major and minor religions. There were handshake alliances, but they were fragile, the balance determined by territorial and volatile creatures.

Killing the soul reaper was a sure way to upset the balance. Pinning it on Aset, Sutekh's ancient enemy, sealed the deal. Despite the inverted ankh tattooed in the reaper's skin, Calliope wasn't convinced that Aset or her Daughters had been in any way involved. Whoever the killer was could have meant to divert attention from the truth.

The video was grainy and dark, jumping around like grease in a hot pan. There were no faces. Only the reaper's chest and two sets of black-gloved hands. Knives with black blades. Blood. An oblong bowl.

Wait.

She paused the feed and stared at the lower-left corner. Ungloved fingers holding the bowl. Short nails, clipped and neat. A ring in the shape of a scarab beetle.

She knew that ring. Kuznetsov wore one exactly like it, as did every Setnakht priest.

Interesting, but not revelatory. She'd already suspected they were somehow involved. This was just confirmation.

She hit Play again and watched a little more, her eyes scanning the corners and the background before returning to the main action. Later, she'd take her time, watch it frame by frame. She'd get a copy to a Topworld tech who would look at anything for a price. He might be able to enhance the video and see things her eyes missed.

For a few seconds, she focused on the blades. One moved into the foreground. The very end of the hilt was visible for an instant, the design unusual.

Again, she paused the feed then glanced at her

watch. Seven minutes and forty-three seconds of her nine minutes were up. The video would have to wait.

She turned off her phone, tucked it into the pocket at her hip and zipped it closed.

Then she moved, little more than smoke in shadow.

MAL TOOK THE STAIRS to the twenty-sixth floor. He was in no rush. In fact, he wanted to let his soon-to-be good buddy Pyotr Kuznetsov settle in and relax.

The hallway was empty, not a soul about. *Soul*. He grinned at the private joke.

Slipping a narrow pick from a black leather case, he applied it to the lock on Kuznetsov's door. Of course, he could simply have turned the handle and torn it free, but he still enjoyed the challenge, the *thrill* of a lock giving beneath his hand.

Besides, he didn't want to leave a broken handle visible to anyone who might walk past. Nothing to alert suspicion. He had no desire to invite human notice. That tended to make things messy.

Within seconds he felt the tumblers turning, the lock opening. He stepped inside, pulled the door shut behind him and locked it once more.

Anticipation hummed. He had a good feeling about this. The High Reverend was going to be a fount of information. They were going to have a friendly, guy-to-guy talk about his role in the killing of three women. Three whom Mal knew of, anyway.

More important, Pyotr Kuznetsov was going to share

intimate details about what role he had played in Lokan's death. Mal meant to get his answers, even if he had to rip out the bastard's heart to do it.

He was going to enjoy helping his new pal Pyotr remember—and share—every second of the night Lokan died.

Mal glanced around, the darkness presenting no impediment to his reaper sight. His senses were attuned to even a whisper of sound. No guards. One heartbeat.

Too easy. No chase. No challenge. Where was the fun?

The sound of water drumming against tile led him to his right. He pushed open the door to the master bedroom. It was dark, but the door to the en suite was cracked open, letting a thin stream of light and steam escape the bathroom.

He turned away and moved through the condominium with preternatural speed, peeking behind paintings, running his fingers along the backs of cabinets and under drawers, checking for hiding spots. Nothing.

Mal returned to the master bedroom. The water was still running. Looked as though Kuznetsov liked his showers long.

Settling in the far corner, he leaned one shoulder against the wall and waited. And waited. That seemed to be his lot tonight. He heard a groan from the shower. A gasp. Then, "Yeah. Ohhhhh, fuck, yeah," the words sounding as though they'd been forced through gritted teeth.

Aw, hell. The asshole was beating his meat.

From the panting and grunting, Mal was guessing it was near the crescendo. He could only hope.

Damn, he should have gone for a latte before heading up here. He could have done without the audio.

Mal straightened and did a quick sweep of the room. Kuznetsov would provide answers, willingly or not, but it never hurt to search for interesting things. He paused by the dresser. It was uncluttered, adorned by a single black ceramic bowl that looked very old. It gave him a split second's pause, then he noticed it was round rather than oblong and he moved on.

He did a quick check of the drawers. Neat and organized. Maybe too neat. Then he moved to the bookshelves and finally the painting that hung as the lone focal point on the wall opposite the window. He ran his fingers around the edges. Bingo. Swinging the picture out a few inches, he peeked in behind. The perfect cliché. A safe peeked back at him.

He froze, an odd sensation crawling up his spine. Glancing back over his shoulder, he slowly scanned the room but found nothing out of the ordinary.

A loud grunt carried from the bathroom, followed by a sharp cry. Then nothing.

Looked like Kuznetsov was done.

The shower turned off. There was the shush of a towel pulled from the rack. Mal settled the painting back against the wall.

A cell phone rang. The door to the bathroom opened,

leaving Kuznetsov standing there, towel in hand, wet and naked.

Mal could have done without the eyeful.

Snagging his phone, Kuznetsov answered the call then listened, his posture growing tense.

"What?" he snapped, eyes wide, nostrils flaring. "When?" His voice cracked. Then, "Dead? Are you certain?"

He waited for the answer then ended the call without another word. His hand was shaking as he tossed the phone on the bed, oblivious to the fact that he had company.

The shadows shifted and moved. Mal froze, stunned by the realization that good old Pyotr wasn't the only one who'd been oblivious.

The woman stepped into view. She was behind Kuznetsov and a little to the right, and she was looking over his shoulder, right at Mal, as though she could see him. Which she couldn't. He was confident of that. But this was the second time tonight that her gaze unerringly sought him. He wasn't one to ignore the strange and inexplicable.

Green eyes—cat eyes—looked right through him. They were bright even in the shadows, almost luminescent, framed by thick lashes, accented by straight-cut bangs. He felt a split second of recognition, and then it was lost. He didn't know her, other than having seen her get out of the cab. The white coat she'd worn earlier was gone. Now, she was clothed entirely in black, covered from neck to wrists to ankles, her catsuit so tight it might as well have not covered her at all.

Mal registered it all in a blink.

Then he noticed the long, narrow leather tube hanging against her back. The strap crossed her chest, lying between the swells of her breasts. Really nice breasts. Perfect handfuls. He stared at them for a second longer than was warranted. There was something about the shape of her body—

Kuznetsov straightened, tensed, started to turn, as though he sensed her presence.

The woman was inhumanly fast as she stepped even closer. She caught Kuznetsov's head between her hands—

Mal leaped forward.

—and gave a sharp turn and a twist.

There was a loud crack.

Impossibly, she was almost as fast as he was. So despite his enhanced speed, he was too late to stop anything because he'd been standing just a shade too far away.

Mal froze midleap and landed lightly, close enough that he could reach out and touch her. Reach out and kill her for what she'd just done.

Pyotr's body went rigid then relaxed. The woman stepped back, loosed her hold and let him drop like a sack of dirty laundry. Her face was smooth and composed, betraying no emotion. Not pleasure. Not remorse.

Dead. She'd killed him. She'd cracked the bastard's neck and destroyed Mal's one solid lead.

For an instant, he felt nothing. Then he felt too much; disbelief, anger, a sense that he'd been cheated. Robbed. That was usually his job. He was the prowler, the pirate, the thief. Yet this woman had robbed *him*.

He wanted to kill her, to take her head and twist her neck and do to her what she'd done to Kuznetsov.

But he didn't move. From somewhere deep inside he managed to dredge some self-restraint and he froze, panting, willing himself to stay cloaked from her sight. He could kill her as easily in a few moments as he could now.

Better to wait, watch and possibly get answers to the questions that hammered him. He wanted to know how she'd gotten in here without him sensing her presence. How she'd killed a man so easily with nothing but her hands. *This* man. *This* kill. Why?

He focused his awareness on her, stretching his ability to detect any hint of the supernatural. And then he felt it. A low energy signature that had hummed under his radar, until now.

Damn it to hell. Damn it to fucking hell. She had her own stealth skills. Impossible. The only beings he knew of who could hide in plain sight were soul reapers. And to a one, soul reapers were male.

She definitely wasn't one of them.

So what the fuck was she?

CHAPTER FOUR

I shall have power in my heart,
I shall have power in my arms,
I shall have power in my legs,
I shall have power to do whatever I desire.
        —The Egyptian Book of the Dead, Chapter 26

THERE WAS SOMEONE WATCHING her. Calliope knew it in her gut, though she had no visual confirmation. Eyes could be tricked. Instinct couldn't.

She looked up from Pyotr Kuznetsov's lax form, letting her gaze slide to the corners and the shadows.

Only one thing she knew of could essentially make itself invisible, hiding in plain sight. A soul reaper. Her gut was telling her that one watched her now, invisible, undetectable, until and unless he decided otherwise.

A rare, sharp thrill of fear arrowed through her. She choked it into submission, holding her ground, alert, wary. Calm.

Panic and fear were her enemies more than any corporeal creature.

Besides, she couldn't outrun him. If he was here and he wanted her, he'd catch her. Better to tough it out.

Keeping her focus, she checked the last call on Pyotr's cell. The Temple of Setnakht. She wondered who was dead and why that death had made Kuznetsov afraid. She tossed the phone back on the bed then cut a veiled glance at the shadows, willing whoever was there to materialize from the ether.

Wishful thinking. She would not see him unless he wished her to, would never know that he approached until it was too late.

A chill crawled up her spine. Bad enough to be stalked. Worse, to be stalked by one such as he. Memories clawed at the lid of the box she tried to keep locked, but she slammed it shut, refusing to let them crawl free.

Surreptitiously, she scanned the dark room. Perhaps he was in the far corner. Perhaps he stood by the open closet door. She thought he was closer, only a hand span away. But she had no proof. There was only darkness and shadow and a thin sliver of ambient light breaking through the crack in the heavy curtains.

She could know nothing with certainty except that he was her enemy. And he was deadly.

Her choices were limited. She chose the option that called for brass balls. The direct approach.

"I know you are here, soul reaper," she said softly, though she expected no reply. Let him wonder how she knew. Let him wonder exactly how vast her power was.

Compared with his…a pebble in a windstorm. He

outgunned her. But she had hopes that she could out-think him.

Thugs—whether human or supernatural—generally didn't excel in the use of their gray matter.

Her gaze dipped to where Kuznetsov lay sprawled on the ground, his arms flung wide, the towel he'd been using inches away from his outstretched hand. His head lolled to one side, eyes closed, mouth open, and his legs were twisted at uncomfortable angles, leaving him naked and bare and exposed. She was disinclined to arrange his limbs in a more decorous position. He was not a man who deserved any consideration.

"How did you know you weren't alone?"

Her head jerked up, her attention shifting to the left. Her words had invited the soul reaper to reveal himself, but she hadn't expected that he would.

And she hadn't expected that voice, rich and low, like smoke and velvet. Familiar, somehow. It made every nerve in her body sit up and take notice.

A part of her had hoped that if he did reveal himself, her suspicion would be proved wrong, that he would be some other creature than one of Sutekh's minions. The fact that he didn't correct her told her that hope was in vain.

The shadows cloaked him. The darkness caressed him. His build was honed and muscular. Broad shoulders. Lean hips. Black jeans. Black boots. Dark, blue-gray shirt.

Her focus lifted to his face.

Her heart slammed against her ribs and she felt dizzy. Sick. He was the supernatural she had mistaken for a human. Worse and worse.

Only years of training allowed her to muffle her panic and continue to note the details as he stepped forward into the narrow band of light.

He was night, his hair so dark it was almost black, falling sleek and straight just past the hard line of his jaw. His eyes were bright, glittering like stars, pale gray, almost luminescent against dark, curling lashes. Straight brows. Straight nose, with a slight bump at the bridge. A thin scar slashed his chin from the edge of his lower lip to his jawline, white against the dark stubble that shadowed his jaw.

Two hoops in each ear. A platinum ring on his right baby finger, and a solid, plain band on his left thumb.

With that one glance she learned a great deal. He liked pretty things. Expensive things. He enjoyed what the mortal world offered.

Not only was he more than human. He was a soul reaper, a breed of supernatural both powerful and vile.

And still, she found him beautiful.

Shame twinged. Anger followed. At him. At herself.

Angry is better than afraid. Cunning is better than angry.

She folded away all emotion and stored it in the neat little corner of her mind that she held at the ready for just such occasions. Emotion was valueless at best, danger-ous at worst. She'd be wise to keep it under tight rein. Best way to win against an enemy was cool, calculated logic.

He was a soul reaper, the embodiment of all that was evil. He was the enemy of her kind.

More than that, *her* enemy.

One such as him had taken everything from her. Memories slithered deep in her thoughts, and she held them back, refusing to set them free.

He was looking at her, with that same puzzled expres-sion he'd worn last night. As if he thought he ought to know her. She could only pray he didn't recognize her, that her disguise last night, combined with the darkness of the club, had been enough.

"Instinct warned me I was not alone," she replied at last, keeping her tone utterly composed, betraying noth-ing. Because he didn't deserve to know he'd surprised her, and because she wasn't foolish enough to add that knowledge to his arsenal.

His lips curled in a lazy smile. Her gaze lingered for a second on his mouth.

At her feet, Kuznetsov twitched.

"He's alive," the soul reaper observed.

"You sound surprised."

"I am. Between the twist and the crackle, I thought you'd broken his neck." Cold anger touched his words.

"What would have been the point in that?" What

would be the point in killing Kuznetsov before she could get him to the Asetian Guard and get answers.

"The point?" He stroked his hand along his jaw. "Tough question, given that I'm not privy to your goals."

"Privy," she echoed, surprised by his word choice. It sounded a bit formal, and he didn't look like the formal sort.

He shot her a calculating look, measuring her as surely as she was measuring him.

"What do you want?" she asked, her gaze steady on his. She was focused now, centered. She was a calm lake beneath a cloudless sky.

And he was nothing more than the supernatural version of a worthless thug in Sutekh's ranks.

His gaze lowered to Pyotr's unmoving form then lifted, his gray eyes bright against his dark lashes. "The same thing you want, darlin'."

"I doubt that."

Where soul reapers went, violence and a river of blood followed. She knew what they did. She'd lived it firsthand, not only once, but again and again in her nightmares. For many years, the horror of what they had done had leached from her nightmares into her waking hours, grabbing her by the throat whenever it chose. She would be doing the most mundane task, and suddenly, she would be dragged under by a sucking tide of memories and fear.

It hadn't happened for a long while. It wouldn't happen tonight. She wouldn't let it.

The soul reaper took a single step closer, doing nothing more threatening than letting his lips curve in that lazy, bad-boy smile.

It was enough to raise the fine hairs at her nape. She trusted his smile about as much as she'd trust an asp rising to strike.

"That usually work for you?" she asked.

"Work—" He shook his head. "What?"

"The smile." Her tone was flat.

"The—" He gave a low laugh that reached inside her and twisted her up in a way she didn't like. "Yeah, it usually does. Not this time though, huh?"

It had worked on her last night. She could only hope he wouldn't realize that.

"You are too late, soul reaper. I claim him in Aset's name." She paused, enjoying the telltale widening of his pupils. She had him. He wouldn't dare challenge her, not this close to the meeting of allies. Stealing a prize marked for Aset would stir up a hornet's nest he could have no wish to disturb.

"And if I ignore your claim?"

"I would think that this close to the meeting of allies, you would have no wish to irritate your leader's enemies. Especially in light of the fact that it was your leader who invited everyone to the party."

"Ah, my fearless leader. Right. Wouldn't want to piss off Sutekh by pissing off Aset, would I? It's not like they don't already have a virulent hate-on for each other. Just one small correction," he continued. His brows lifted then lowered. "Sutekh's not merely my leader. He's my father. Which gives me a little more leeway to break the rules."

Father.

"Do you tell me this to warn me off? Do you think that because you are Sutekh's son, I will bow and scrape and surrender my prize like a small beast relinquishing its kill to a larger predator?"

"Nice imagery." He stepped closer, looming over her. "Will you?"

"Relinquish him?" She shook her head. "No."

"Surrender," he corrected her with a leer.

"No."

"Disappointing."

"Disappointment's a bitch."

He blinked. Then he threw back his head and laughed, full and rich.

"What's your name, pretty girl?" he asked as he stepped even closer.

She had a thing about personal space at the best of times. He was invading it. Purposely. She ignored the incursion, refusing to offer him the satisfaction of a reaction, or a reply. Instead, she stepped over Kuznetsov's unconscious form so she straddled his torso, feet firmly planted on each side of his waist, her stance solidifying her claim.

"Shy, are you?" Sarcasm dusted his words. "I'll

introduce myself first, then. Malthus Krayl, at your service. You can call me Mal." He grinned, more predatory than pleasant.

Malthus Krayl.

"Dagan Krayl's brother?" she asked.

The soul reaper tipped his head to the side, and a flicker of surprise crossed his features before he masked it, though whether at her actions or her question she couldn't say.

"And I'm guessing you know my brother's name because you know his mate? Roxy Tam? Her being a Daughter of Aset and all." The grin widened. "Like you."

Smug bastard.

"Your ability to think in linear sequence is admirable." She let none of her emotion leak into her tone. The words came out flat as a Kansas prairie. There was no cleverness involved in his deductions. She'd offered that information, gift wrapped, when she'd mentioned that she claimed Kuznetsov in Aset's name. It was more than enough for even a fool to connect the dots.

"Ouch. Kitty has claws," he said in a perfectly amiable tone. "I can think of better ways to use them." His gaze raked her. "I'd be happy to serve as your scratching post."

For a second, she stared at him blankly, not registering his meaning. And then she did. Was he…*propositioning* her? The possibility was appalling. Doubly so after the mistake she'd come so close to making with him last night.

She offered no reply. He deserved none. He was a soul reaper. He deserved nothing but the endless agony of the lakes of fire. Out of respect and affection for Roxy Tam—her one-time acolyte, her dearest friend—Calliope had an understanding of sorts with Dagan Krayl, at least, as close to an understanding as she was willing to get with a soul reaper. He had stood against his own kind, saved Roxy's life, and—for Roxy's sake—Calliope's.

In that act, he had given birth to an uneasy truce. Calliope stayed away from him. He stayed away from her. Roxy was welcome in her home. Dagan was not. That was the most she'd been willing to concede.

At her feet, Kuznetsov released a small moan.

"I am not a kitty. I am not your darling."

He tipped his head. "I'm guessing you're Calliope Kane, Roxy's mentor in the Asetian Guard. Dae mentioned you." He widened his eyes. "Never said you were quite the hot little number, though." His voice trailed away and his eyes narrowed as he studied her face, as though by mentioning a hot little number, he had started his brain along that track like a train.

She offered a tight smile. "I've been slapping the hands of lecherous—" she looked him over dismissively "—little *boys* for a very long time."

"That I believe, darlin'." He laughed off the insult. "That I believe."

Kuznetsov twitched again. Time was slipping past. She needed to move before he awakened, and she needed a plan for exactly how to accomplish that. Scenarios played out in rapid-fire succession in her thoughts. None was satisfactory.

Her options were limited. Her directive was to retrieve Kuznetsov and question him.

The soul reaper caught her eye. "Shall we flip a coin?"

"Flip a—"

"To see who gets him, since we both want him."

"And if I win?" she asked, only to buy a few more precious seconds.

The reaper widened his eyes and raised his brows, the picture of mock innocence. "I'll take him anyway."

That, she believed, and his honesty surprised her. "Not the type to play fair?"

"Never." He paused. "Step away. I have no wish to harm you. You can walk away from this untouched." His gaze slid over her in leisurely perusal. His voice lowered. "Unless you wish to be touched."

Ignoring that, she focused on her options, mentally tallying her strengths against his. The scale was heavily weighted in his favor. If only she could siphon a fraction of his power.

She blinked as the thought registered. There was a possibility…slim and *repulsive,* but there nonetheless.

Excitement stirred. She couldn't kill him, but perhaps she could slow him down enough to facilitate her escape.

With Kuznetsov. She had no intention of leaving the High Reverend behind.

A series of events and counterevents played through her thoughts.

Then the soul reaper reached for her and time spun away. *Gray eyes, pale and clear and bright.*

Eyes like his had haunted her for a century and a half.

She shook her head, clearing the memory, focusing on the moment. It was not the same man. That man was long dead.

But the images refused to go, the past blending with the present and the future.

A hand extending toward her. The sliver of light from between the curtains. The faint hum of the fan from the bathroom.

That was the future.

Her breath caught. She'd lived this scene before and would again; she had seen it in her mind's eye, a portent of things to come. She'd seen him thrust his hand deep in her chest and tear out her still-beating heart.

Was that moment to be now?

Not if she could help it. Her fate was not set in stone. Her prescience did not account for all choices individuals could make, and that meant outcomes could change.

Arching back, she avoided his touch then kicked out at his knee, hoping for a distraction. For whatever reason, he didn't go for her throat. Or her heart. He appeared to be considering his next move. That fraction of a second was enough.

In a practiced and perfected move, she bent her knee sharply, kicking her heel against the bottom of the long, stiffened leather sheath that hung down her back. The force was exactly enough to send her gleaming sword flying out the top, blade first.

Flicking her hand up, she caught the hilt as gravity drew the sword down. With her free hand, she snatched her knife from the sheath at the small of her back.

The soul reaper's head came up and he moved. Fast. But not fast enough.

She spun and slashed horizontally through the curtains that covered the window. As the severed cloth pooled on the ground, she was already completing the arc, bringing the blade down toward the soul reaper's shoulder.

Again, he moved, his hand little more than a pale blur. This time, he was almost fast enough.

She'd wanted to get his shoulder. His reflexes made that impossible. She barely managed to slice his forearm. Good enough. She hadn't meant to maim or kill—not that killing him was even possible. She'd aimed merely to draw blood. And she'd succeeded.

"What the fuck?" he snarled, that pretty smile gone now, replaced by a grimace that bared his teeth and etched his features with pain and anger. "Do not make me hurt you."

Blood welled in a thick line as the edges of his skin

parted and the white of his bone shone through. That had to hurt. Soul reapers might not die, but they did feel pain—a fact that brought Calliope pleasure, despite her tenuous circumstance.

He wrenched her sword from her grasp and tossed it against the far wall. She offered no resistance. When he reached for her, she made no effort to evade, letting him close his fingers on her wrist, effectively blocking her from using the knife she still held. She didn't need it now; her sword had done the job.

The smell of his blood was rich and thick in the air.

As he yanked her closer, she pretended to struggle, diverting his attention. He twisted the knife from her grasp even as he caught hold of her shoulder with his free hand, clearly expecting her to try to break free.

Instead, she launched herself against him, revulsion bubbling in her gut as she sealed her lips to the gaping wound on his forearm.

His blood filled her mouth.

Here was the reason she had seen him in her future. Not for sex, but for blood.

With a roar, he shook his arm as though trying to shake off an insignificant bug. She sank her teeth in, holding on like a pit bull.

The blood. There was only that. Horrible and beautiful. Repulsive and lush. Copper sweet. Salty. As always, she found the taste both vile and wondrous.

Conflicting emotions warred inside her: loathing, the

thrill of victory, rage and hate. She locked them down. Let herself feel nothing. She focused only on the necessary task.

She was a pranic feeder. She sipped the life force of others to enhance her own.

At the moment, she didn't see him as the most powerful supernatural the Underworld had to offer. Instead, she saw him as food.

She was old enough—and disciplined enough—that she usually fed by tapping into a being's prana and taking a small sampling of what she needed. Without taking blood.

But right now, there was no other way to access the reaper's life force. He was far too strong and adept to let her feed from him any other way.

Her course decided, she did not allow herself to waver. Holding tight, she fought his efforts to dislodge her, barely hanging on as she pulled a second mouthful of his blood from the wound.

Her knees almost buckled as the power of his life force hit her like a tsunami. Wild. Uncontrollable. Beautiful and terrifying.

Pure, luscious energy from the fount.

Throughout her entire existence, she had fed only from mortals. Never from a supernatural; certainly not from a soul reaper. Had never even considered it.

But only a fool dismissed opportunities, regardless of how repugnant they might be. Calliope's orders were to bring in Kuznetsov so her superiors could find out how and why a soul reaper and three Daughters of Aset had been murdered. She was willing to squelch her revulsion in favor of a successful outcome to her mission.

She'd worry about the cost later; everything in life, and death, had a price.

His fingers tangled in her hair. He jerked her head back, the pain making her eyes water. Her teeth tore free of his flesh, and her skin tingled where his blood trickled down her chin.

Teeth bared in a feral snarl, he held her at arm's length. His chest rose and fell. His eyes narrowed to slits.

Gone was the good humor and the bad-boy grin. Here was a beast, a warrior, a predator who was used to being at the top of the food chain.

And she'd just taken a bite out of that.

CHAPTER FIVE

*Pay attention, to the decision of truthfulness
and the plummet of the balance according to
its stance.*

—*words spoken by He who is in the embalming chamber*

THE ENTIRE ENCOUNTER lasted only seconds. Calliope's actions, and the soul reaper's, had been fueled by preternatural speed.

"What the fuck?" he snarled. The moonlight cast his features in hollows and shadows, handsome still, but harder, sharper. Now, he looked like what he was, a fearsome creature, dangerous and volatile.

One she needed to escape with her prize in tow.

She felt his power in her cells. She tasted his blood on her tongue. And she didn't let herself think about anything but that.

His blood, his life force, fed hers. She was stronger already. Her vision was sharper, her hearing clearer. Suddenly, she could smell the faint trace of citrus on the soul reaper's skin, hear the beat of his heart.

His eyes darkened, the pupils dilating. His nostrils flared.

"Did you just *feed* from me?" he asked, his voice low and flat. Dangerous. The calm before a storm. "Didn't anyone ever teach you manners? Wait until you're invited before you eat."

With her gaze locked on his, she dragged the back of her hand across her lips then licked his blood slowly from her skin. Waste not, want not. Once the Matriarchs found out what she had done, she would pay a heavy price for this night's actions. She might as well get full benefit while she could.

He stared at her, eyes glittering, and the way he looked at her made her shiver. There was threat there—which was expected—and interest—which wasn't.

It was the interest that made her wary.

"Not so nice being the prey, is it?" she asked and then lunged at him, ready to take a final pull if she could.

As though her actions lit a fuse, he thrust her from him with enough force to make her body jackknife so her legs and arms came up straight in front of her. She flew through the air. Her back slammed against the wall with a thud, her head rocking back a second after her shoulders hit. She felt the drywall give. And despite that, she knew he'd been gentle, that he could have used far more force.

His power was so great it made the air hum. She could feel that now in a way she hadn't earlier on and hadn't last night. He was incredibly adept at hiding the vast well of energy that cycled through his inhuman cells.

She slid down the wall, got her feet under her and came down with knees bent. And...*yes*...there was her sword. She dove, grabbed and bounced to her feet to find him watching her, features taut.

As fast as she could, she darted to the right. The air stirred and he was there before her. Undeterred, she moved left, only to find that, again, he was faster. Which told her everything she needed to know.

She'd hoped that with her temporarily enhanced agility and speed, she'd be quick enough to dodge him. Of course, that made no sense because it was his agility and speed she'd borrowed.

Plan B, then. Soul reapers might be nearly impossible to kill, but they bled. They felt pain. She would use that to slow him down. All she needed were a few seconds.

His lips pulled back in a feral smile. He was enjoying the game. He thought he was the sure winner.

"I could have snapped you in two. But what a waste," he said. "Give it up, darlin'. I'm a forgiving sort." His gaze raked her. "We can kiss and make up."

"I'd rather kiss a week-old corpse."

He waggled his brows. "Don't say that till you've tried it."

No. He couldn't mean that he'd—

"Put down the sword, darlin'. You can't win. You know that. Cut my heart right out and lay it on the floor, and I still won't die. Trust me, I'm far more pleasant to be around when I'm not angry. Your sword's not going to do much more than piss me off."

Actually, it would do much more than that.

Time to act. She surged toward him, harnessing the power she'd stolen from him, channeling force through her arm, through her blade. She stabbed at his gut.

As expected, he was faster than she was. His arm came up to deflect the blow, and she ended up thrusting her sword through the left side of his chest instead of his belly. That was fine. She wasn't finicky. Her only regret was that her blow wasn't positioned to skewer his heart.

Thanks to the power she had siphoned from him, her blade sank through skin and muscle, clear through his back and deep into the wall. The hilt vibrated as she let go, leaving him impaled.

Everything felt as if it moved in slow motion, when in truth they were both moving with incredible speed. He looked down. His mouth fell open. Then his head lifted once more. Gray eyes, pale and bright and cold, pinned her as her blade pinned him.

His hands came up to close on the hilt of her abandoned weapon.

She dipped, shoved her shoulder into Kuznetsov's belly and flipped him up into a fireman's carry—she didn't want to think about where his naked dangly bits were at the moment. At least she had the comfort of knowing they'd be shriveled by the cold.

With the reaper's blood surging through her veins,

the maneuver was no more challenging than slinging her purse over her shoulder.

She hated to lose her weapon, but she hated to lose Pyotr Kuznetsov even more. A sword could be replaced. The information his brain held couldn't.

The Asetian Guard wanted his secrets.

And so, it seemed, did the soul reaper.

From the corner of her eye, she saw him pulling on her sword, the blade inching free, dripping fat drops of luscious blood.

The smell taunted her, lured her.

That was the risk. She'd tasted him. Savored him on her tongue.

She wanted to taste him again.

But the bigger risk was that he was almost free.

The blade was longer than his reach. He took a breath and switched his grip so he could pull the final half of her steel from his chest.

He made not a sound, though she had little doubt he felt pain. Deep, searing pain.

His gaze met hers, cold, angry. But still, that interest lingered, as though by breaching his defenses, she'd earned even more of his awareness.

His gaze shifted to Kuznetsov, who hung heavy across her shoulder.

The sand in the hourglass had run out.

She spun, snatched up the marble statue on the nightstand, hauled back and used the strength she'd stolen from the soul reaper to amp up her throw.

Stone slammed against glass.

The window shattered, a thousand glittering shards arcing outward into the night and raining down to the ground below.

She didn't hesitate, didn't flinch.

Head bowed to protect her face, arms tight around Kuznetsov's naked back, she launched herself through the jagged hole into the star-tossed night.

And she fell, the cold air stinging her skin, the ground rushing up to meet her.

MAL DRAGGED THE LAST FEW inches of the sword free of his flesh, wincing at the raw pain. She'd stabbed him. She'd fucking pinned him to the wall like a bug.

She'd *fed* from him and used his own blood and power against him. He hadn't seen that coming.

He was both affronted by—and admiring of—her resourcefulness. Calliope Kane had brass ones the size of cantaloupes.

The wound in his chest hurt like a bitch. His pride stung almost as much. She'd bested him, for now. The outcome of a small skirmish did not a battle decide.

Pressing the side of his balled fist tight to stanch the blood, he staggered to the window, cursing and snarling and wishing her to every territory of the Underworld that had fire. Hot, unforgiving, devouring fire.

At the same time, she'd left him feeling exhilarated.

Calliope Kane was a riddle. Cool. Calculating. She'd

jumped out the damned window without a second's hesitation. He'd have liked to make the jump alongside her. Doubly so, given that she'd taken the damned High Reverend with her.

He looked down at the terrace a few stories below. An empty terrace. She was already gone, moving with uncanny speed. Thanks to her little snack of reaper blood.

His blood.

Which was currently leaving his body in steady spurts.

His next move depended on hers, and he was no mind reader. He mentally calculated the options she could choose from, using that as a template to chart his own course. She'd need to get to the elevator or the stairs, get Kuznetsov to ground level and get him out of the building. All Mal needed to do was make certain he was there ahead of her, waiting. With open arms. His lips curved in a dark smile.

He could leap out the window after her, but while that might have appealed were he not bleeding like a gutted boar, it didn't appeal given that he was.

Crimson drops dripped off the edge of his fist. He thought of the way she'd licked his blood from the back of her hand. And why the fuck that made him feel the first stirrings of a hard-on, he had no idea.

Maybe because she was one hell of an adrenaline high.

Looked like this wasn't his week when it came to the ladies.

On a sharp exhale, he snagged Kuznetsov's discarded towel from the floor, folded it into a bulky square and pressed hard on his chest. He'd heal. He'd hurt, but he'd heal. He always did.

He ought to be pissed. And he was. But there was something else in the mix. A bubbling stew of admiration and attraction that he didn't want to look at too carefully.

Females were fun. Even the deadly ones were fun, given the right set of circumstances, along with a set of clean sheets. Sometimes, they weren't even that finicky about the sheets.

Handle a woman right and even a succubus or a fire genie could be stroked into submission.

His encounter with Calliope Kane hadn't been fun. She definitely hadn't been remotely submissive. The events of the last two nights had left him with a flicker of doubt about his ability to cajole, caress or charm a female into acquiescence.

But only a flicker. He was nothing if not innovative. Yeah, given the right set of circumstances, and possibly a pair of fur-lined handcuffs, Ms. Kane might be brought under his hand.

The image was far too appealing.

He crossed to Pyotr's walk-in closet, sifted through the contents and paused at a black silk robe. He laughed—talk about cliché—then winced at the pain.

But the robe was perfect for his purposes. He dragged it off the hanger.

As he turned, the built-in storage caught his eye. The top had open shelves and the bottom a set of six narrow drawers. He went through them quickly. One for underwear. One for socks. One for silk handkerchiefs in a rainbow of colors. He pulled the top drawer open to find an array of neatly aligned watches on the velvet lining. Movado. Piaget. Tag Heuer.

Mal gave a low whistle. Looked like the High Reverend business was lucrative.

He helped himself to the Rolex. Shiny.

As he settled it on his wrist, he couldn't help but wonder what the good Reverend would lock away in a wall safe behind a picture when he left such treasures out in a drawer. He wondered if the contents of that safe had monetary value or some other importance. He had time to find out. It would take him less than a minute to take the stairs to the ground floor and head off Ms. Kane before she left the building with Kuznetsov. It would take her a good deal longer than that to figure a way to get the naked Reverend downstairs.

Mal had the benefit of being able to pass unseen by human eyes. She didn't.

Tossing the silk robe on the bed, he then went to the painting, swung it back and stood contemplating the safe. The High Reverend had sprung for the more expensive electronic locking system over combination or key, but he hadn't gone all out for fingerprint identification. In less than a minute, Mal was in.

And he had his answer as to what Kuznetsov would deem worthy of locking away.

Pulling out his cell, he dialed Alastor. After several rings, his brother answered with a snarled, "What the bloody, fecking hell do you want?"

"I had Kuznetsov."

Alastor was silent for a second, then, "*Had?* Past tense?"

"Yeah."

"But have him no longer?"

Pulling the towel away, Mal stared at his blood where it flowered dark crimson on the off-white terry cloth. He pushed the towel back against the wound. "That'd be a yes."

"And you're calling me instead of haring off after him because…"

"I need you to come pick something up." His gaze flicked to the safe.

"Bloody hell." Alastor heaved a sigh.

He could hear the murmur of a woman's voice and the sounds of Alastor shifting on something that had springs. A couch? A bed? Shit.

"Bad timing?" Mal asked, fairly certain that the woman was his brother's mate, Naphré, and that the springs belonged to a bed.

"Incredibly," came Alastor's clipped reply. "Naphré and I just had a rather harrowing but successful adventure, the details of which will be of interest to you."

"Yeah? I'm having a bit of an adventure myself. The details of which will be of similar interest to you and Dae."

"But not on the phone."

"No."

"What exactly do you need me to do?" Alastor asked.

"That video Dagan got his hands on… You remember the blades?" Rhetorical question. They'd all watched that video enough times that they'd memorized every frame as they searched for clues.

"Black. I'm guessing obsidian volcanic glass," Alastor replied, his voice tight.

"Good guess," Mal stared at the black-bladed knife that was one of the two items in the safe. There had been a second knife in that video. But it wasn't here. And his earlier investigation of the other rooms hadn't revealed anywhere that Kuznetsov could have hidden it.

"You there, mate?" Alastor asked.

"Yeah. And so is one of the knives." His head jerked up as he heard sirens in the distance. No doubt the broken window had set off some alarms, or perhaps a neighbor or a passerby on the street below had called it in. The safe wasn't wired, so it hadn't triggered any alarms. He rattled off the condo's address and described the location of the safe. "You'll probably have to make your way through some cops. They'll be here to investigate a shattered window."

"Why don't you just bring it along yourself?"

Mal smiled darkly. "I'm going hunting, and I don't want to risk losing this in the scuffle."

"Hunting?" Alastor asked, his tone dusted with amusement.

"What?" Mal asked.

"Dae said something similar to me not too long ago."

"Yeah? What was he hunting?"

Alastor laughed. "Roxy Tam. And you?"

Choosing to ignore the question, Mal ended the call. He stared at the knife. Volcanic glass. The hilt was metal, intricately wrought with dragon scales and at the very bottom, a dragon's head. He was no expert on weaponry, but he knew enough to hazard a guess that the knife was old. And it was Japanese.

Mal took a deep breath. He'd recently had occasion to visit the Japanese goddess of death, Izanami, in her Underworld realm. He'd found himself liking her during the brief time he'd spent in her company. He'd liked her all the more when she'd set his brother Alastor, and his mate, Naphré, free.

He'd hate to name himself her enemy, for a whole boatload of reasons. So he didn't want that knife to have anything to do with her. Didn't want her involved in his brother Lokan's death.

But a Japanese knife used in the kill ceremony made that a strong possibility.

He took the second item from the safe. A cartouche, the insignia of pharaohs and kings—living gods. It was old gold. And it shouldn't be here because the name inscribed within the sacred oval was not Sutekh's, but Aset's.

"Fuck." Every time he turned around, the lineup of suspects got longer. Setnakhts. Xaphan and his concubines. Traitors from within Sutekh's own ranks. Izanami by dint of the obsidian knife, and now Aset's cartouche.

Kuznetsov, a Setnakht priest, shouldn't have either of these items in his possession. The fact that he did muddied the mix because the only way Mal could see one of Aset's Daughters working with Sutekh's priest was if she was a traitor.

Instead of finding answers, Mal's digging was only turning up more questions.

He locked the knife in the safe for Alastor to recover, but the cartouche he put in his pocket. Then, to prevent anyone else from trying to open the safe before Alastor got here, he crushed the external apparatus.

Alastor would retrieve the knife. He had the strength to rip the door of the safe clean off. Not too many other beings did. He'd get it analyzed using Topworld forensics and their own Underworld techs. They'd find its secrets, preferably sooner than later.

Mal crossed to the bed and snagged Kuznetsov's

robe, then he used Calliope's blood-drenched sword to slice the sleeves off. He wrapped the blade with the remainder of the cloth before creating a makeshift sling from the sleeves. Then he tied the sword she'd skewered him with across his back, much the way she'd worn it earlier.

He had a feeling that Ms. Kane would want her little toy back. While he hadn't yet decided *what* price he was going to demand for relinquishing it, two things he did know: it would be steep. And she was going to pay it.

He was definitely going to enjoy that.

CHAPTER SIX

I ally myself with the divine Aset.
—*The Egyptian Book of the Dead, Chapter 78*

THANKS TO THE SOUL reaper's blood, Calliope managed to land on her feet despite the four-story drop and the weight of Kuznetsov on her shoulder.

She rose and shot a quick look overhead. He hadn't followed. Yet. But it would be only a matter of moments, perhaps seconds, before he got free of her blade and came after her. He wouldn't let her get away that easy. He wouldn't let his prize slide through his fingers without a fight. Which meant she needed to get out of here, the quicker, the better.

She strode across the terrace and tried the balcony door. Locked. She almost kicked in the glass, but then she paused, aware of the reaper's life force cranking through her like a drug. She tightened her grip and yanked with all the force she could summon. The metal twisted and shrieked as the lock gave way and the glass slid open. She stepped through.

Standing in the darkened living room, she did a quick scan of her surroundings. She could clearly make out the sofa and love seat, the end tables, even the individual tassels on the cushions.

Sharper vision, hearing, increased strength, all because of a few drops of blood. Reaper blood.

A shiver chased up her spine.

She could still taste it on her tongue. Rich. Delicious.

She didn't want to think about it. Didn't want to acknowledge that even as she had been revolted by what she had chosen to do, she had reveled in the taste of him and the feeling of power that slid through her veins. Roxy had never mentioned it was like this.

Of course, disgusted by the thought of drinking a soul reaper's blood, Calliope had never asked for details. She realized now that her prejudices might have cost her. Information was power, and she'd denied herself some key knowledge. It was a mistake she'd take care not to repeat.

She kept moving, focusing on the benefits rather than the revulsion she felt for having drunk from him. It had been the surest path to success, and she was trained to succeed at all costs. She had no idea how long the enhancements would last, but she intended to use them to her greatest advantage while they did.

The dining room was dead ahead, then the breakfast bar, then the kitchen. A hall to the left likely led to bedrooms. A hall to the right probably to more of the same.

Thoughts spinning, she strove to weave a new plan

from the severed threads of the one she'd been forced to abandon by the reaper's unexpected appearance in Kuznetsov's bedroom.

As she moved, she unzipped the pocket at her hip and pulled out her cell. Her direct superior, Sarita, answered on the first ring.

"I have the item," Calliope said. "But delivery may be a problem." Her intent had been to have dinner with the High Reverend of the Setnakhts, ply him with drinks and questions, and if his answers didn't satisfy, hunt him in his home. He'd evaded and deflected all through dinner, so the hunt it had been.

"Was the patch not effective?" Sarita asked, the innocuous words in fact asking a different question entirely: Was Kuznetsov unconscious?

"It melts in water," Calliope replied. When she'd embraced the High Reverend before she'd left in the cab, she'd placed a patch on his skin that would leach a drug into his system to make him sleep.

But he'd gone into the shower and washed the tiny patch down the drain, so she'd been forced to subdue him by physical means. Her plan from that point had been to loop his arm around her shoulder, take the elevator down and walk him out the front door. If anyone asked, she'd say he was her inebriated date.

Of course, he wasn't supposed to be naked when she got there. And he wasn't supposed to be keeping company with a soul reaper. Both of which had thrown a bit of a monkey wrench into her plans.

"But the item is inert, for the moment," Calliope said.

"Do you require a pickup?"

"Unclear at this time." Turning her head, Calliope listened to the sound of approaching sirens. Unwelcome, but not unexpected, given that she'd broken a window in a high-security building. She'd have preferred to leave humans out of the mix. The police would be a complication.

"I will put a team on notice in the event they are required," Sarita said and ended the call.

Calliope zipped her phone back into her pocket and then froze as she heard a faint shush behind her. She spun, her body vibrating readiness. With one hand, she steadied Kuznetsov on her shoulder. With the other, she grabbed the blade from the sheath on her thigh. She'd noticed the reaper carried one there, as well. Only now, with her own blade in her hand, did she wonder why he hadn't used it on her.

Her hand was dead steady, her breathing slow and even as she scanned the shadows looking for threat. This was second nature to her. This was who she had become.

There was no one behind her, but the fine hairs at her nape were standing on end.

She usually knew when trouble was coming for her, and even who—or what—that trouble might be. Except she hadn't known the soul reaper would be there tonight. And other than an unpleasant feeling of premonition, she was coming up blank as she tried to see what would come next. She was getting a whole lot of gray static and not much else.

And the reaper's blood seemed to be making her a bit paranoid, her heightened senses reading threat into every sound and every shift in the breeze.

Plan. She needed one. Now.

In the span of a second she weighed possible options, seeing the scenarios as though watching them on a screen.

The sound of the sirens was louder now as they drew nearer.

She picked up her pace, and when she reached the foyer, her options clicked like a camera, snapshotting her plan: a lovely Bokhara carpet stretched over the travertine tile. One problem solved.

Working quickly, she moved the rug, flopped Kuznetsov on the underpad and rolled him snug as a bug, so he was cushioned and muffled. Then she rolled the rug on the outside. She hefted him onto her shoulder with only moderate effort, thanks to the soul reaper's generous donation of red cells, plasma and life force.

A stack of mail on the console table caught her eye as she passed. She grabbed the first letter, memorized the name and address, then tossed it back on top of the pile. She owed these people for a balcony door and a rug.

She moved to the front door, paused and reached deep inside herself, searching for calm. The soul reaper—she didn't want to give him the courtesy of using his name, not even in her thoughts—might well be out there, waiting for her. She closed her eyes, let her senses search for him and found nothing.

Which meant nothing. She already knew exactly how good he was at concealment.

Besides, whatever heightened abilities she had at the moment, she'd stolen from him. He was still stronger, faster and able to hide in plain sight. But she was out of time. She'd have to take the risk.

Unsettling. She was used to being in control, knowing the way any scenario would play out.

She was not fond of sliding by on the seat of her pants. Twice in two days was unbearable.

Tense, ready to bolt, she hauled the door open, knowing without a doubt that she was about to encounter *something*. But her ability to read upcoming events was crackling like static, pushed out of whack by the soul reaper's blood.

The murmur of male voices came from her left. She dropped the carpet and took a defensive crouch, knife in hand. At this moment, she truly regretted the loss of her sword and its longer reach.

Two men rounded the corner of the hallway that cut at right angles to this one. Humans, with a faint whiff of supernatural clinging to them. They were Topworld grunts, mortals who did jobs for supernaturals. Some did it purely for money, believing they were working for the mob. Some did it because they knew the score and hoped to earn a supernatural's favor, and with it, eternal life.

They had no idea what price they'd pay for that.

The man on the right was slower, lagging a half step behind the one on the left. The possible ways this scene might unfold played out in her mind. She calculated her options, analyzing her wisest course in a matter of seconds.

The rug lay at her heels.

They didn't so much as glance at it, just kept their eyes locked on her. And she kept hers locked on them.

"Hello," she greeted them.

They stopped dead and exchanged a look, clearly not expecting that. The one on the left had stopped first, which meant he'd be the one to move on her first.

She was already stepping aside as he lunged like a bull.

She spun, ramming her elbow into his solar plexus. Then she kicked back, nutting the guy on the right with her heel. They both doubled over, breath rushing out, knocking heads on the way down. She caught one by the throat and pressed hard on his carotid sinuses. The color drained from his face and his eyes rolled up as he closed his thick fingers around her wrists. Finally, he went out like a snuffed flame. She let go and he dropped with a meaty thud.

"I just killed your friend," she lied to the second guy as he lifted his head, wheezing from the pain of getting kicked in the scrotum. She grabbed his throat and pressed, taking care not to overdo it. "Tell me who you work for, and I won't kill you."

"Big Ralph," he croaked without even a hint of reluctance.

Calliope sighed. Loyalty was such a rare commodity.

Big Ralph was a Topworld grunt who ran prostitutes for Asmodeus, the Underworld demon of lust. Calliope had never met him, though his name had come up during conversations with Roxy a time or two. He was one of her sources.

"What did he send you to do?"

She tightened her hold. He clawed at her wrists, but he would have been no match for her at the best of times. He didn't have a hope in hell while she was amped on reaper blood.

"Is today your day to die?" she whispered.

His eyes widened and he made an effort to shake his head, though her grip on his throat constrained him. She eased up enough to let him talk.

"There's supposed to be a guy here who Big Ralph's boss wants to talk to."

"And you were generously going to play escort. Who's Big Ralph's boss?" she asked, not because she didn't know, but because she wanted to see if *he* did.

"Don't know. I swear it."

"Who's the guy he wants to see?"

"Kuznetsov."

Of course. It was just that kind of night. "You're on the wrong floor."

The guy brightened. "You know which floor he's on? We weren't sure."

"So you were what? Going door-to-door?"

The expression on his face said it all.

With a shake of her head, she pressed until he passed out. Then she dragged them both into the condo she'd just left and closed the door once more with a soft snick.

She checked her watch. The whole exchange had taken less than three minutes. But they were three precious minutes that she could ill afford to lose because she had no idea where the reaper was, or why he hadn't followed. That was making her uneasy. The fact that he hadn't come after her right away. The lack of a frontal assault heralded a sneak attack.

She hauled the rug with Kuznetsov's dead weight onto her shoulder once more and hit the button for the elevator. A glance told her it was stopped on the twenty-sixth floor.

Kuznetsov's floor.

Where she'd left the reaper pinned to the wall.

Her pulse ramped up as the car began its descent. She shifted to the side, knife in hand, held out of sight behind her thigh.

The doors slid open.

A birdlike, white-haired woman stood dead center of the enclosed space, blinking at her. Calliope kept the

knife exactly where it was and didn't jump to conclu-
sions based on the woman's appearance. Badass things
often came in innocuous packages.

And the reaper could be in there, hiding in plain sight.
She wouldn't see him unless he wanted her to.

Her gaze dipped to the floor. No blood trail. While
he might be able to hide himself, she doubted he'd be
able to make his blood disappear once it left his body.
So odds were that he hadn't hitched a ride with the tiny,
wrinkled virago who was glaring daggers at her.

"You can't come in here with that," the woman
snapped, stepping forward to bar her way and pointing
at the carpet. "You need to get the padding from the
moving room and hang it. You can't just use the elevator
for moving furniture whenever you feel like it." She hit
the close button and muttered, "Rules are rules," as the
doors slid shut.

Calliope let the car go then hit the button again, mentally ticking off seconds. The goons were going to wake
up and get their bearings. Worse, the reaper could show
up at any time. She mapped the exit sign on her left. The
stairs would be—

The doors opened. The second elevator was empty.
She checked for blood drops and, seeing none, stepped
inside, angling herself so the rug stretched corner to
corner in order to fit.

High-end building. High-end security.

Keeping her head bowed to obscure her features, she
cast a sidelong look at the far corner and, sure enough,

there was the camera. She could throw something, smash the lens. But that would only alert security to a problem. Better to forge on, act as if she had nothing to hide. She dipped her head and kept her face hidden by the massive roll of rug and man on her shoulder.

As the car descended floor by floor, she willed it not to stop, not to let anyone on. The fine hairs at her nape stood on end and unease buzzed through her like bees through a hive. The lower the elevator went, the stronger the sensation grew.

Five floors…four…three…

Finally, the doors slid open.

She tensed. Someone was out there, and it wasn't a low-level supernatural or Topworld grunt.

Her bet was on the soul reaper. It was a bet she'd prefer to lose.

The lobby appeared empty, except for the red-coated concierge behind his desk. Appearances could be deceiving.

She took a quick look but saw no traces of blood on the ground. How fast did a reaper heal? Fast enough that blood from his wound would no longer give him away?

Spinning, she took three steps toward the back of the building, aiming for the rear exit. The buzz turned brutal, as though a thousand fire ants crawled all over her, taking tiny little bites.

Plan C, then, which would be—she shot a glance

at the concierge who was halfway around his desk now—brazening it out.

She headed for the doors. Attention fixed, she didn't even glance at the concierge, though she picked up his movement in her peripheral vision.

He was scowling at the rug.

She walked faster, all her senses telling her the soul reaper was close. Too close.

The fact that she could sense him was bad. Very bad. She shouldn't be able to. Soul reapers were impossible to detect, unless they wanted to be.

Which left two possibilities. He could be *choosing* not to dampen himself, wanting her to recognize, and fear, his presence.

Or taking his blood had created a connection between them. That possibility was one of the main reasons the Asetian Guard had rules about drinking from supernaturals. Because the connection could run both ways. Which meant that the reaper would be able to track her no matter where she went.

Either way, she needed to move quickly.

"Hey," the concierge called just as she reached the glassed-in front of the lobby. The revolving door was a no-go; the rug wouldn't make it through.

"Hey, you," he called again, louder, closer. "You can't just bring that rug down like that."

The concierge was bearing down on her. The sirens outside were far too close now. The sensation that she was being stalked was crawling over her skin.

Her heart slammed against her ribs. Her senses hummed with the need to get Kuznetsov the hell out of here.

It had been a very long time since she had allowed emotion to shoehorn aside logic. This was not like her. Her responses were out of whack. She could almost believe that the reaper's blood was messing with her mind, like a bad drug.

In a strange way, that possibility decreased her agitation. It offered a logical explanation. She could work with that.

The glass door and freedom beckoned. She slammed her palm against the auto-open.

Almost there.

"Hey!" The concierge's hand closed on her wrist. She turned her head to the right, ready to hurt him if she had to.

Someone shouldered between them.

The weird, wired feeling that had set her skin prickling ramped up into overdrive.

"Hello, Calliope," the soul reaper said.

Instinctively, her hand dropped to the knife at her thigh, only to find the sheath empty.

Steel flashed as he flipped her knife in his hand so the blade tucked up against his forearm, out of sight of the human who was buzzing beside them like a gnat.

Wonderful. Now he had her sword and two of her knives.

She lifted her head and met his gaze.

His eyes were the pale gray of metal so cold it burned the skin.

And his lips peeled back in a smile that promised retribution and blood.

CHAPTER SEVEN

The blood which dropped from
them was captured...
—The Egyptian Book of the Dead, Chapter 18

"HAPPY TO SEE ME?" Mal asked, careful to keep his body angled so the human wouldn't see the bloodstain on his shirt or the knife tucked against his forearm. Most mortals tended to be disturbed by blood, and he'd prefer to get the hell out of here without further mayhem.

"Thrilled beyond measure." Calliope's gaze lingered for an instant on her sword, which hung down his back in its makeshift black silk sheath. He bet she wanted that back, but her expression gave nothing away. In fact, her features were completely serene, offering no clue as to her emotions.

He clamped his hand on her upper arm, enjoying the flare of anger that turned her eyes from cat green to darkest jade. He'd like to see her eyes change color while she was under him, or over him, or up against a wall, naked and wild.

And he had a feeling she *would* be wild, once he stripped away the heavy layers of her control.

He blinked as the thought hit him with a feeling of déjà vu. As though he'd had her under him or over him. But he'd remember those eyes if he'd seen them before…

Except, yeah, he kept thinking he had seen them before. Not crystal green. Not cool and reserved. Those eyes in a different face. Or maybe that face with different eyes.

"You brought that down without signing up for a move time." The concierge distracted Mal from his thoughts, poking his index finger into the rug in choppy bursts, like a woodpecker going at a tree. "I'm going to have to check the elevator for damage. And you're going to have to sign the appropriate paperwork now."

"How much damage could a rug do?" Mal asked, enjoying the secret irony. In Calliope Kane's hands, no doubt a great deal. But the concierge wouldn't know that.

Mal held out a C-note, folded between his second and third fingers, then blinked as he realized Calliope was mirroring his movement. His gaze slid down her catsuit-clad form, and he wondered where she was hiding her wallet. The only curves and bumps he saw were the ones that ought to be there.

Ah, there, a zippered pocket on her hip.

There was silence for a heartbeat.

"I guess not much damage." With a smirk, the guy took Mal's offering then plucked the bill from Calliope's fingers. He backed off a bit, his expression going from belligerent to almost friendly. "But she should have followed proper moving protocol."

"Absolutely. She should have followed protocol—"

"*She* is standing right here," Calliope said, her tone devoid of inflection.

"Sisters—" Mal shook his head and shot the concierge a *mano-e-mano* look "—gotta love the way they call you at all hours. To help with a rug." Turning to Calliope, he winked. "And it looks as though you don't even need me after all. You've already done the tough job. Got everything rolled up nice and tight."

He waited with anticipation for her to stiffen up like an overstarched collar. He liked the idea of getting under her skin.

She denied him that pleasure. She didn't even blink.

"She's your sister?" The concierge was the picture of confusion. "That's—" He grimaced. "I don't look at my sister like…" His voice trailed away as Calliope shot him a look that would shrivel a man's balls.

She shifted the rug on her shoulder.

"Must be heavy," Mal murmured, all solicitous concern. "Why don't you let me help y—"

"Touch it, and lose a finger," Calliope said, her tone low and flat.

The concierge laughed and nodded. "That's exactly how my sister talks to me."

"Sibling rivalry," Mal offered. But his gaze never left Calliope's face. He could almost hear the wheels turning in her brain as she planned and plotted and tried to figure an angle that would get her out of here without bringing him along. Fat chance. He'd underestimated her once tonight. He wasn't the sort to repeat his mistakes.

"My car's around the corner," he said. "You coming along for the ride, *sis,* or you want me to take it from here?"

He was certain she understood the warning. Either she chose to accompany him, or he'd go without her. Her choice. But the rug, and Kuznetsov, would stay with him.

"You can carry the front." Her tone was bland and even, her message clear. She wanted him in front of her where she could keep an eye on him.

"Nah." With a grin, he lifted the back end of the carpet. "I've got your back, *sis.*"

The very idea of having her behind him made him antsy. She'd stabbed him. Bitten him. Swallowed his blood. Impaled him and pinned him to the damned wall. He had no desire to find out what other fun and games she had in mind.

Even though he'd gained possession of three of her lethal weapons, he couldn't ignore the possibility that she might be hiding a fourth, though where she'd hide it in that skintight outfit, he had no clue.

"After you," he said.

The corner of her mouth tipped up in the faintest hint

of a smile. One that promised retribution and more of his blood.

And damn if the sight of it didn't make him want to grin in return. This girl was danger wrapped in one hell of a pretty package. He had every intention of hanging on for the ride.

Without a word, she turned, hit the automatic open button and walked through the door. She was one cool player.

"Cat got your tongue?" he murmured once they were outside.

"I prefer to converse with higher life forms."

He almost let that pass, almost made himself behave. But it was just too tempting. "Then maybe we should put your tongue to other uses."

She stopped dead, glanced back at him over her shoulder, pinning him in a universe of crystal-cold green.

"Does everything always come so easy to you?"

He didn't even pretend to misunderstand.

"Always." The not-quite-a-lie slid from his lips like honey. In his early years, he'd known more than a fair share of abuse, hardship, despair. But that was a long time ago, and the more recent past had been far kinder. Which was why he preferred to dwell in the present.

He sent her a lecherous grin, letting his eyes tell the story his mind was conjuring. Imagination was a wonderful thing.

"Silly. Little. Boy," she said, dismissing him as she turned and started walking once more.

There was no point taking offense or protesting the facts. Truth was, she reduced him to, if not quite a silly little boy, definitely a randy teenager.

He watched her hips sway in front of him and grinned, looking forward to the challenge of showing her that he was no boy. He was going to have Calliope Kane; that was a given. Have her under him, over him, beside him. He was going to have her every way he could. The only question was, how fast he would get her there?

Not too fast. Anticipation…the chase…those things were usually denied him. He meant to savor them now that they were being served up on a lovely, dark-haired, ivory-skinned, green-eyed platter. With legs that wouldn't quit and a nice, perky ass that was so grabbable his hand was itching to do exactly that.

He stared at that ass, and again that odd sense of déjà vu hit him.

They were maybe ten feet clear of the door when her head snapped up and she glanced through the high, glass front into the lobby. He followed her gaze in time to see…nothing.

A few seconds later, two men staggered out of the elevator. He didn't recognize them, but he knew their type, could sense the faint energy signature they threw off like a bad smell. Topworld grunts.

The way Calliope had just acted, she'd known they were coming before they arrived, which prompted him to ask, "Yours?"

"No. They work for Big Ralph."

"Who works for…"

She ignored him.

He figured they were here for the same reason he was. Same reason Calliope was. Whatever Underworlder they worked for wanted a piece of Kuznetsov. The man was mighty popular.

Glancing back through the window, he noticed that both men looked a little worse for wear, which made him think they'd already tangled with Calliope Kane at some point this evening. He almost felt sorry for them.

Since she wasn't into answering that question, he asked another. "Can you usually jump four stories?"

She kept walking without a word.

"I'm guessing you can. I'm guessing the terrace was your backup plan all along. Before you knew I was there. Before you fed from me." He paused. "You can contribute to the conversation any time, darlin'."

She skirted a puddle on the sidewalk, her pace set slow and easy so as not to attract attention. As though walking down the street with a rolled-up carpet sometime near midnight was the most normal thing in the world.

But she didn't say a word.

"I'll just keep talking, then," he said. "Those first-date silences are so…uncomfortable."

Was that a slight tension creeping into her shoulders? A stiffening of her spine?

Flashing lights appeared at the far end of the street. He shook his head. There were Topworld grunts in the lobby, mortal cops on the street, and with the way this night was shaping up, Calliope Kane had reinforcements on the way. What should have been a straightforward hit-and-grab was turning into one big clusterfuck.

And he'd be a liar if he tried to pretend he wasn't enjoying the chaos.

"You don't strike me as the type to leave anything to chance," he continued as the police car sped past. "I'd say you're a planner. So I doubt that it was just a lucky break that the terrace happened to be there, four stories below the penthouse. You planned that escape route well in advance, and you knew exactly how far you'd be falling if circumstances demanded you use it."

Another set of flashing lights appeared at the far end of the street.

"In my mind," he continued, "that means a three- or four-story leap is something you can usually handle, even when you're not hyped on my blood."

She stopped dead and turned her head toward him, her expression unreadable.

"Your mouth is extremely attractive—" she said, her tone devoid of inflection "—when it's shut."

He laughed. He couldn't help it. She turned and resumed walking, but her reaction told him he'd hit the nail on the head as he'd speculated about the scope of her power.

Nice to know. He stored the information for future reference. Next time he ran into her, he'd make sure they were at least five stories up, and he'd make sure she didn't snack on him.

He preferred to have the upper hand.

The cop car slowed. Made sense. They were jogging through the night with a rug.

"Turn here," he ordered, and Calliope surprised him by following his instructions, ducking into a shadowed niche as the police cruiser crawled past.

"Can you simply make us disappear?" No sarcasm in her tone. She meant that as a sincere question. Her voice was modulated, beautiful. Like a song.

Damn, her voice did things to him.

"No."

The car moved along. She started walking again. He glanced to the left and watched her reflection in a glass-fronted building. The way she moved was a thing of beauty, all grace and sinew. And legs and boobs and ass.

And icy-cold control.

How long would that last if he started at the bottom and licked his way to the top?

He wanted to make her shatter.

On some level, he knew that his fascination made no sense. He never lacked for female companionship. Each one was beautiful. Each one was special. For a night. Then, the next one was special. That was just the way he rolled. He rarely encountered a woman who said "no," and when he did, he simply turned to the one beside her who invariably said "yes."

But something about Calliope Kane was extraordinary. What?

Damned if he knew. But he meant to figure it out.

"Why not?" she asked, and it took him a second to remember what they'd been talking about. If one-word answers could be considered a conversation.

"Thought you preferred my mouth shut…"

"I'll make an exception for a coherent and concise explanation."

"I'll trade an answer for an answer. Take a look at this."

She paused and glanced back at him over her shoulder.

He pulled the gold cartouche from his pocket and turned it so it caught the light of the streetlamp. But he kept his gaze locked on her face.

She was good. He'd give her that. Her eyes didn't widen. She didn't gasp. But while she might consciously control any overt reaction, she couldn't stop the color from draining from her cheeks.

"Belong to anyone you know?" he asked.

"No."

Reaching behind his neck, he undid his chain, slid the cartouche on, then refastened the clasp. She watched his every move, and he was careful to keep one arm looped around his end of the rug where it rested on his shoulder. He didn't want to offer her even the whisper of an opportunity to take off on him.

"See—" he scrubbed his palm along his jaw "—I'm a very good liar. I'm even better at spotting other liars."

She fixed him with a frigid look. "You asked. I answered. Your turn. Can you make us disappear?"

She *had* answered. In fact, she'd told him far more than she imagined. She definitely knew whom the cartouche belonged to, and the fact that he had it in his possession troubled her.

"Fine. I don't *disappear.* I merely prevent others from seeing me." Three centuries back, when he'd first learned the trick, Mal had accepted it as magic. Now, he gave the credit to science. "The key is molecular vibrations. I can bend the bonds between atoms, rock them into different orientations. That alters the visible spectrum that reaches the viewer's eye."

It was as simple, and as complicated, as that.

When she made no comment, he continued. "I can bend the atomic bonds in my own molecules, but not yours. Or the rug's. Or the High Reverend's, and if the cops spot you walking down the street with the invisible man holding up the opposite end of this carpet, it'll have the effect of drawing rather than deflecting attention."

"Agreed."

Wasn't she chatty? Her tranquility made him itchy. She had to be pissed as all hell that he'd foiled her clean getaway, but there wasn't a thing in her expression or tone to indicate that.

"I didn't see your clothes," she said.

"Beg pardon?"

"When you were bending your molecules in Kuznetsov's apartment, I didn't see you, or your clothes."

"I can extend the ability a short radius around my body."

She glanced to the left, then the right. "We're exposed here. Can you summon a portal?"

"Not the best moment for a portal." He was little surprised that she knew about them. Soul reapers could grab the energy that surged between Topworld and the Underworld and momentarily combine them to create a fracture between the realms, an icy portal that would allow them to travel directly to a place of their choosing. The ability wasn't exactly common—or common knowledge—among other supernaturals.

Then he recalled that Gahiji had disgorged in her living room through a portal, chasing after Roxy Tam. That explained how Calliope was aware of them. "Unless I want the whole world to know that I can open a hole between dimensions, I need privacy—"

"We need to move," she ordered sharply and led him into a narrow, dark alley between buildings as a third cop car sped past, proving his point about privacy. They both held still, blending with the shadows as the reflection of red lights danced along the wall.

He expected her to press for more information. When she didn't, he asked, "You're not curious?"

Her only answer was a one-shouldered shrug.

"You always this placid?"

She glanced back, eyes green and cool. "As a lake on a summer's day."

He thought about that for a second. "One filled with piranhas."

Her lips curved in a cold, hard smile. "Watch out. Piranhas have a wicked bite."

"Bite me any time, pretty girl."

She made a dismissive gesture. "I already did."

"Yeah. You did." He wasn't into pain, not giving it or getting it, but for some bizarre, twisted reason, the memory of her mouth on his forearm pulling his blood from his vein turned him on.

They kept moving, Kuznetsov and the rug that wrapped him joining them in a silent, fraught alliance.

Despite having been spotted with the rug, there was no hue and cry behind them. Which suited Mal just fine tonight, though usually he would have enjoyed a bit of a chase. But his forearm was stinging like a bitch. His chest felt as though someone had hammered a stake through it. Or a sword. And his shirt was damp and sticky with blood.

And speaking of blood, what hadn't dripped, or been sucked, out of him was currently pooling in his groin as he watched Calliope Kane's pretty, perky ass.

"Wait," he ordered, figuring they were far enough from the building now that he could pause for a quick call.

She kept walking.

He tightened his grip on the rug and yanked back hard enough to fortify his message. She stopped but didn't look back at him, just stood, staring straight ahead.

It was like a tug-of-war, each of them barking orders, pulling, tugging, vying for supremacy. He'd win, but it might be fun to let her think she had, just for a while.

The thought of how that would play out in bed didn't help the direction of his blood flow.

He hauled out his cell, vaguely uneasy because she had given in too easily. He'd expected her to argue, to ignore his directive, maybe even to go for him, tooth and nail. He expected her to try to get the rug and Kuznetsov and hightail it for safety.

A reasonable expectation, given the damage she'd already managed to inflict on his person with exactly that objective in mind.

But she just stood there, not even asking why he'd wanted to stop. He thought that if he took his eyes off her even for a second, she'd pull a hidden weapon from—his gaze raked her from crown to toes—*somewhere* and gut him.

She turned to face him and cocked a brow. Caution made him keep his eyes on her, but his gaze dipped to her breasts as he hit speed dial. He could see the outline of her taut nipples. He stared for a second then forced himself to look away.

Damn, there was something about her that had him thinking with the wrong head. But that wasn't the worst of it. There was something about her that made him curious. He wanted to take her apart like a clock, figure out her inner workings. Funny…his curiosity about what made things tick didn't usually extend to women.

"I need cleanup," he said when Kai Warin, Sutekh's new second-in-command, answered. Kai had been fast-tracked up the ranks when Gahiji, Sutekh's former second-in-command, had suffered an unfortunate incident that left his head separated from his body. The unfortunate part being that Mal hadn't been the one to do the separating.

Mal and his brothers had been surprised when they heard the news of Kai's promotion. He wasn't a choice they might have expected Sutekh to make; he wasn't at all like Gahiji. But then, given Gahiji's betrayal, maybe that was the point.

Now, he gave Kai the address of Kuznetsov's building and a brief rundown of events.

"I sent Alastor to get a package," he said with a glance at Calliope, unwilling to offer more than that for her to overhear. "But I need you to deal with the concierge and any witnesses, direct or indirect—"

Calliope interrupted him. "Will he hurt them?"

"What? Hold on, Kai… Hurt them? No. It's a benign process that simply makes them forget the significance of having seen us. They'll remember it as a dream, or something they imagined. It's like—" he spread his hands "—a superstrong form of hypnosis."

She gave a short nod, then said, "There was a witness

in the elevator. An older woman. Tiny. White haired. She came from Kuznetsov's floor."

Mal relayed the information then continued. "Wipe the security tapes. At this point, you might even need to deal with the cops. It would be best if my companion and I were forgotten."

He left out any detailed description of his companion, or any mention of the fact that she'd skewered him like a kabob. That information was for his private rumination. And his personal payback. Only, the sort of skewering he meant to do in return had a whole different definition.

Ending the call, he looked up to find Calliope watching him, her expression far too serene for his comfort. He didn't trust her composure. She ought to be pissed that he'd crashed her party, because he was absolutely positive she'd wanted Kuznetsov to herself. Just as he did. Yet she was going along with him. For now. He had no doubt it was a temporary acquiescence.

"Which way?" she asked. And when he didn't answer, she clarified, "To your car. I don't know where you're parked."

Tight-lipped, she smiled. It didn't reach her eyes.

He smiled back, certain he looked every bit as predatory as she did.

She was planning something, and if he wasn't on his toes, whatever plot she hatched just might succeed. He'd already underestimated her more than once this evening. He wouldn't do it again.

"All the way to the end of this alley, then take a right at the corner, then a right at the lights. I'm parked in the public lot on the north side of the street."

She waited as he put away his phone and shifted the rug on his shoulder.

"Ready, now?" she asked.

Again, he had the sensation that she was far too amiable. Which sent his alarm bells clanging.

He tipped his head to the side. "You're in a pleasant mood."

"I am always in a pleasant mood."

"See—" he wagged his index finger "—that's the thing. I think your mood's pleasant on the surface, but scratch a little deeper…? I think I might find a bit of venom."

"You would not need to scratch very deep. And you would find far more than a bit." Her face was serene, her posture relaxed. She tapped her palm against the rug. "Let's go. He won't stay asleep indefinitely. And, for the moment, I'd rather deal with him unconscious than awake."

Without waiting for a reply, she set off. The rug was maybe eight feet long, which put Mal in a perfect position to follow. And admire. Damn. The view from back here was perfection.

They took a right at the corner, then another. His chest still ached where she'd skewered him. His forearm still stung. He focused on both, letting the pain ground him. It reminded him that however luscious she looked, Calliope Kane was his enemy.

A dangerous, adept enemy who would try to slice him to shreds if he gave her half a chance.

He had no liking for pain, but the adrenaline high he got from sparring with her was almost worth it.

She stopped dead when they hit the parking lot. There was a rusty blue van parked in the far corner and a white convertible Boxster Spyder under the lamppost. The lot was otherwise empty.

"Tell me the van is yours."

"The van is mine."

She dropped her end of the carpet and turned to face him. He peeked in his end, saw feet and winced. Looked like she'd just dropped the good Reverend on his head. He almost felt sorry for the guy. Almost.

"*Now* tell me the van is yours," she said, a trace of steel in her tone, "and say it in a way that makes me believe you."

"I never was very good at lying," he admitted.

"You said you were a very good liar. You said you were good at spotting other liars."

He lifted his brows. "Guess I must have been lying."

She shot a glance at the Porsche, then looked at the carpet. "It won't fit." Before he could vocalize his agreement, she hunkered down, grabbed the edge of the roll and gave a hard tug. The underpad and rug spun out until they lay flat, leaving Pyotr Kuznetsov naked under the star-flecked sky.

"If I fold him, will he fit in the trunk?" she asked.

"Fold him?" He laughed. She didn't. She was serious. He shrugged. "Doubt it. But you can try."

CHAPTER EIGHT

As for eternity, it means daytime;
As for everlasting, it means night.
—The Egyptian Book of the Dead, Chapter 17

The Underworld, the Territory of Sutekh

DJESERIT BAST FOLLOWED the female servant along the sandstone gallery. Below them a long line of people snaked through the courtyard and beyond. They were silent and still, and Djeserit thought that the sight of them was important, but she couldn't seem to recall why.

She pressed her thumb and forefinger against her closed lids, the pain behind her eyes so sharp and strong it made her stomach roll. She was dangerously close to throwing up.

"Wait," she said.

The servant stopped but did not look back.

Glancing around, Djeserit searched for somewhere to sit, but there was no chair or bench in sight. She swallowed against the bile that crawled up the back of her throat and the panic that surged in a sudden powerful wave.

She had no idea where she was or why she was here. Wispy memories danced beyond her reach, without shape or form. Had she been in an accident? Had she been injured? She—

A slow, deep breath allowed her to master her fear enough that she could think. She was a High Reverend of the Temple of Setnakht, worshipper of Sutekh. She was a leader, a woman of strength and power. She knew her convictions. And her enemy: her fellow High Priest, Pyotr Kuznetsov.

These bits of information, flickering in her thoughts like strobe lights, gave her comfort. And confidence.

She had the feeling that she was here—wherever here was—on Setnakht business. What business? As she tried to recall, an obsidian wall shot up in her mind, blocking her way. The pain came back stronger than before. Dizziness overcame her and she struggled to remain standing. The servant shuffled back toward her, head bowed, and offered her arm for support.

Ashamed of her weakness, Djeserit took it, because falling flat on her face on the cold, stone floor was even worse.

She wished she could see the girl's face. Her eyes. But the woman kept her chin tucked and never looked up or said a word.

Leaning heavily on the servant, Djeserit walked on. What seemed an eternity, but was likely only moments later, they reached a pair of double doors. The woman stepped forward and pushed them open then withdrew to one side without lifting her head.

From this, Djeserit understood that she was to enter.

The room was cavernous, with a high ceiling and two sets of columns running down the center. Brightly colored scenes were painted on them, but she was not interested enough to look carefully at the depictions.

Urgency burned in her belly, and cold fear. She could explain neither.

She glanced back at the servant, who had silently entered the room and drawn the doors shut. But her head remained bowed, her chin tucked down to her chest, and she only made a small shooing motion for Djeserit to move along.

There seemed little choice.

Where to go?

At the far end of the room was a small group of chairs, one of them raised on a dais like a throne. For lack of instruction, she headed in that direction then paused as a noise sounded behind her. She spun to see her escort drop a heavy wooden bar across the doors. Wariness slithered through her, and the panic that had threatened her earlier came back full force.

She turned back toward the dais and saw a man sitting on the throne. Graying hair. Weathered skin. He looked familiar, someone she had seen before. He was…

Abasi Abubakar.

She had never met him, but she had seen his picture every day at the Temple of Setnakht. He had been the High Reverend years ago, before her time. He had murdered six young women in a locked room, painted the walls with blood and locked himself in with their rotting corpses.

Until he died.

As she stared at him, a sharp pain twisted in her breast. Her breath came in short gasps. He was dead.

Which meant she was—

"Come," he said and extended one hand toward her.

She shuffled forward, her feet sliding along though she didn't consciously will them to move. And then memories flew at her like angry wasps. She had been in her office. She had turned and seen a man in the shadows. He had asked her questions, and she had answered. But he had wanted more. Information that she did not have.

Wrapping her arms across her belly, she tried to still her feet. But they kept moving. Against her will.

She remembered then that the man had reached for her, his hand shooting forward from the shadows. She had felt pain, horrific, indescribable pain, and when she had looked down she had seen the man's hand buried in her chest and her blood dripping to the ground.

A soul reaper had come for her.

Her gaze jerked down. Her clothing was not blood-stained. She lifted her hand to her chest. There was no wound there.

"Sit," Abasi Abubakar ordered, his voice soft.

Panting with fear and horror, she moved to the chair directly before him and sat.

He rose and went to a table that held an ornate Middle-Eastern teapot and small glass cups.

"You are pale," he said and then poured tea in a glass. He added cubes of sugar then carried the glass to her and stood over her, holding the steaming cup. "Drink."

She took the glass and sipped, her hand shaking so badly that liquid sloshed over the sides, burning her fingers. The sensation sent relief cascading through her. She could not be dead if she felt pain. Yes. That was surely true.

"Do you know why you are here?" Abasi asked, resuming his seat on his gold-inlaid throne.

No. Yes. She had done terrible things. Killed innocents. And participated in the murder of… Someone important. She could not recall, and as she pushed and strove for answers, terrific pain slammed through her skull. It was as if every time she drew too close to remembering some forbidden truth, a wall stopped her and no matter how hard she tried, she could not get around it.

"You participated in the murder of a soul reaper," he said, his voice cold now, his words clipped. "Do you remember now?"

The pain in her head intensified.

"No," she whispered, confused and appalled by the very thought. She was Sutekh's worshipper. She would not kill one of his minions.

"My son," he corrected softly, and before her horrified gaze Abasi Abubakar's features melted away, to be replaced by a young and handsome man. Fair-haired. Familiar. She had seen that face. Where?

On the dead soul reaper.

"No," she whispered again, the word broken and hoarse.

Yes. She remembered flashes. Blood. Knives. A black bowl.

The glass fell from her hand, shattering into a million shards on the stone floor. Because she *did* remember. She and Kuznetsov had made a pact. They had been there when the soul reaper was killed. She had held the bowl that caught his blood. But they were not the killers. It was—

With a cry, she grabbed her head, the memory bursting into such pain that she let loose a wild howl that went on and on. She fell to the floor and rolled from side to side, whimpering.

She saw the faces of young girls. Daughters of Aset. She had been part of their deaths. She and Kuznetsov.

"What do you remember?" His voice was gentle, luring her to trust, to tell all.

She stared at the being before her, his features

changing again and again, melting between forms with incredible speed. And she knew he was her master.

"Sutekh," she whispered and then rolled until she was on her knees, her forehead to the floor.

"Tell me," he ordered, his tone almost kind.

"For you," she gasped. "To bring you back. To let you walk in the sun."

"How?"

"The prophecy. The blood of Aset. The blood of Sutekh. And the God will pass the Twelve Gates and walk the Earth once more." She lay on the cold stone floor and sobbed as he stood over her. She wanted to touch him. To reach out and lay the tips of her fingers against his sandaled feet.

She dared not.

"A mortal could never kill a soul reaper. You had help. Underworld allies. Tell me," he coaxed, so gently. "Surely you remember."

She wanted to. She wanted to tell him everything. But she could find nothing of value in her thoughts. She babbled Kuznetsov's name and the names of the Marin brothers, mortals who had been there that night. But they were dead. Killed. Who else?

"A child," she whispered. "A little girl was there. She left before anything began."

"The child is not important to you. Tell me who killed the soul reaper." There was something commanding in his tone and something so frightening it iced her blood.

As she reached deep inside her mind for that memory, she came against that smooth, obsidian wall, and the pain exploded like an overripe tomato slammed by an angry fist.

A scream tore free, and another.

"Nothing coming to you?" Sutekh asked softly. "Nothing at all?"

The pain was so terrible she could not even form a reply. How long she lay there, sobbing and suffering, she could not say.

She only knew that suddenly, the pain was gone. She could breathe. She could think.

Pushing up on all fours, she caught her breath.

"Leave us," Sutekh ordered.

Djeserit turned her head and saw the servant, bowed at the waist. The woman straightened, and Djeserit gasped. The servant's ears had been removed, her eyes and lips sewn shut.

"She is still able to perform her duties quite nicely," Sutekh said and then slanted a glance toward Djeserit, who huddled on the floor. "Perhaps you would serve me in a similar manner. Is that not your wish, Djeserit Bast? To serve your master?"

In horror, Djeserit scuttled back on all fours. Her every sense became hyperaware. She smelled lotus blossoms and heard the burble of a brook. She felt the stone, cold under her hands.

Sutekh came toward her and hunkered down before

her. Now, he wore the face and form of a young Pharaoh with eyes dark as coal, flat and soulless.

"You are dead, Djeserit Bast. Your mortal remains already bloat and rot."

She made a desperate sound.

"And you claim to remember nothing of the night my son was killed, save for the names and faces of worthless mortals."

Not merely a claim, she wanted to scream. *The truth. Only the truth. I remember nothing more.* But she could not speak; she could only sob.

"I will keep you here, with me," Sutekh said, gentle, firm, and despite all she had seen and knew, she took comfort from his voice. "Right here. Not in a distant place, but close to me, as close as can be. Do you want that, Djeserit?"

So kind. After what she had done, he offered her this.

"Yes. I beg of you. Yes."

And only when his jaws unhinged and she felt a terrible unraveling did she understand. She looked down and saw a part of herself separating from the rest. It was dark and slick and looked like an overfed slug. Her darksoul.

Her head jerked up. The gaping maw before her was dank and deep, and it smelled of death and rot and putrefaction.

She felt herself coming undone, tearing apart at the

seams. The pain was indescribable, agony that went on and on.

With a cry, she tried to tear herself away. But it was too late.

CALLIOPE APPEARED TO TAKE some mental measurements of the Porsche's trunk, then she made a sharp motion that negated that option.

"Unlock the door," she prompted.

Mal hit the automatic lock, watching her to see what she'd do next. Not surprisingly, she opened the passenger door, hefted Kuznetsov, dragged him over and shoved him in.

"You might have helped." She glanced around, then, with a moue of distaste, dusted her palms against her thighs as though wiping away something unpleasant.

"Looked like you had everything under control."

Turning back toward him, she rested one hand on the open passenger door.

He took in the pretty picture she made with the Porsche stretched out behind her, and he noted the details. Two seats, one of them occupied by the naked Kuznetsov, the other the driver's seat. She meant to escape him, leave him behind. How did she imagine she'd accomplish that? He wasn't about to smilingly turn over his keys. "Where're you planning to sit, darlin'? On his lap?"

She cocked a brow. "The very thought is repulsive."

"On my lap, then?" He liked that idea. Her sitting on him while he drove. Now that would be interesting. More interesting if neither of them were clothed and he kicked the engine into overdrive. Sex at 200 mph. Nice.

"That option is no less revolting. Possibly more so." She meant every word.

Why? Yeah, she was a Daughter of Aset—okay, actually a member of the Asetian Guard, probably fairly high in the ranks if he had to guess—and he was Sutekh's son, which meant they had oceans of hate between their kinds. But that hadn't stopped him or his chosen bedmates from having a little fun in the past, a sort of temporary cease-fire that all parties enjoyed.

Not that he'd ever romped with a member of the Asetian Guard—if he thought about it now, he realized that he hadn't. But he'd had more than his share of Xaphan's concubines, several of Asmodeus's girls, members of Osiris's household, and…yeah…pretty much an endless list of those who would stand against him in a fight.

But the way he saw it, when they weren't making war, why not make love? Or, at least, fuck. His bed—or any one of theirs—worked well as a neutral zone.

So what was it with Calliope Kane and the ramrod welded to her spine?

He prowled closer, stalking her, taking his time with each step, waiting to see if she would step back as he moved toward her. Not Calliope. She held her ground, her eyes on his, her features composed.

"You must spend hours practicing that look," he murmured.

They were a foot apart now. He reached out, closed his hand on the open car door and slowly pushed it shut. Which brought him closer still, his body flush with hers, mere inches between them.

Something stirred in her expression in the fleeting, unguarded instant before she slammed it down and corralled it. Attraction. He'd seen it. And something else. Rage. Hate. Utter and complete revulsion.

Damn.

She was attracted to him and didn't want to be.

"You know, I find the thought of the Reverend's naked ass on my brand-new, pristine leather pretty repulsive," he said, his gaze dropping to her mouth. Pretty pink lips, full and lush, just begging to be kissed. He leaned a little closer. "You've killed—or at the least, forever tainted—my driving enjoyment of this vehicle."

That earned him a dismissive snort and a flat-toned suggestion. "Then buy a new car, soul reaper." Her gaze dipped to his mouth, and he felt a momentary thrill of success before her next words squelched it. "And if you move even a millimeter closer, I will bite you. Not merely hard enough to draw blood. Hard enough to tear a chunk of flesh from your face."

The words were at odds with the musical sound of her voice, like water flowing over smooth rocks. For a second, he didn't register her meaning, and when he did, he blinked, withdrew and looked into those gorgeous cat-green eyes. Cold as a glacier lake.

Like a bolt from the sky, the realization hit him that while he was sparring—flirting, really—she wasn't. She was dead serious.

He was playing the game of approach and retreat, two steps forward, one step back.

But he was playing it alone. She genuinely despised him to the marrow of her bones.

He was mystified and more than a little offended. He'd been scathingly turned down by two women in two nights. He didn't know quite what to make of that. He almost lifted his arm to take a sniff, just in case.

"I'm the injured party here. It isn't as though I stabbed and fed from you," he pointed out, sounding perfectly reasonable. When she offered no reply, he continued. "These one-way conversations are becoming tedious."

"Then stop talking." She looked away, her gaze slowly sweeping the parking lot. Perimeter check.

"Because my mouth is more attractive when it's shut?"

She met his gaze and there was no hint of teasing in her eyes. "Precisely."

He blinked. His charm invariably worked at breaking down barriers, but in this case, it seemed to be building them higher. He wasn't accustomed to that.

Which only made him more interested.

What would it take to get past her defenses? He

suspected that was a riddle he'd have no easy time solving.

Again, his gaze paused on her mouth. A taste. One taste. For the low, low price of a little more of his blood and a chunk of his flesh.

"It might be worth it," he murmured.

Her gaze snapped back to his. Tension hummed between them.

One dark brow lifted a fraction of an inch. Her pupils dilated. Her posture stiffened.

He leaned closer and brushed his lips over hers. It was the most chaste—and the briefest—kiss he'd ever had. Barely a kiss at all. But he felt it zing through him like an electric charge.

With a gasp, she pulled back at the same instant he did, the two of them recoiling like magnets of the same charge.

For a split second, he thought he read many things in her eyes. Anger. Confusion. Perhaps a little bit of attraction.

Her expression locked down, her lips parted, and he thought she actually *might* bite him.

Or kiss him back.

Hard to tell.

CHAPTER NINE

He shall emerge from every fire,
Nothing evil shall encircle him.
A matter a million times true.
— *The Egyptian Book of the Dead, Chapter 18*

THE AIR AROUND THEM began to hum, sparking like a live wire in the rain. Mal could feel the energy on his skin and deeper, in his cells. As though he'd cranked a full case of Red Bull and it'd hit all at once. He knew that energy vibe, and he knew it meant they had mere minutes before unwelcome company came calling.

Calliope stiffened and lifted her head.

"You feel it?" he asked.

"I do."

"You know what it is?"

"A threat."

Right.

Flattening both palms against his chest, she shoved him away. Again, the sensation that he'd been through these motions before, that she'd had her hands on his chest—

"My sword?" She dipped her chin toward the black silk sheath he'd fashioned.

He raised his brows. "I think it's safer if I say no."

"My knives, then?" She held out her hand, palm up.

He laughed. "Don't think so, darlin'. I'd much rather have them hanging from my belt than embedded in my gut."

"You would leave me to face my adversaries without a weapon." Her tone implied that she expected no different of him.

"Given that you clearly view *me* as that adversary, and your weapon is likely to end up somewhere I won't enjoy...that would be a yes." He leaned close enough that he could breathe in the scent of her skin. The faintest hint of vanilla. It made his mouth water, luring him to take a taste.

He dipped his head just a little, breathing in. Damn, she smelled good.

"Just stay behind me, pretty girl," he murmured. "I'll keep you safe."

"I haven't relied on someone else to keep me safe since I was a child." The words dripped ice.

And that pretty much used up any opportunity for conversation because the smell of brimstone carried on the wind, confirming his suspicion about the identity of the new arrivals. The air crackled, electric and wild.

"The guy you mentioned earlier. Big Ralph. He have any connection to Xaphan?" Mal asked. Because brimstone meant they were about to face off with the keeper of the lakes of fire. Or his minions.

"I have no knowledge of any such connection. Big Ralph is Asmodeus's man." She shrugged. "But it's not outside the realm of possibility that he's done work for Xaphan."

He waited a beat for her to ask why he'd asked. She didn't. Which annoyed him. Why didn't she act like most other females he knew? Chat. Ask questions. Demand answers.

With most females, he felt as if he was in the comfort zone, as though he knew what to expect and how to play them.

With Calliope Kane, he felt as though he didn't.

"I ask because we're about to have company."

"About to?" Her tone was so dry that he half expected her to spit sand. Her gaze shifted to a point over his shoulder. "I'd say they're already here."

"Hello, Mal," another voice purred.

A voice he recognized. With a sigh, Mal turned. The creature before him was female. She had been born human but was no longer. Now she was a fire genie, one of Xaphan's concubines.

Nerita was incredible, in her own terrifying and lethal way. And she had once been his lover. With *once* being the key concept. He'd come away from that encounter scorched in the most literal sense. It had taken him two days to fully heal from his burns. And having been with a fire genie before, he knew they could dampen their flame if they wished. Which meant Nerita had turned him into barbecued roast on purpose. Not his thing…so he hadn't gone back for a repeat. Unfortunately, she was one of the few females he'd hooked up with who hadn't been willing to accept the fact that it was a one-time event.

"Nerita," he greeted her and offered one of his slow, lazy smiles. He sensed Calliope moving closer to him, almost touching his back. Maybe she'd decided to take his advice to stay behind him, but somehow, he couldn't make himself believe that. Great. That meant he had to watch his back as carefully as he was watching his front.

Nerita wasn't smiling; in fact, she looked downright pissed. An annoyed former lover was never a good thing.

She strode forward, her body sleekly muscled, a predator's form. Her skin was a deep burgundy red, smooth and supple as the most expensive leather. Her feet were bare, and her toes and fingers sprouted long, black, lethal talons.

Behind her was a cadre of fire genies, all of them fairly humming with anticipation. They were spoiling for a fight.

"What can I do for you lovely ladies?" Mal asked.

"We want Kuznetsov. Turn him over, and we leave."

"What makes you think we have Kuznetsov?"

Nerita waved a hand toward the Porsche. "He's sitting naked in the passenger seat."

There was that.

Nerita strode closer, hips swaying. Her gaze flicked beyond him for an instant then returned to his face. Which told Mal that she'd assessed Calliope and determined that he was the greater threat.

He felt Calliope's hands on both sides of his waist, then lower, along the curves of his hip bones, her fingers sliding forward. Give the lady top marks for effort. She was making a play for her knives. With a grin tugging at his lips, he closed his fingers on her wrist, stopping her quest. Her other hand dipped forward, her fingers snagging on his pocket. He caught that wrist as well and squeezed tight enough to offer a warning, but not tight enough to hurt.

Then he felt her breath against the back of his neck as she spoke in a whisper. "Silly. Little. Boy."

He was about to correct her when Nerita pulled a fireball out of thin air and balanced it on the palm of her hand.

"Neat trick," he said. "Nice to know you've still got a bit of fire in you."

"Give me the Setnakht, Mal. Xaphan told me not to return without him."

"I have former claim. And if I didn't, Aset does—"

Obviously uninterested in his explanations, Nerita sent the fireball straight at his head. He deflected, fast, but not fast enough. The flames licked his sleeve and reached out to fan his face. The heat was incredible. Not just fire, but the white-blue core of the flame, like a welder's torch.

Damn, what was it with him getting injured tonight?

From the second he'd laid eyes on Calliope Kane, he'd been in for nothing but trouble.

But he didn't want her injured. If anyone was going to lay a finger on her, it'd be him. And not in anger.

He spun, just to make certain the fireball hadn't sent stray sparks to burn her.

Only she wasn't there.

She was in the car—*his* car—and she slammed it into gear and tore away to the end of the parking lot.

As he fended off another fireball, he watched the car from the corner of his eye. Then he turned his head for a split second. She cast him a single glance, met his gaze and looked away. He wanted to think it was because she felt a little guilty for taking off on him, but more likely she was laughing at how easily she'd made her getaway.

The fire genies were slinking toward him now, and he turned a half circle, waiting for them to make their move.

Silly. Little. Boy.

Yeah, he was.

Calliope hadn't been going for her knife at all but rather his keys. And she'd succeeded. Not because he hadn't clued in.

Well, no, actually, he hadn't. Not at first. But then he had, and he'd let her take them, preferring to know she'd gotten away safe. With Kuznetsov. He'd find her again. And with her, his prize. If they'd all three hung around here, more than one of them would have been singed. And Calliope or Kuznetsov wouldn't heal the way he could. He wanted them both alive and healthy for the moment, for completely different reasons.

Two of Xaphan's concubines went after her as the Porsche tore out of the lot. White-hot fireballs flew from their fingers to bounce across the roof and hood, leaving scorched, black trails on his brand-new paint. Damn.

On instinct, Mal dove and rolled toward the two that were after Calliope, knocking their feet out from under them like bowling pins. Protecting her seemed immeasurably important. Which made absolutely no sense. But then, nothing had made sense since the second he'd seen her step out of the cab in front of Kuznetsov's building.

He told himself it was because he wasn't about to let the fire genies burn her to a crisp and rob him of his payback.

She was *his*.

All he needed to do was find her again.

The fire genies rounded on him, a feral pack working in synchrony, faces etched with rage and malice.

"We can talk this through," Mal said, spreading his hands and aiming for *nice*.

Nerita rounded on him, her lips peeled back in an ugly snarl, baring very white, small, pointed teeth.

"I called you," she said, her voice low. "I waited at the places I know you like. But you never even thought of me, did you? *Did you?*" The look in her eyes wasn't quite right.

In that second, Mal realized this wasn't just about Kuznetsov. This was personal. "Shit."

His clothing sparked and multiple tiny flames flared. The temperature edged from hot to blistering. He slapped at the flames as he advanced on her.

"Nerita," he began but never got to finish. Extending her right arm, she opened her fist with a sharp movement and fire came at him in a stream.

Gritting his teeth against the pain that screamed through every nerve in his body, he fought a losing battle, slapping at the fires as they grew and merged until everything he wore went up like a torch, the cloth melting into his skin.

He dropped. Rolled.

The pain cranked higher, his clothing gone, the fire cooking him like a spitted roast.

Then it stopped altogether as his nerve endings burned away.

Healing from this was going to be hell.

With a snarl, he lost all his charm. He surged to his feet, clawed his fingers and drove them straight through the chest of the nearest fire genie, tearing through flesh and shattering her ribs. She screamed as he tore her heart out, blood spurting from the severed vessels to spatter over him and the concrete at his feet.

Then he spun and did the same to a second fire genie who leaped at his back.

Nice only took you so far.

CALLIOPE HIT THE GAS and tore out of the parking lot. In the rearview mirror she watched Malthus Krayl go up like a torch. Her gut clenched, and she had the fleeting thought that she ought to go back and save him, that she owed him that. Which was so out of character that she actually felt her stomach churn.

Or maybe she felt sick because he was burning like a log in a fireplace. She wouldn't have wished that on him.

The second the thought formed, she squelched it. He was a soul reaper. The enemy of her kind. *Her* enemy. She wanted all Sutekh's reapers dead. Shouldn't matter to her how that was accomplished.

Besides, a reaper who'd been charred like an overcooked burger wouldn't be coming after her. Which meant she'd have to contend only with the fire genies.

But somehow, she couldn't make herself hang any confidence on that thought. Her gut was telling her that no matter what she'd just seen, the soul reaper wasn't gone for good. He might be in a world of hurt, but if it was that easy to kill a soul reaper, every member of the Asetian Guard and most Underworld armies would walk around with a gas can and a lighter in hand. Or better yet, a flamethrower.

No. Malthus Krayl wasn't dead. And she didn't doubt for a second that he'd be coming after her just as soon as he could.

Good luck with that. The destination she had in mind was reaper-proof.

And dangerous, because she'd be held accountable for tonight's choices and because the cartouche the reaper had shown her made everything suspect. A chill crawled up her spine.

The only good thing was that he hadn't appeared to recognize her as the woman who'd left him in the club's basement with his arms bound by his shirt and what likely had ended as an unpleasant case of blue balls.

Be thankful for small favors.

She geared down, easing up to a red light. Every instinct was screaming for her to take off with the Porsche in redline. Instead, she took pains to signal and drive according to the rules as the light changed to green. The last thing she wanted was for mortal police to get involved.

Keeping a close eye on the road behind her, she headed toward the lake. There didn't appear to be anyone following, but that didn't necessarily mean someone wasn't. The skin on the back of her neck prickled. She hadn't seen the last of Xaphan's fire genies. She doubted they'd forfeit the prize without a fight.

She glanced at Kuznetsov, still unconscious on the seat beside her.

"Aren't you a popular guy?"

The question was, why? She knew what she wanted from him—information about three dead girls with traces of a bloodline linked to Aset—and she could explain the reaper's interest because Kuznetsov was a Setnakht priest, and Setnakhts were the mortal worshippers of Sutekh. Also, Roxy Tam had discovered a link between the Setnakhts and the dead soul reaper. It made sense that Malthus Krayl would want information about his brother's death. But there were a number of unaccounted-for players in the mix. Xaphan and his fire genies. Asmodeus via the Topworld grunts Big Ralph had sent. So many puzzle pieces that didn't quite fit.

At the moment, the answers didn't matter. The priority was getting Kuznetsov to her superiors in the Guard. She would take him to the Matriarchs and let them discover his secrets. It was the wisest course, despite the fact that on a personal level, it was her worst choice.

She'd broken rules tonight, and she was going to pay a heavy price for that. Best to have her core mission deemed a success so at the very least she had the satisfaction of a job well done.

Or, if not *well* done, at least done.

If she drove straight through, she could reach her destination in a day and a half, maybe two if she got stuck behind a slow-moving convoy of trucks on the single-lane section of Highway #1.

The soul reaper's Porsche was too conspicuous. She needed something nondescript. Lucky for her, she was ever prepared.

Rounding the corner, she took a sharp left down an alley so narrow there were mere inches on each side of the car.

Kuznetsov groaned. His eyelids fluttered. Not good. She was running out of time. He'd regain consciousness very soon, and she'd have to be ready to deal with him.

Choices. She had them, but they were damned few, and none was completely satisfactory. She was still way too close for comfort to where she'd left Xaphan's concubines and Malthus Krayl, but she'd have to take the risk. She had a loaded vehicle parked nearby, one she kept for just such emergencies. All she needed to do was get there, transfer Kuznetsov and disappear before the fire genies managed to follow.

She turned onto a one-way street and headed down the ramp to the underground garage. It wasn't the best of its kind; it was poorly maintained and the security cameras were there just for show. They didn't actually record a thing. That was the reason she'd chosen this place. It was perfect for her purposes. Pay the owner cash each month, and he never asked questions.

Pulling the Porsche into an empty spot in a shadowed corner beside a silver SUV, she killed the engine and got out. She bolted around the car and hauled open the passenger door. Kuznetsov was deadweight as she dragged him out, his feet hitting the concrete with a thud. But not enough of a thud.

Something was wrong.

She lurched back as he slammed both his fists back toward her kneecaps.

He was fast. She was much faster.

He missed her entirely, the momentum of his failed blows sending him off balance. He went down hard and skidded on the concrete. Then, lips peeled back in a feral snarl, he pushed to his feet and lumbered away.

"Not so fast," Calliope said as she tore after him, grabbed him by the hair and yanked back, hard.

He went down on one knee then came up swinging, a rock clutched in his fist. Despite the weapon, they were nowhere close to evenly matched.

"Sorry. No time to play," she murmured then hauled back and hit him, coming up from below to connect with his jaw. She didn't put full effort into the blow, well aware that she was still hyped on reaper blood, her strength far greater than usual. Even so, his head rocked back, and for a second she thought she'd actually packed enough of a wallop to snap his neck. His gaze locked on her for what felt like eternity, then his eyes rolled back in his head and he slumped to the ground like the sack of shit he was.

Breathing hard, she stared down at him.

"Serene," she whispered. "I am serene. I am calm," she continued, each word spoken with firm conviction. "I am a blue lake beneath a cerulean sky. I am—"

She gritted her teeth and shook her head. "I am so fucked."

Because she'd noticed something as soon as Kuznetsov went for her. She should have *known* he was going to do that, but the gift she'd relied on for centuries was still missing in action. The reaper's blood had affected her ability to sense what was about to happen. The gray static she'd been subject to earlier had morphed into vast patches of…nothing. She was getting strobe-like flashes of unease, but no real sense of prescience. And that cost her her edge.

Her hope was that, as her body used up what she'd taken of the reaper's life force, the effects would lessen.

She dragged Kuznetsov to the SUV and hauled him inside, not paying particular attention to gentle handling. Any bumps and bruises he got along the way were the cost of doing business.

Once he was settled and buckled in all nice and legal, she rounded to the back and pulled open the door. To the casual observer, a glance would reveal an empty trunk. But look a little closer and the floor of the trunk was too high. She yanked out the false bottom, revealing neatly separated compartments that held her emergency stash. Winter gear. A thermal blanket. Food. Water bottles. Basic climbing equipment: harness, rope, carabiners, nuts. A wallet containing fake ID and cash. Everything ready in anticipation of her destination.

She grabbed the blanket, two bottles of water and the

wallet, slammed the door and got into the driver's seat. There were a pair of sweatpants back there, and though they would be a bit snug for him, she could have grabbed them to offer Kuznetsov once he made the return trip from dreamland.

Could have, but didn't.

His nakedness made him vulnerable, so that was how she left him. But she did toss the blanket over him. She didn't want him hypothermic.

She peeled out of the lot, leaving the Porsche behind. Minutes later, she was almost at the ramp for the expressway. From there, she'd head to the parkway and go north, then west. The more distance she put between her and the fire genies, the tougher it would be for them to track her.

Not so for Malthus Krayl. No matter how she might wish it wasn't so, the reality was that he'd probably be able to find her. Eventually. Soul reapers could move like the wind. They could make themselves invisible to both human and supernatural eyes. They could kill without weapons and heal from any wound.

And they always found their prey.

The second she'd stolen Kuznetsov from under his nose, she'd made herself the reaper's prey. Taking his blood, using his own power against him, had only added insult to injury.

He would come after her. And he would find her.

Her best hope was to stay well ahead of him until she

got to the one place a reaper couldn't go. The reinforced fortress that the Asetian Guard called home.

But if he caught up to her before that, things would get dicey.

Sirens sounded from a nearby street, heading in the direction she'd just left. A glance in the rearview mirror revealed a flare of light and, above that, a thick curl of smoke twirling up to stain the night sky. The parking lot.

The fire genies had found the abandoned Porsche.

But despite the fact that she'd seen them take down the soul reaper, they weren't the ones who worried her.

He was.

She had a feeling that for all his laid-back, bad-boy veneer, Malthus Krayl was one hell of a predator.

CHAPTER TEN

I go on the road I know in front
of the Island of the Just.
— *The Egyptian Book of the Dead, Chapter 17*

DAGAN KRAYL REACHED for the bowl on the bedside table and rummaged for a lollipop. Beside him, Roxy stirred. He was naked, sated and his mate had just finished pulling mouthfuls of his blood out of his body into hers while he moved deep inside her.

Which suited him just fine.

What didn't suit him was the bone-deep unease that was suddenly crawling around inside him. He'd thought maybe he just needed a sugar hit, but as the sucker dissolved on his tongue and the sugar rushed through his system, feeding his half-human, half-god physiology, he was forced to acknowledge the truth. Something was wrong.

"Dagan?" Roxy's voice was low, drowsy and incredibly sexy. "What is it?"

"Not sure," he said, leaning over the side of the bed to reach for his boxers and jeans where they lay in a heap on the floor. When he'd taken them off, *tidy* had been the furthest thing from his mind. "Might be Alastor. Might be Mal. One of them's in trouble."

"Is it bad?" Roxy pushed to a sitting position, her dark ringlets tumbling over her shoulders. She was a gift he'd never expected—and certainly didn't deserve. And she was his.

He felt her eyes on him as he reached into the pocket of his discarded jeans for his phone, but she didn't ask questions. She knew that he and Alastor and Mal— and before his murder, Lokan—shared an unbreakable connection. They couldn't climb inside each other's thoughts, but they could sense when any one of them needed the others. Sort of a psychic 911.

And right now, Dagan's gut was telling him that one of his brothers was dealing with something less than pleasant.

His gaze slid back to Roxy. The sheet was tangled around her hips, leaving the endless length of her sleekly muscled brown legs and all of her torso, including her luscious breasts, bare. He made a vague gesture. "Could you…ah…"

With a laugh, she prowled across the bed, pressed her mouth to his then rose, taking the sheet with her.

"I'll do better than just covering up. I'll remove the distraction entirely," she said and padded toward the bathroom.

The fact that she instinctively understood his need for privacy—no questions—warmed him. A second later he heard the shower turn on. Which meant she hadn't removed the distraction entirely because he had inordinately fond memories of that shower. He was building quite a repertoire of them, in fact.

His phone rang before he could dial.

"You okay?" Dagan asked.

"Peachy," Alastor replied, his voice tight. "I'm okay. You're okay. Which means Mal isn't."

"Yeah." Dagan was already on his feet, holding the phone in one hand as he dragged on his jeans with the other.

He froze as the discomfort crackling along his nerve endings ramped from a simmer to a rolling boil. Whatever shit was going down with Mal, it was getting worse fast. He was in trouble. In pain. Both Dagan and Alastor had sensed it, and given the timing of Alastor's call, he'd felt it first, which meant he was closer to the source.

"He's alive," Alastor said. *Unlike Lokan,* he didn't say. "And it's probably something he can handle himself. He might not like us bursting in like a couple of anxious babysitters."

Dagan inhaled sharply, the agony of Lokan's murder far too fresh. Each of them had felt his brutal death, in vivid Technicolor detail.

"I'd rather have him pissed at us than dead." He zipped his fly and reached for his T-shirt. "Where are you?"

"At Kuznetsov's condo. Mal called me to come and retrieve an item of interest. I have it with me now." Alastor paused. "And I have another item of even greater interest that Naphré and I retrieved earlier this evening."

There was an edge to his brother's voice that made Dagan sit up and take notice. Whatever Alastor had to tell him, it wasn't something he'd risk on an unsecured line.

Alastor gave him an address. "We'll discuss it when you get here. And by the way, Kai's in the lobby doing cleanup."

"Why'd he call Kai?" Dagan asked, immediately on edge. It wasn't like Mal to call one of Sutekh's minions without calling his brothers first.

"No bloody idea," Alastor replied. "You at Roxy's?"

"Yeah." Dagan trapped the phone between his ear and shoulder as he pulled on socks and boots. "Can you get a general fix on Mal? A direction? I'm picking up a world of pain, but not much else."

"That's what I'm getting, along with the feeling that he's freezing. Cold enough to cry ice cubes. And since I'm sensing more than you are, logic follows that he's closer to me than he is to you."

"When he called you, he didn't say where he was going?"

"No idea. He said he was following up on a lead and didn't want company." Alastor paused. "But I feel as if he hasn't gone far. He's downtown somewhere. Probably not more than a few blocks away. Hang on. Kai's ringing me."

Dagan dragged on socks and boots as he waited for his brother to come back on the line.

"Right, then," Alastor said a moment later. "Kai was a bloody fount of information. Apparently, Mal had company." Alastor paused. "A woman. They left carrying a rug."

"A rug," Dagan repeated, trying to keep the *what the fuck* from his tone. "Anyone happen to see what direction they went?"

"East. And one woman claims she saw them turn south down an alley."

"Not much to go on."

"No. I'll wait for you here. You have three minutes before I head out on my own."

Disconnecting the call, Dagan acknowledged his brother's subtle meaning. *On my own.* It was his way of saying he wasn't bringing Naphré along and his way of asking Dagan to leave Roxy behind. They had no way of knowing what they would find, what shape Mal would be in. And if they needed to deal with things— soul reaper things—by taking Mal to Sutekh's realm, their mates could not join them. Both Roxy and Naphré were Daughters of Aset, previous members of the Asetian Guard, though neither of them had ascended very high in the hierarchy. It was reason enough for Sutekh to bar them from his realm. Add to that the fact that as a rule, those who went to the Underworld didn't get to come back, and Dagan had no intention of taking Roxy anywhere near the Underworld.

He crossed to the bathroom and yanked open the door just as Roxy stepped from the shower. Wrapping her in the towel, he pressed a kiss to her lips.

"It's Mal," he offered, and Roxy nodded, her bronze-green eyes full of sympathy. At the same time, they were full of questions. Though she wasn't part of the Asetian Guard anymore, old habits had to die hard.

The two of them were still dancing around this *mate* thing, and trust was meant to be built over time, not forced. So he offered her everything he knew, an olive branch, because if they didn't have trust, then they didn't have a hope in hell of making it together.

"Alastor and I both sense that he's hurt, but we have no idea how or why. All we know is that he called Kai for a cleanup at a downtown condo, that he wasn't alone and that he stole a rug."

"A rug?" she asked and shook her head. "Can I do anything?"

"Good question. One I don't have an answer to. Yet." He let the assurance hang, unspoken but understood, that as soon as he had a task to give her, he would. He knew exactly how competent she was. If he needed information, he'd ask her to find it. Her network of Topworld grunts and contacts was probably more extensive than his own.

She'd been an excellent soldier for the Asetian Guard, and while her exit from the ranks was recent, she was no slacker. She'd already begun to lay the groundwork for her own Topworld investigative agency, dancing around

Alastor's mate, Naphré Kurata, to see if a partnership might be possible. Naphré had her fair share of skills as a trained assassin and Topworld enforcer.

Dagan pulled Roxy against him, amazed and awed that she was his, that after years of dreaming about her, she was actually in his arms every night. He kissed her, his mouth hard and hungry. Hers was no less so. Roxy Tam met him in the middle in all ways. She stood toe to toe with him, nose to nose.

"I'll call you."

"Do that," she said and stepped away. "I'll be out on a job. A little freelance work I picked up from Calliope."

He nodded then turned and focused his attention on summoning a portal—

"Outside," Roxy ordered and shoved hard at his back. "Last time you opened a portal in my house you left marks on the floor."

True enough.

"Our house," he corrected softly.

"What's mine is mine—" she shot him an arch look "—and what's yours is mine."

"And you are mine, so I guess that makes this my house."

She rolled her eyes. "Go."

He went.

He heard Roxy's cell ring as he opened the front door, and the surprise in her voice as she answered a question the caller asked.

He crossed the wide porch and vaulted the wooden rail. Before his feet hit the ground, the air before him began to undulate and twist, and then it became a great, black, gaping hole with tendrils of smoke that writhed at the edges.

The cold hit him like a roaring breaker, the air flaying his skin like a thousand tiny blades and shearing his lungs as he breathed in.

"WHERE ARE WE?" Kuznetsov asked.

They'd been driving for over thirty hours straight, stopping only for gas.

Calliope glanced at him. "Bugaboo Provincial Park."

She doubted he knew where that was, and even if he did, it wouldn't be much help to him. Where they were heading was accessible only by climbing or helicopter. Naked and wrapped in a blanket, he wouldn't get far if he tried to run off alone—not that she'd let him—and she doubted he had a helicopter hidden up his butt.

She turned off Highway #95 and headed west along the gravel road. Wouldn't be long before a team came down from the mountain to meet them.

"Ready to tell me about the phone call?" she asked. "Who died, and why did it make you afraid?" Like every other time she'd posed the same questions in the hours they'd been together, he ignored her, which only served to bolster her conviction that the phone call he'd received when he came out of the shower was significant. Otherwise, he'd give a flip answer and blow her off.

A few moments later, he said, "I have to take a piss."

This time she didn't even bother to glance at him.

"Use the jug," she said. "That's why I gave it to you." She'd had no choice but to stop for gas along the way, and each time, before she pulled into the station, she'd bound and gagged him and covered him with the blanket after pushing him down on the floor of the rear seat, releasing him only when they were clear of the gas station.

There was no way she'd let him get out of the car to use the facilities, so she'd picked up a milk jug and emptied it for his comfort.

"It's embarrassing."

She did look at him then, and she let the disgust she felt seep into her expression. "I wonder if the women you killed found what you did to them embarrassing. I know Marie Matheson was embarrassed. Horrified. Afraid." Marie had been lured to the Temple of Setnakht, singled out by Kuznetsov for his benevolent attention. And then he'd drugged her, intending to kill her. Maybe intending to rape her first.

The only reason she'd escaped was because Naphré Kurata, a former trainee of the Asetian Guard, had stumbled on her by accident and hauled her out of there. And Calliope knew this only because somehow, Marie had ended up in Roxy Tam's care.

"How do you know Marie?" He fidgeted in his seat and pulled at the bonds she'd kept around his wrists as a precaution against his early exit. "You're a member of the Asetian Guard, aren't you?" he asked, his tone pitched high with stress. He'd asked the latter question more than once on their trip, and she hadn't offered answers.

"You'll know everything you need to soon enough," she said.

He would. Because they were heading into the heart of the Asetian Guard. And chances were good that neither of them would be leaving alive.

As she'd expected, a team met Calliope on the road; four silent, black-clad women took Kuznetsov from her. She didn't argue. There was no point. With her arms folded across her chest, she watched as they shoved him into the Hummer. At least she'd done this much, delivered him to the Guard.

She found it faintly amusing that as they pulled away and he realized she hadn't been invited to come along, Kuznetsov sent a panicked look at her out the back window. She supposed there was some logic in that reaction. Better the devil you know.

Moments later, she heard the chop-chop of the helicopter blades and saw the shadow move across the sky, flying dark, no lights. She'd been left to make her way on foot. A message. The Matriarchs weren't particularly pleased with her.

Which meant they knew what she'd done. Again, no surprise. Even the newest acolyte would have been able to sense the soul reaper's prana flowing through her. The Matriarch's could probably feel it from miles away.

She headed back to the gray SUV and got her sleeping bag out of the back. Then she climbed in the backseat and made herself as comfortable as she could. She had one hell of a long climb ahead of her, and she'd just driven halfway across the country without sleep. Best thing she could do was grab a half hour now before she set out. Because she had a feeling that once she got where she was going, sleep would be the last thing she had a chance to do. So she set her watch alarm and closed her eyes.

Years of experience and training had taught her to sleep when she could. Within seconds, she was out.

SHE JERKED AWAKE, FEELING hyperaware, listening for her watch alarm. Nothing. Which meant the half hour she'd set it for hadn't passed. Something else had woken her.

Pushing open the door, she climbed out of the SUV and looked around. She kept the hood of the vehicle at her back and turned her head from left to right, scanning the perimeter. Then she turned around and did the same in the opposite direction.

The sky was darker than it had seemed earlier, the air warmer. The sensation of being watched prickled along the back of her neck.

Her breath hitched. She didn't need to turn to know he was behind her.

"Calliope." He said her name as if he was savoring it, and she closed her eyes at the sound of his voice. Smoke and warm brandy. She didn't want to find the sound of it appealing. "Took a bit of effort to find you."

She heard him step up behind her and felt the heat of his body. She smelled the scent of his skin, bright and clean. Like sunshine.

He wasn't here. Couldn't be here. She knew that. If she turned, she would find herself alone. If she turned, he would be gone.

She turned.

And he was right there, gray eyes locked on hers, stormy. Angry. And something else.

"How did you find me?" she asked, her voice even, though inside she was a roiling turmoil of nerves. The night was dark, the moon only a thin sliver, but her vision was enhanced by the blood she'd taken from him. She could see him clearly. The long curve of his lashes. The stubble that darkened his jaw. The shape of his mouth, his lower lip a little fuller than the upper.

"I summoned a portal. The exact thing you were questioning me about last time we met. What sort of a gentleman would I be if I didn't grant the lady her deepest desires?"

She lifted her brows, feigning calm. "But how did you know where to exit? It isn't as though there's a subway stop, is there?"

His lips curved. "You showed me."

"No."

"'Fraid so, darlin'." His mouth curved in a dark, sexy smile. "Happy to see me?"

Calliope huffed a sharp exhalation through her nose. She couldn't help it. The question was so absurd. And if a tiny part of her was glad to see that he was unharmed by the fire genies' inferno, it was only because she'd had a measure of guilt for sacrificing him in order to escape. Just because she despised his kind didn't mean she had to sink to their level.

"Ah, think so highly of yourself, do you, darlin'? Like we aren't the same, deep down inside?"

The same? No. They weren't. They never would be.

He was a monster. A killer. He ripped out the heart of innocents.

She killed only when there was absolutely no other choice.

That made them different.

She went for her knife. It was not there. Somehow, he'd taken it from her.

The soul reaper stared at her, and his mouth turned in a faint, knowing smile. His eyes were like molten silver against the fringe of dark lashes, his gaze focused. Greedy. Like he meant to swallow her whole.

Awareness danced across her skin and made her blood thick and hot, her limbs heavy. She was mortified by her reaction. He was her enemy. He was a soul reaper, the darkest, most vile denizen of the Underworld, a creature that barely qualified as having slithered from the primordial sludge.

Then his lips curved even more, a pirate's smile. White teeth bright against dark stubble.

In that second, she acknowledged the truth, because to lie to herself was dangerous. She might despise all his kind. She might be disgusted by who and what they were. But on a purely physical level, she found him beautiful. Sexy. She wanted to touch him, taste him, put her hands on his naked skin. And from the way he was looking at her, he wanted to do the same to her.

She'd wanted him that first night at the club, before she'd known what he was. She still wanted him now, with eyes wide open.

What sort of a creature did it make her that she could want what she reviled?

He moved so fast she didn't even have time to gasp. One moment, he was in front of her, more than an arm's length away. And then he was plastered against her, his thighs flush with her own, his chest against hers.

His fingers laced with hers and he drew her arms back behind her then turned her palms so they pressed against cold metal. She didn't acquiesce, nor did she struggle.

Leaning in, he brought his lips to her ear and spoke so low that she had to strain to hear. "I'm going to kiss you now. And you're going to let me."

She had a flash of memory, the feel of his lips on

hers in the parking lot before the fire genies came, and to her utter horror, she realized she wanted more than just a fleeting taste. She wanted him to kiss her hard and deep.

There was something wrong. She had more control than this. She reached for the smooth lake that grounded her, the place inside her that was ever calm. Panic swelled when she couldn't find it, couldn't touch it. There was only the scent of his skin and the feel of his hands holding hers, spiced with the lingering regret that she hadn't kissed his mouth when she'd had the chance in the club's basement.

She hadn't wanted to then because it seemed far too intimate with a nameless man she meant to use for her release.

She shouldn't want to now that she knew what he was.

But she did. She wanted it so badly, it made her ache.

The soul reaper did nothing more threatening than draw back to study her through narrowed eyes. But her panic escalated, as though he threatened her somehow.

Because he did. Something about him threatened the things she believed about herself.

She felt hot, out of sorts, herself, but not herself.

His hands were on her thighs, running up the outsides to her hips, holding her as he pressed forward against her, pressed her to the cold metal of the SUV's hood.

With a sharp inhalation, she closed her eyes as he lowered his face to the place where her neck met her shoulder. She could feel the rub of his day-old stubble against her skin, abrasive, erotic. Feel the brush of his lips and then the sharp nip of his teeth.

She wet her lips. *Kiss him.* An insidious whisper in her thoughts. *Kiss him once and get it out of your system. Kiss him once and prove to yourself exactly how repugnant he is.*

His fingers skimmed the undersides of her breasts. She gasped.

He lowered his head. She stayed perfectly still, her lips already feeling puffed and swollen and aching for his kiss. And when he brushed his lips against hers, she let her mouth open, let her tongue slip out to taste him, know him.

Electricity ramped through her, hot and bright.

His weight came full against her, his chest flattening the swell of her breasts, his thighs hard against her own. He traced his fingers along her collarbone, his touch so light she barely felt it. Then he tunneled his fingers through her hair to splay across the base of her skull. His touch was not so gentle now as he tipped her head back, making her open to him. Exactly the way he wanted.

He smiled. Hungry. Knowing.

And then he claimed her, his mouth open, his tongue pushing inside her. The feeling was lush, his kiss hot and wet and deep. Teeth. Tongue. The pleasure swelled like a wave, crashing over her. Pulling a moan from deep inside her.

She dragged the hem of his shirt from his waistband, raked her nails along the hard ridges of his belly. His skin was warm and smooth, and she remembered the taste of him from the club.

Moving her hands to his belt, she undid the buckle, freed the button, grabbed the zipper. It went down with a faint rasp, and then she had her hand on the taut skin at the base of his belly, following the thin line of hair that arrowed down.

The sound he made, low in his throat, animal need and masculine pleasure, set a torch to the kindling of her lust. And then the sound changed to a series of short, high-pitched—

She surged upright, her breath coming in hard gasps, her body shaking, her heart slamming against her ribs. The lingering image of him burned her eyes and then flickered out like a match.

She was alone. Her knife was in her hand. Her watch was beeping.

Time to go.

CHAPTER ELEVEN

O you keepers of the gate, make a way for me,
For I am one like you.

—*The Egyptian Book of the Dead, Chapter 86*

MAL JERKED AWAKE, TRYING to hold fast to an image that danced at the edge of his thoughts. He felt as if he was leaving something behind, losing something important.

Then the image was ripped away completely as agony came at him with the power of a sledgehammer. Every inch of his body twitched. He barely held back the scream that tried to claw its way free.

He drew a breath through his nose and blew it out through his mouth. Again. A third time. He wrestled the pain under control and took stock of his situation. He was flat on his back. His eyes felt as though they were glued shut. His mouth tasted as if he'd been licking sand.

And he had a raging hard-on.

Right.

For a disoriented second, he thought he was in the ship's hold, held by chains, the skin of his back raw from the flogging, the fire eating the wooden planks and the ribs of the ship with incredible heat and speed. Drown or burn—

Then he heard the soft burble of water over smooth rock, not the roar of the ocean tearing through the hull.

His eyes felt as if they'd been sewn shut or weighted in place, refusing to obey his will as he tried to open them. Then the smell hit him. Lotus blossoms. And... something else that triggered a major *this-is-not-okay* recoil in his brain.

It smelled like burning hair. Charred cloth. Burnt... Him.

He was the source of that smell. Or at least part of it. The lotus blossoms were a whole different deal.

In that second, he knew two things. He'd been charbroiled like an overdone roast, and he wasn't in the hold of a ship in the year 1742, but rather in the Underworld in Sutekh's realm.

"The Rolex was melted. I had to slice it out."

Dagan's voice.

"Bloody hell." Alastor's voice. "The bag's empty again."

Dagan's words made sense. Mal remembered Kuznetsov's Rolex on his wrist. But he had no idea what bag Alastor was talking about.

"We've got a glucose IV drip running," Dagan explained.

Ah…an IV bag, a sugar hit straight to his cells. Mal definitely felt as though he needed it. He heard the scrape of a shoe on stone, then a suctioning pop like someone pulling off a plastic cap.

His thoughts drifted and floated away, closer to sleep than wake, though he was still peripherally aware of his brothers' voices. In his relaxed state, he remembered what he'd thought he'd left behind when he first woke up, an image that had seemed both important and far beyond his grasp.

He'd been dreaming about kissing Calliope Kane. And she'd been kissing him back. With tongue. While she shoved her hands down his pants.

Nice. That explained the hard-on.

Two small problems.

Ms. Kane would sooner cut out his tongue than tangle it with hers.

And soul reapers didn't dream.

He opened his eyes, then slammed them shut as light stabbed clear through to the back of his skull.

An arm circled around his back and his shoulders were lifted. Then a glass was pressed to his lips and Alastor commanded, "Drink."

He drank.

Sorting through the tangled skein of questions that twisted through his thoughts, he picked out one. How long—

"I'm guessing you want to know how long since you

had your little run-in with Xaphan's fire genies," Dagan said. "Measured in Topworld time? Days."

Days. An enormous gulley of time between him and what he wanted: Calliope Kane and, through her, Kuznetsov.

Except that if he was brutally honest with himself, he wanted them both.

Kuznetsov for the secrets he held.

Calliope Kane for reasons of a different sort, only one of which was payback.

She'd stolen his damned car. She'd stolen a nice helping of his blood. She'd stolen Kuznetsov.

No. Not true. He'd *let* her steal the High Reverend, and he had no way to explain that. He could have sacrificed her to the fire genies. But he hadn't. He'd taken the hit himself so she could get away.

What the fuck was wrong with him?

Altruism had never been his thing. Especially not for an enemy of his kind, which she was, given the whole son of Sutekh, Aset's Daughter/Otherkin thing.

But that was just it. He didn't want to be her enemy.

He wanted her for more than just her link to the High Reverend.

Which made about as much sense as snow in July.

He opened his eyes again, the light still so bright it blinded him. All he saw were vague, dark shapes.

"The knife…" he rasped.

"Got it," Alastor said. "And you were right. The blade is volcanic glass. It appears to be from Hokkaido."

"Japan," Dagan clarified.

Which could either mean that Izanami had been involved in Lokan's murder, or that someone had covered their tracks very well, setting up the origins of the knife as a red herring.

"The knife had traces of blood," Dagan continued as Alastor tipped the glass against Mal's lips once more. Mal focused on his brother's words rather than the fact that the water moving down his throat felt like ground glass. "The Topworld techs say the traces were human. Female, for the most part. At least four different women. And one man. Alastor offered up some blood as a control. The tech's tests indicated that the male's blood was a match for having the same paternity as Alastor."

Which meant that the knife Mal had found *had* been used on Lokan, one of the two blades they'd seen in the video. Find the second knife and they'd have a direct line on the supernaturals Kuznetsov had been working with, maybe even a lead on the bastard who'd masterminded the entire scheme.

"Our Underworld techs are looking at the knife now."

Mal nodded. At least, he thought he did.

The knife. The blood. Lokan's blood. Hope flared. He knew that Roxy Tam had the unique ability to track humans through their blood, sort of a supernatural GPS. If she took a taste of Lokan's blood, would she be able to find him?

"Blood," Mal croaked. Then, "Roxy."

"We were a step ahead of you," Dagan said.

Mal's breath hitched as hope surged.

"But so far, she hasn't come up with a thing. I'm not sure if the blood was too old or the amount too small. Either way, Roxy hasn't been able to find him."

Disappointment was a stiletto plunging deep.

Alastor gave him another drink. It went down far easier than the other two, more like gravel than ground glass.

"Genies?" he asked, the single word coming out as a barely intelligible croak.

"Four of them were lying on the ground when we got there. You were working on the fifth. The one who was still intact was running around shoving hearts into chests. We almost bloody well turned around and left since you didn't appear to need any help," Alastor said.

Yeah, he'd needed help, but not because he couldn't take care of business himself. He could do that, too well—that was the problem. When they'd turned him into a living torch, he'd been caught in the moment. Instinct and centuries of training kicked in until he wasn't thinking, just acting, thrusting his hand through skin and bone, deep in their chests to rip their hearts free.

He'd been a breath away from harvesting their dark-souls and feeding them to Sutekh as a meal of pure power.

And that would have been a disaster. It would have cost Sutekh any hope of maintaining pleasant relations with Xaphan, the keeper of the lakes of fire. While a brawl between sides would be tolerated, darksoul harvests would not.

Soul reaping 101. Don't harvest from your allies. It tended to piss them off.

"Why'd they attack?" Dagan asked.

"They wanted Kuznetsov." Mal took another sip of water. He closed his eyes tightly then opened them wide, trying to get his vision to clear. The light bored into him, as though someone was jamming a nine-inch nail through his pupil. "Nerita said Xaphan told them not to come back without him."

But there was more to it than that. For Nerita, it had been personal.

The moments before she lit him on fire played through his thoughts. She hadn't been thinking. She'd been acting on pure emotion. He hadn't seen it coming. He'd thought that during their brief entanglement, they'd been on the same page. She'd acted as though she wanted the same thing he did—a little fun for a night. He hadn't realized that he'd hurt her.

He didn't feel particularly good about that.

Between the glucose IV and the water, Mal's energy was slowly reviving, his thoughts clearing, his vision growing sharper, losing the haze.

First thing he saw, dead ahead, was an oasis of palm trees overhanging a tranquil pond.

Second thing he saw was a man's back. He was wearing loose-fitting linen shorts, cut off at the knees, and not much else. His exposed skin was puckered, with fluid oozing from the raw patches.

"Nice," Mal muttered, closing his fist on the linen that covered his own thighs. He noticed that the skin on the back of his hand was pink and shiny, a freshly healed scar.

The man turned and Mal might as well have been looking in the mirror, a little worse for wear. The face was singed red along the jaw but relatively unmarked above that. He couldn't say the same for the rest of the body. Arms, legs, chest…all were marked by healing burns.

"Malthus," his doppelganger greeted him.

Mal had no idea what his father really looked like because Sutekh could choose to take on any form. Kemetic art showed a creature with a doglike head, the snout of an anteater and a forked tail. At the moment, Mal wished his father would have chosen that form. It would have been far more appealing than the one that he'd taken—one that Mal had no doubt reflected the sorry shape he himself was in.

"Do I look that bad?" he asked.

"You did when we first brought you in. Not so much anymore." Alastor glanced at him. "At least they spared your ugly face."

Sutekh's gaze flicked from Mal to Alastor, and back again like he was watching some fascinating but confounding species of insect. It was those eyes, flat black and soulless, that marked the difference between them. Mal's eyes were gray. And human.

"Do you mind changing?" Mal asked with an attempt at a grin. "Bad enough I have to experience my injuries. I'd prefer not to have to look at them, as well."

Sutekh stared at him, and Mal saw a tiny telltale tic beneath his father's right eye, so minute it was almost imperceptible. But Mal knew what to look for from long years of purposefully aiming for exactly that reaction.

Only today, he hadn't been aiming to irritate his father. But he'd definitely said something—

He'd asked him to change his appearance.

Mal mentally sorted through the possibilities of why that would piss him off and could come up with just one that made any sense. His father had chosen to take the form of his injured son as a show of...what? Empathy? Mal had no idea if Sutekh could feel pain, if he felt the burns because he'd chosen to mirror Mal's form. Did he know Mal's suffering? Was this a way to offer some fatherly support?

The thought was bizarre.

But Mal couldn't come up with a better explanation.

Unless Sutekh's goal was to make him more uncomfortable than he already was. Which was a more likely possibility.

He exhaled through his teeth. Maybe he shouldn't bother trying to figure out the machinations of his father's Machiavellian mind. He hadn't had any luck at that for nearly three centuries.

"You are healing," Sutekh said. Impossible to know if he thought that was a good thing or bad.

"Yeah." Mal pushed to a sitting position and looked at his brothers. It was then he noticed that they'd paid a price for his rescue. Alastor's forearms and hands were pink and puckered, fresh burn scars marking his skin. The left side of Dae's neck and face were similarly marked. The fact that the scars remained days after the incident meant the damage had been significant.

"Sorry," he muttered.

"Everything was on fire. Them. You. No way to pull you out without diving into the inferno," Dae said with a shrug. "Not the first time one of us took a hit for the other."

No. Not the first time. And, no doubt, not the last.

"We'll heal," Alastor said.

Yeah, they would. And the fact that they'd been there for him, stepped up and put themselves in harm's way for him, made Mal feel both incredibly guilty and nauseatingly touched.

"Right." Mal cleared his throat and changed the topic. "So, uh, you've got my sick bed set up in the garden because…?"

"What…you don't like the ambience?" Alastor asked.

"Just not sure why I'm in the Underworld instead of my own bed."

The fact that they'd brought him to Sutekh's territory was odd. But given that they were here, the garden-as-recovery-room wasn't. This was Sutekh's favorite place in his entire territory. He would sit for hours—hell, maybe even days—watching the exotic fish he'd had imported from the river Nile.

Mal figured he missed them. The Nile. The fish. The Topworld he'd been ejected from millennia past.

"Your bed wasn't safe. At least a dozen of Xaphan's concubines know where you live." Dagan paused and lifted a brow, as though waiting for confirmation of the number. When Mal said nothing—mostly because he wasn't sure of the exact number—Dae continued. "We didn't want to take a chance on one of them leading the rest in for a little payback. You roughed them up pretty bad."

Mal gave a harsh bark of laughter. "They roughed *me* up pretty bad. And you, as well. But I see your point. So why didn't one of you take me to your—" He cut himself off, not bothering to finish the question. He knew why. They both had mates now. Neither of them would bring danger to his mate's door.

"You are fortunate that your brothers arrived so precipitately." Sutekh glided closer until he stood over Mal, filling his vision.

"Yeah." Mal scrubbed his palm along his jaw. "How *did* you find me so quickly?"

"Roxy got a call," Dagan said, his tone carrying just a hint of question.

"A call." Mal shook his head. There was only one person who could have made that call.

Calliope Kane hadn't appeared to have any qualms about leaving him to burn like a torch while she made off with the prize. But apparently, she had. Fascinating. It brought a new layer to the game. He'd expected her to nab Kuznetsov. He'd expected that he'd find them both when he went looking.

He *hadn't* expected her to do anything to save his ass, and he didn't trust the fact that she had. There had to be an angle to that.

And from the faint question in Dagan's tone, he was wondering about it, as well. But it wasn't something they'd talk about in front of Sutekh. He was prickly about the fact that two of his sons had mated with his enemies. No reason to stick pins in the already enraged bull.

"Speaking of calls," Mal said. "Kuznetsov got one right before everything went south. He asked who was dead, and if the caller was certain. Whatever the answer was, it made Kuznetsov damned jumpy. I think we need to find out who died."

"We already know," Alastor said. "Djeserit Bast."

"What?"

"Djeserit Bast is dead."

"How?" Mal held up a hand, palm forward. "Forget it. Doesn't matter. Who claimed her?" Whoever had claimed her soul would have access to her memories and the secrets she harbored. He wanted those secrets.

She had to have information about Lokan's death. "Can we get her darksoul? Get answers?"

"No," Sutekh said, and when Mal opened his mouth to protest, continued, "I claimed her. And she had no answers to give."

CHAPTER TWELVE

I have gone to make inspection and
I have returned to speak; let me pass,
that I may report on my errand.
—*The Egyptian Book of the Dead, Chapter 86*

CALLIOPE LEANED HER HIP against the stone balustrade
and looked out at the moon-drenched garden. The entire
estate was surrounded by a ten-foot-high wall, topped
by electrified wire. Outside of that was a second barrier,
made of electrified high-tensile steel. The only break
was the front gates. They were massive doors of solid
steel, and they too were electrified. Dogs and guards
patrolled the perimeter, both inside and out. Security
cameras covered every angle. And the compound's location was in itself a defense, the mountaintop perch
inaccessible for any but the most tenacious.

But the Guard did not rely merely on physical boundaries and deterrents. There were wards in place and
spells and magics of which only the oldest among their
kind had knowledge.

Isolated and inaccessible, surrounded by wilderness
and danger, this place was the bastion of the Daughters

of Aset, the hidden and protected headquarters of the Asetian Guard.

Twenty hours ago, she'd taken rope and gear from the SUV, a bottle of water and a couple of protein bars. The climb might have taken three or four days under other circumstances. Only the fading high of her serving of reaper blood made it go faster than it should have, but it hadn't been any less grueling. She'd reached the compound, exhausted, hungry, only to be met with another challenge.

While she was allowed through the gates, the doors of the house were not opened to her. She was left here, on the stone balcony, to wait on the pleasure of her superiors.

Either they were occupied with things of greater import, or they meant her to worry. To stew. To weaken. And thus to spew all her secrets the second she was summoned into their presence.

The funny thing was, she intended to have no secrets. She meant to acknowledge her crime. There was no other way. Get within ten feet of her and even the lowest acolyte in the Guard, a foot soldier with no standing, would sense the reaper's blood flowing through her, fading or not.

She'd fed from a supernatural, something that was frowned upon. And not just any supernatural. A soul reaper. Which was frowned upon in the extreme. Were she merely an acolyte or low-ranking soldier, her lapse might be forgiven. But she was not, and the fact that she had sipped the life force of a reaper was not something her superiors would be pleased about. For a multitude of reasons.

She stared out at the grounds. She knew the perimeter was impenetrable, yet her gut was telling her nowhere was safe.

Exhaustion gnawed at her. Other than that half-hour nap—which thanks to her dreams had been less than restful—she hadn't slept in…how many hours? Sixty? Seventy? She'd lost count between the cross-country drive and the mountain climbing. Every cell in her body was weighted with fatigue. She leaned her hip against the balustrade, the chill of the stone seeping through her clothing. Closing her eyes, she let her head rest against the column that rose to the overhang. She had no idea how long she stood there. Maybe she even slept for an instant.

Sensing someone behind her, she jerked upright and spun.

A woman stood a few feet away, her face both stunning and serene. Her skin was dark, her hair a tightly curled cap cut close to her head, her cheekbones high and curved.

"Zalika," Calliope greeted her, taking comfort in her familiar face. It had been far too long since she had seen her mentor.

"You are tired," Zalika said, moving to stand beside her and lean her hip against the stone railing. She was tall and slender, her posture military straight. She was a warrior and a politician. And Calliope regretted that this woman whom she both respected and loved had been assigned the less-than-pleasant task of advising her of her fate. "Why did you not stop along the way for rest?"

"Perhaps I should have." She smiled thinly. "But I didn't. It was imperative that I get Kuznetsov here as quickly as possible. I left the soul reaper lying on the ground, surrounded by Xaphan's concubines, writhing in pain, consumed by flame. That, coupled with our impenetrable security, should be enough to put me at ease, no?"

"But you are not at ease."

"The soul reaper will come after me." Calliope resisted the urge to tighten her fingers on the cold stone. Serenity was her customary defense. She would be wise to stick with the familiar. "A handful of fire genies might be able to turn him into a torch, but they could not terminate him. He will heal. Perhaps he already has. And he will look for me."

"For *you?*" Zalika stressed the final word, and Calliope only then saw the trap in her own reasoning. She had personalized this. A mistake.

"For Kuznetsov," she amended. But it was too late. She had already made the assertion and it hung between them, heavy in her thoughts and, no doubt, in Zalika's.

But her mentor let it pass. For now. "Why does the soul reaper want him?" she asked.

Calliope weighed her words, uncertain of exactly how much Zalika knew. The Asetian Guard was a secretive and paranoid group; they shared as little information as possible with the soldiers who comprised the ranks. By this point, just about every supernatural and Top-world grunt knew about the butchered reaper, but there was no way to know if Zalika was aware that he was Sutekh's son. Finally, Calliope chose the neutral path. "The reaper and his brothers seek information about the one who was killed," she said. "And the one who killed him."

"As do we." Zalika paused. "Do you believe your precautions were not enough to obscure your trail?"

"I don't know." She'd thought she knew a great deal about soul reapers, the enemy of her kind. *Her* enemy. But Roxy Tam's association with Dagan Krayl had proved that she did not. She wasn't about to make assumptions that might put members of the Guard, or even the Matriarchs, in danger. "He is a soul reaper. He will want payback. I stole his prize from beneath his very nose, and I stole his power to use against him." There. It was out in the open. What she had done.

"You fed from him."

Zalika's tone betrayed none of the horror and disgust she most assuredly felt. Calliope knew what that felt like. She'd experienced it when Roxy had revealed that she'd fed from Dagan Krayl.

But Calliope had been partially to blame for that debacle. Believing that Roxy knew the lore and rules of

Daughters of Aset, she had failed to clarify the rules of feeding. By the time she'd discovered her error, it had been too late.

No, in truth, it had been too late before she ever met Roxy Tam, because Dagan had met her first. He had been Roxy's first blood, a year before Roxy entered the Asetian Guard.

And that was another thing that Calliope must divulge. Her failure to properly train and teach Roxy Tam.

Calliope turned fully to face her mentor. "What of Kuznetsov?" she asked, changing the subject because there was nothing left to be said. Her shortcomings would be picked over by the Matriarchs. No need to tell the full story before she must.

"He was offered rest, a bath and clothing, as well as refreshments."

Of course he was. While the Matriarchs might leave Calliope to stew out here on the stone balcony in the cold, they would not treat a captive less than humanely. It was their way.

"What do you know of Djeserit Bast?" Zalika asked.

"She is a High Reverend in the Toronto branch of the Temple of Setnakht." She knew that from Roxy, and she'd done a bit of poking around on her own, as well. But her focus had been Kuznetsov. "She was involved in an attempt on a Daughter of Aset, a former trainee for the Guard who never took first blood."

Zalika's brows rose. "Naphré Kurata?"

"One and the same."

"And Kuznetsov? Did he reveal anything during your journey?" Zalika asked.

"Nothing. And…" She shook her head, uncertain how to explain what she'd felt each time she'd questioned Kuznetsov during the long drive. "I had this odd conviction that he wasn't simply keeping the answers to himself. I felt that there was some sort of block in place, as though he couldn't access his own memories. He knew they were there and what they pertained to, but he didn't know the details of what he had experienced."

Zalika looked at her sharply. "What makes you say that? You are not a soothsayer. That is not your talent."

"No, it isn't. I don't know what makes me think that. Perhaps his expressions. He looked—" she paused, searching for the right word "—perplexed."

"What you say is in keeping with what Meharet described," Zalika said.

Meharet had the gift of freeing one's tongue. She could lure even the most taciturn individual into conversation and steer that conversation along the path she desired. Her abilities were strong. She could touch secrets, the buried darkness that people swept into the dusty corners of their minds. Meharet could draw out the things that people wanted to hide, even from themselves. Most especially from themselves.

"She learned nothing?" Calliope asked.

"Even she could find nothing of value in Pyotr Kuznetsov's mind."

"I have spent some time with him," Calliope murmured. "I believe he has a great deal in his mind. Much of it evil."

"It is possible that someone purposefully tampered with his thoughts and left nothing to find."

"Who? It would take power and skill comparable to that of the Matriarchs' to perform—" her voice trailed away as she thought of the cartouche that Malthus Krayl had held in his hand then threaded on the chain about his neck "—such a delicate task," she finished.

"A question I wish I had an answer to. It appears that someone has taken the memories of Pyotr Kuznetsov's actions and hidden them even from himself. He knows he committed murder. He knows he was part of a ceremony, that he took blood and life from one who should not die. But he cannot remember details. Not a single detail."

Calliope stared at her. "Took blood and life—" She could not contain her astonishment, didn't even try. She'd suspected that Kuznetsov was involved in Lokan Krayl's death, but Zalika was saying the involvement was more than peripheral, as she had assumed. That he had participated in the kill. How was that even possible?

She was a supernatural, a blooded Daughter of Aset, one who had sipped from Malthus Krayl's life force. She knew what flowed through his veins and powered his cells. Even that small bit of blood and prana had ramped her own power up immeasurably. The remnant of that power was the only thing keeping her on her feet after so many hours without rest. Still, she would have been no match for him. Whatever small victories she gained in their brief skirmish had been thanks to the element of surprise and quick thinking. But a skirmish wasn't a war. She didn't delude herself into imagining she could have killed him. So how could Kuznetsov, who was purely mortal, have murdered Malthus Krayl's brother?

"How could a mortal kill an unkillable soul reaper?"

Zalika offered a faint smile, accenting the high curve of her cheekbones. "A question we would all like answered."

"He couldn't have done it," Calliope said. "Whatever information of value he might reveal, it will not be a confession of personal guilt. We can only hope that he manages to remember, and name, those he allied with."

Zalika raised a brow. "Or we can hope he does not."

The words were softly spoken, but their message was clear. If Kuznetsov's allies that night had been Daughters of Aset, members of the Asetian Guard, then to remember them would put them all at risk. The only members of the Guard with enough power to even contemplate such a deed were the Matriarchs. If they had killed Lokan Krayl, if Kuznetsov somehow remembered that and the information got out, Sutekh would come for them with a vengeance.

All of which would explain the Matriarchs' directive that the dead reaper must stay dead. They said it was because Lokan Krayl's reanimation would lead to a war of apocalyptic proportions when he named his killers and Sutekh drew the entire Underworld into his vengeance.

If it was the Matriarchs who had done the deed, all the more reason to ensure that their victim could not name them and that any witnesses were removed. If Kuznetsov could attribute the deed to a blooded Daughter, then he had sealed his fate.

"Zalika, the cartouche of Aset. Who wears such a one?"

"The Goddess herself. The Matriarchs. No other." Zalika stared at her. "You know that."

The urge to tell all, to seek her friend's guidance, was nearly overwhelming. But decades of training and habit were not easily overcome. In the end, she said only, "Yes. I'm sorry. I'm just very tired."

Zalika laid her hand on Calliope's arm and gave a gentle squeeze.

At that moment, the front doors swung open, held by two members of the Guard.

"Come," Zalika said. "The Matriarchs are ready for you now."

But was she ready for them?

"How is it that her soul told him nothing? How is that even possible?" Mal paced across Sutekh's greeting chamber and snagged a piece of baklava from the table laden with sweets. His father always kept a ready supply of food brought in from Topworld because if Mal and his brothers consumed the food of the dead, they would be permanently consigned to the Underworld, never again able to move between realms.

"I'll tell you the same thing I told you the last ten times you asked," Alastor said. "Dad says he sent Kai Warin to harvest Djeserit Bast. She offered nothing when Kai questioned her. He did his thing. Sutekh claimed her and worked his charm on her intact soul. She didn't seem to know a bloody thing about Lokan's death, other than the names of the humans we already knew were involved. So he swallowed her darksoul—"

"And it was blank as a wiped hard drive," Dagan finished.

"Now there's a question," Alastor said. "Can you really wipe a hard drive? I mean, doesn't something always stay on it?"

"There are programs—"

"She offered no names?" Mal interrupted.

Dagan shrugged. "Yeah. She offered names. Ones we already knew. All human."

Mal stared at them, his thoughts churning. What they were describing was impossible. Sutekh should have been able to read every dark deed Djeserit Bast had ever done. That was what happened when he took a darksoul and fed on it. He got a megashot of pure power and all the knowledge of his victim's soul.

Except, in the case of Djeserit Bast, he hadn't. And in the case of Joe Marin. And in the case of pretty much anyone linked in any way, shape or form to Lokan's murder.

Each one had come up a blank slate.

Like someone had wiped them clean.

All soul reapers could wipe the conscious memory of a human who happened to see too much. It was a sort of hypnosis that left the individual certain it had all been a dream. But the human still retained the memory. It wasn't as if they could go in and cut it out of the gray matter.

"Who has that sort of power?" Mal asked. "Who could obliterate any hint of memory?"

He munched another piece of baklava, craving the sugar hit. He was almost completely healed from his burns now, but his half-god metabolism was still screaming for glucose.

Turning, he strode toward the table that had been set up in the center of the room. It was draped in gold cloth and guarded by a phalanx of soul reapers. And smack-dab in the middle was a lead box covered in symbols. Among them was the Amenta, the symbol for the Underworld. An ankh with wings and horns, the symbol of Aset's Daughters, the Otherkin. A shenu, or cartouche, surrounding Aset's name. The flail and crook, the symbol of majesty and dominion.

"They seem to point to Aset, or possibly Osiris, as Lokan's killers," Dagan said, following Mal's gaze.

"They do, don't they?" Mal moved closer, shooting a quelling look at the guard who shifted to block his way. "You think you need to protect him from me?" he asked softly. The soul reaper met his gaze, held it and finally backed down. He stepped aside and Mal moved closer to the lead box.

He knew what was in it. Lokan's partial remains.

Seven parts.

Hands. Feet. Arms. Torso.

The other seven were still unaccounted for. Including Lokan's heart. And they had no leads on his soul.

"What made you think of looking for him between realms?" he asked Alastor.

"Bloody brilliant of me, wasn't it?" Alastor replied.

Dagan grunted.

Alastor ignored him. "After Naphré and I escaped Jigoku, I kept thinking that if there was one null place, why not others? And since they didn't seem to be something anyone gave much thought to, what better place to hide Lokan's body?"

"I just don't get why there are seven parts in this box. I thought his body parts had been scattered across the earth. It's as if someone other than us has been searching for Lokan, gathering his parts in one place." Mal laid his palm on the lid, as though physically touching the casket that held part of his brother's butchered body would offer a clue.

"And having far better luck," Alastor said.

Dagan was silent, contemplating the box. "Why'd we think that, though? Why did we think his body parts had been scattered? Who originally told us that bit of information?" he asked.

They stared at each other for a minute.

"Got no fucking clue," Mal said.

"And maybe we need to get a clue," Alastor said.

With his hand resting on the lid of the lead casket, Mal closed his eyes, picturing Lokan as he had been. Fuck. He missed his brother. He wanted him back. He kept expecting to feel someone punch his shoulder, to turn and find Lokan standing there, laughing his ass off.

Something flickered against his palm, a faint spark of energy. It sparked brighter, a tiny flame in a sea of inky blackness. He reached for it, tried to tease it free, wanting with all he was for it to be a link to his brother. They could all sense each other's pain. They'd all felt Lokan die. He wanted to be able to feel him still.

But they had lost him. His soul was gone. His spark gone. They were left with nothing but a burning desire for vengeance.

Just as he was left with nothing now as the spark sputtered and was lost. Likely, it had never been there at all. Wishful thinking did crazy things to the imagination.

He glanced at Dae, then at Alastor. *We're not going to find him. We're not going to be able to bring him back.* A part of him wanted to say the words, wanted to start the healing by putting it out there, naked and indescribably painful. But he knew they both wanted to believe, and so he held his silence and let them.

Pulling his hand away, he let his fingertips skim the etched symbols. He thought he ought to recognize some mystic clue there. He thought, too, that he ought to recognize the box, its origins, its significance, that he'd seen something like it…somewhere.

He shook his head, unable to quite nail down where or when. Maybe he hadn't. Maybe it was just one of those quirks that left him thinking he had. Just as he kept thinking he ought to know Calliope Kane. That he'd seen her before.

But thinking about her only brought a slew of emotions he didn't want to acknowledge at the moment. Yeah, he was pissed at her. Yeah, he was attracted to her. Yeah, she kept crawling through his thoughts when he'd prefer she didn't. Because every time he thought about her, his dick got so hard it hurt.

Which probably meant he ought to stop thinking about her.

He shot a glance at his brothers. "We're missing something. We're fucking missing something." Mal still couldn't wrap his head around what. He wanted names. He wanted someone to pay for what had been done to Lokan.

"Yeah, we are," Dagan agreed. "And we need to figure out what before we run out of time."

Time. Dae and Alastor viewed the contents of the

box as a step closer to getting Lokan back before time ran out. Mal viewed his brother's remains as proof that he was gone.

He knew better than to hope. He'd played that game before, held out hope for almost a decade back when he'd still believed he was mortal and believed he had a right to his happy ever after.

He'd searched for Elena for ten years, only to find she'd been dead for all of them.

It had almost destroyed him. And it had taught him not to hope, to live each day, to grab what enjoyment he could. To live for the adrenaline high.

He'd learned not to regret the past or dream of the future. Instead, he lived for right now, squeezing every drop out of every moment.

"It had to have been a sodding supernatural," Alastor muttered.

"Take your pick," Dagan said. "We have a fuckload to choose from. Aset. Osiris. Asmodeus. Xaphan."

"Izanami," Alastor offered. "Though my bets are against her."

"We're going around in circles," Mal snarled, anxious to go to Topworld and *do* something. But they were waiting on Sutekh for a nice little strategy meeting.

The double doors at the far end of the greeting chamber opened, and a soul reaper entered. Kai Warin. He was a hair under six feet, dark eyed, dark haired. His features were handsome and hard.

Mal jerked his head toward the far end of the room

and Kai headed in that direction. Alastor and Dagan followed.

"Thanks for cleaning up after me at Kuznetsov's condo," Mal said.

Kai's expression was impassive. "I owed you."

"Three whole words," Dagan observed. "That a record for you?"

Kai slanted him a look, moving only his eyes, but said nothing. He wasn't much of a talker, more of a thinker. Maybe that was why Sutekh had made him second-in-command, fast-tracking him up the ranks after Gahiji's betrayal. They might have wondered at their father's choice—Kai had been a soul reaper for less than fifty years—but Kai hadn't fucked up even once in those fifty years. Not once. He was solid as a brick shithouse.

Still, Mal was wary of trusting anyone, especially in light of the fact that there was likely still a traitor in their midst. Gahiji and his two new recruits might not have been the only ones to betray Sutekh. Until they knew with one hundred percent certainty, Mal wasn't inclined to trust anyone other than his brothers.

"You spoke with Djeserit Bast before you took her heart and soul?" he asked.

Kai gave a short nod.

"She say anything?"

"Already told Sutekh everything," Kai said.

"She didn't give up any names?"

"Humans. No Underworlders."

"Making us work for it, aren't you, Kai?" Alastor

clipped, his English accent more pronounced with his impatience.

Mal had had an accent, too. But unlike Alastor's mostly upper-crust diction, Mal's accent had been born in the gutter. Like him.

He'd lost it over the centuries, preferring to pick up new speech patterns and slang in order to blend in. It was a handy ability for a thief to have.

"Tell us everything Djeserit Bast said before you took her heart," Mal suggested.

Kai stared at him for a long moment then blew out a breath. "She babbled Kuznetsov's name. Described Gahiji. Offered up the Marin brothers on a platter. And just before I took her heart, she whispered shit that made no sense."

"What sort of shit?"

"Something about a prophecy."

When Kai said nothing more, Mal prodded, "Wanna share?"

"The blood of Aset. The blood of Sutekh. And the God will pass the Twelve Gates and walk the Earth once more."

They all stared at him for a heartbeat, then Alastor said mildly, "Well, that's a whole hell of a lot of help."

CHAPTER THIRTEEN

Save me from all kinds of harm and injury,
From the trap with painful knives,
And from all things bad and harmful
Which may be said or done against me
by men, gods, spirits or the dead.

—*The Egyptian Book of the Dead, Chapter 148*

WITH A GASP, HE BROKE the surface. The night sky was a dark saucer above him. The water pulled at him like a sucking bog. Barely did he fill his lungs before he was pulled under again. Something had his ankle. His wrist. He felt like he was being pulled apart, sucked into a vacuum.

Not all of him. Just parts.

He fought and strained and managed to break the surface once more.

Icy rivulets cascaded down his neck, his back. Above him, the night sky held no stars, not even one.

Panting, he fought to stay afloat, and then he shook his head, fear clutching his gut.

There was no sky. There was no water.

There was only the sensation of something tugging at

him like an undertow, leaving parts of his body numb. His hands. His feet. His arms. The pressure was enormous, a suctioning pull.

Part of him wanted to let the vortex take him, suck him away, until he was both here and there. Wherever *there* was.

A spark of recognition ignited. He felt a connection, someone out there whom he ought to recognize, ought to know—

It flickered. Vanished.

He felt bereft. Betrayed. *Come back.*

No—

Help me *find my way back.*

Yes. That was it. He needed to go back to—

The knowledge, so powerful and clear a second past, was gone. He couldn't remember what he needed to go back to.

It struck him then. He had no idea who he was. Where he was. There was only emptiness, a vast universe of nothingness.

His thoughts were leaden, mired in fog. Desperately, he reached for his name. Just that. Let him remember only his name. And then he did. Lokan. He was Lokan Krayl. He was mortal and immortal, half human, half god.

Immeasurably pleased with his success, he rolled to the side and pushed up on all fours. The movement left him feeling dizzy and sick. And then he realized he wasn't up on all fours. Disoriented, he tried to differentiate up from down. But this place had no such limitations as direction. And he remembered now that he was in a place of confinement, a prison of sorts, one without walls or boundaries.

He was confined by his own lack of substance.

Fear bit at him with sharp rat teeth. Because he was suddenly infinitely sure that he had regained this knowledge more than once, only to lose it again and again. This place did that to him. It robbed him of himself.

That realization brought him pain. Not physical. Something else. An ache of longing that made him gasp.

They were looking for him.

Who?

His *brothers*. He remembered them, hazy recollections that undulated and twined like smoke. He had brothers.

Malthus. Alastor. Dagan.

And a daughter. Dana. Precious Dana. He'd sent her to his enemies to keep her safe.

No, that couldn't be right. But it was. He had sent his daughter to his enemies because his allies could not be trusted. Betrayal was too close.

Gahiji, his father's second-in-command, had watched them carve the skin from his chest. Black blades. An oblong bowl, filling with blood. His blood.

But there was more than one traitor. Not just Gahiji. Someone else. Someone closer still. It was—

Cold horror settled like a lump of ice in his chest.

The one who had butchered him could butcher those he loved. So easily. Like snapping a twig.

He surged to his feet and battered at the confines of his cage.

There was no cage.

There was no Lokan.

There was nothing save the echo of his scream.

And then there was nothing at all.

WITH EXHAUSTION DRAGGING at her, Calliope lowered one foot then the other, concentrating on descending into the bowels of the earth without tripping and tumbling head over heels. Above her was the mansion with its hundreds of rooms and hundreds of women, all members of the Asetian Guard.

But other than Zalika, not a single one had greeted her. She had passed through the front doors and the long hallways, and the women she passed did not so much as glance her way. They would have been told not to. They would have been given no reason, only an order. And none would even think to disobey.

Such was the way of the Asetian Guard. Secretive. Private. Even longstanding members of the Guard, those of fairly high rank, were often told almost nothing of their mission or purpose. Protection, the Matriarchs said. One could not betray what one did not know.

That rule had worked to Calliope's advantage when she'd made the choice to release her acolyte, Roxy Tam, from her post. Roxy had been so low in the hierarchy that she'd been allowed to muster out because she'd been privy to no sensitive information.

Privy. She sucked in her breath, thinking of Malthus Krayl and her secret amusement at his word choice. Images flashed through her thoughts. The way he'd told her to stay behind him. The way he'd brushed his lips over hers, gentle, almost…sweet. And the way she'd left him, fire licking at his skin. She locked down the tiny flicker of regret. He was a soul reaper. Her enemy. She felt nothing for him.

He'd been a necessary sacrifice to her mission.

She had no idea why she was thinking about him at all. Except some tiny kernel inside her felt that he'd gotten a raw deal since the first second she'd approached him. She hadn't exactly been his good-luck charm. The thought made her lips shape a rueful smile.

As her boots rang against the polished oak of the staircase, Calliope glanced at Zalika.

"The night I took Kuznetsov," she said, "there were others there."

Zalika met her gaze. "The soul reaper."

"Him. But others, as well. Xaphan's concubines. And before that, a couple of Topworld grunts who work for Asmodeus."

"So many guests to the party." Zalika pressed her lips together. "I wonder who invited them all on the same night."

"Yes. Exactly," Calliope said. It was highly unlikely

that happenstance had so many supernaturals show up at Kuznetsov's building.

"Who knew of your plans?" Zalika asked, vocalizing the unease Calliope had been living with since she'd first sensed the reaper outside Kuznetsov's building. In retrospect, she should have aborted. But then, perhaps not. Had she waited to take the High Reverend another night, the soul reaper would have him now.

"No one."

They reached a landing, and Zalika paused, studying her.

"I've replayed every aspect of the evening in my mind," Calliope continued. "I spoke with Roxy Tam from the taxi but gave no indication of where I was or what I was about to do." She didn't bother to add that even if she *had* known, Roxy would never betray her, despite having taken a soul reaper as her mate. Best to stick only to the facts. "I told no one that I was planning to take Kuznetsov that night."

Zalika shot her a measured look. "You spoke with no one in the Guard?"

"Yes. Of course. I spoke with Sarita." Her direct superior. "It was a secure line from a secure location. There was no chance that I was overheard. And later, from my cell, but that was after my encounter with the reaper, and we spoke in only general terms at that point."

"Your direct superior. No one else knew of your intent?" Zalika's voice was so low, Calliope had to strain to hear her.

Again, Calliope ran through the events of that evening in her mind and came up with the exact same answer she had arrived at as she'd mulled it over again and again on the long drive here.

"No." She thought of the gold cartouche with Aset's name that Malthus Krayl had had in his possession. She knew what she'd seen, and it led to a possibility that was both unlikely and obscene: that there was a traitor here in the Guard, allied with the soul reapers.

"You will need to investigate the possibility of a—" She broke off, unwilling, or perhaps unable, to say the word "traitor" aloud. "Zalika, all is not right with this. We are days away from the meeting of allies. There is evidence of at least three, likely more, murdered Daughters of Aset. There is a dead soul reaper whom no one should have been able to kill. We have Xaphan and Asmodeus poking into places they have no business being."

"I have heard through a secondary source that even Izanami has stirred herself to have dialogue with Sutekh and the soul reapers," Zalika said.

Calliope sent a quick glance around, judging the privacy of their conversation. Though they were already speaking in whispers, she lowered her voice even further. "I have confirmation that Izanami sent one of her *Shikome* to Sutekh's realm."

"How do you know this?"

"Because she went there to lay claim to the soul of Naphré Kurata."

Zalika's brows rose. "An odd coincidence. Roxy Tam is the only acolyte you have ever trained, and Naphré was the acolyte you would have trained had she not left the Guard before she was blooded."

"An odd coincidence," Calliope agreed. Odder still that both were now mated to soul reapers. There had to be some significance to that.

Yet, Calliope's prescience had offered no forewarning; she had never seen a whisper of that outcome, and she had to wonder why.

"There are strange alliances unfolding, and they can all be traced back to the dead soul reaper," Calliope said. "I have only my instincts on this, Zalika. No proof. I must rely on you to follow the trail…in the event that I do not leave the Hall of the Matriarchs."

Zalika offered no denial to that. They both knew it was a possibility. Calliope had made her choices. If those choices had brought danger to them all, then she would pay a heavy price.

"Contact Roxy Tam," Calliope said. "She can put you in contact with Naphré Kurata."

Zalika stared at her. "Naphré long ago left the Guard, and Roxy has recently made that unfortunate choice as well. Neither can be trusted."

"I trust Roxy. With my life," Calliope said. "With the lives of my sisters in the Guard. With the lives of the Matriarchs."

"Be that as it may, she is no longer one of us."

"You need not trust her with our secrets, only ask her to share hers," Calliope pointed out.

"My duty and my emotion are at odds in this," Zalika whispered, her dark eyes shadowed. "My loyalty, as ever, is to the Guard."

"As is mine. And that is all the more reason to pursue the possibility of a traitor. A viper within the nest is more dangerous than one attacking from without."

Zalika closed her eyes and pressed her lips together. When she opened her eyes once more, her gaze was clear. "Yes," she said, and in that word Calliope had her assurance.

They continued down into the lower levels of the compound. The mansion above them was enormous, but the levels belowground were all the more vast.

The Asetian Guard had laid out the headquarters with a careful eye to detail and respect for ancient Egyptian numerology.

Seven flights of seven steps each, then the polished wooden stairs ran out, replaced by stone.

"I must leave you now," Zalika said. "You know the way."

"I do." Calliope had been called before the Matriarchs once before.

Zalika embraced her then, a brief instant of warmth and connection before she took her leave.

CALLIOPE CONTINUED DOWN the stone staircase. Seven flights of seven steps each, and with each flight the space narrowed. At this point, if she shifted inches to either side, her shoulder would touch the wall. Cold stone. Cold air. And the smell of earth all around her.

Seven. The symbol of perfection. Effectiveness. Completeness.

Seven. The symbol of the vile betrayal Sutekh had perpetrated when he hacked Aset's husband, Osiris, into fourteen pieces—seven for each of the two regions of Egypt, Upper and Lower. The hatred between Aset and Sutekh had started then, leading to generations of war and tensions, both open and concealed, that followed.

Rumor stated the dead reaper's body had been hacked into fourteen parts, and those parts were scattered to ensure they were not brought together to offer a vessel for the reaper's soul to inhabit once more. That in itself seemed to point to Aset or Osiris as the killer. How convenient. Any Underworlder wishing to start a war might well create such an obvious clue. But why would Osiris or Aset be so careless?

The stairs ended. Calliope paused in the small, cave-like reception area with walls of weeping gray stone. Before her was a heavy steel door, guarded by the latest biometric security.

A scan of her retina. A check of her fingerprints. She said her name and the system evaluated her voiceprint. The door swung open with a faint hydraulic hiss.

She had three seconds, only that, before it would swing shut once more.

Those who sought entry to this place had best be nimble on their feet.

Calliope stepped forward, staying perfectly still as the door swung shut behind her. She heard the faintest click, almost inaudible, and she knew the self-destruct had been engaged once more. If enemies tried to force their way past, the door would explode, the charges set to seal this path and at the very least slow—but preferably kill—those who tried to breach security.

She held still, waiting. Technology was not the only challenge that lay in her path.

Tendrils of ancient magics reached out and swirled around her limbs, testing her, tasting her. She resisted the urge to squirm away from the damp, cloying touch. They were not spells wrought of light, and not precisely of darkness, but rather some twisted combination of the two. Such spells were risky, but the Matriarchs of the Daughters of Aset would do anything to protect the line. Security was paramount, and those who had set these defenses willingly took the blight for the conjuring on their souls.

They made that sacrifice for the common good.

Such was ever the expectation of members of the Asetian Guard. Sacrifice for the common good. The collective before the individual. The single irrefutable fact: the line must continue.

The sensation of being probed by tongues of magic she could not see receded, and she continued along the narrow stone hallway that sloped down at a sharp angle.

Beautifully wrought symbols were etched in the stone walls, ancient hieroglyphs that told a story of the way to rebirth. They depicted the Twelve Gates of Osiris, one for each hour of the night.

Some ancient texts spoke of twenty-one gates. She was familiar with the concepts of both.

Again, she paused. Before her was a second steel door, and she repeated the entry process before stepping into a second chamber, this one bearing hieroglyphics that told the story of Aset and her brother/husband Osiris, and the birth of their son Horus.

Calliope had been to this underground place once before in her life, which made her a rare breed. There were many in the Guard who would never enter the presence of the Matriarchs.

She remembered the first time she had passed through these doors, just over ten years ago when she had been promoted to the position of mentor, entrusted with the rare and wonderful opportunity to guide the growth of a new member of the Asetian Guard. Roxy Tam.

On that previous occasion, she had been invited to enter.

This time, she had been ordered.

Still, she would not choose her actions differently were she able to go back and change them.

The collective before the individual. The choice she had made had kept Kuznetsov in the hands of the Guard and prevented the soul reapers from having access to his knowledge. The outcome was desired; only the method was questionable.

If she was to be punished, so be it.

Taking a deep breath, she stepped through the second door. Soundlessly, it swung shut behind her.

Lights came on, so bright they hurt her eyes. Calliope blinked against the glare, not fighting it, merely waiting for adjustment to occur. Once it did, she stared straight ahead. The lights illuminated a defined circle, perhaps ten feet in diameter, and she was at the center of it. Beyond the sharp boundaries of light was utter blackness.

If she reached out, she would encounter thick, fortified glass: a cage of glass. She had discovered that on her previous visit. She didn't bother to confirm its existence now.

The lights came up all around her, first taking on a faint glow, like a single candle, then growing brighter and brighter until the space beyond the circle was as bright as that within.

Three identical chairs stood on a raised stone dais at the far end of the massive chamber. Made of fine wood from Lebanon, each was engraved with the knot of Aset, also known as the "blood of Isis." Each chair back was set with a deep red cushion embroidered with gold thread, and similar cushions formed the seats.

There was no chair within the cage of thick glass that surrounded her, but there was a silk carpet in tones of red and beige and brown beneath her feet, a small concession to her comfort.

She had no idea when the Matriarchs would see her. It would be wise to take this time to rest. Despite her exhaustion, she knew she wouldn't be able to curl up here and sleep, but she could meditate and offer her mind and body a small respite. Sinking to the floor, she crossed her legs and let go of the tension in her frame. She sought—and found—the warm light inside herself, a place of harmony and ease.

After a time, the energy in the chamber shifted, growing sharper, molecules vibrating faster. She opened her eyes and rose, knowing that substantial time had passed, but uncertain of exactly how much. She didn't bother to look at her watch. She knew from experience that it had stopped the second she was sealed in the glass cage and would begin to run again only once—*if*—she left.

A dozen armed guards entered and formed a living wall around three women dressed in flowing red robes with cowls pulled up to hide their faces. It was ever this way. The elders were not to be seen. Their identities were guarded as carefully as their physical bodies. Calliope had always wondered about that. Why guard them so carefully when they were the most powerful and ancient of all Aset's Daughters? Should it not be the other way around? Should they, the strongest, not be guarding the weakest among them?

On the other hand, she understood the need for the Matriarchs, above all others, to survive, no matter what.

They were the mothers, Amunet, Beset and Hathor, the vessels of millennia of knowledge, the keepers of history.

They glided forward, postures erect, their movements so graceful that they appeared to levitate. Perhaps they did, in fact. The long gowns obscured their feet, so she had no way to tell with any certainty. Once they seated themselves, the other women—who were dressed in dark, supple clothing much like Calliope's own—moved to flank them but stayed slightly behind, a mark of respect.

She was their kind. She was their sister. What were they all but Aset's Daughters, gifted with the blood of the goddess and the ability to feed from the life force of others to live eternal?

Yet a cold slither of fear iced her veins.

CHAPTER FOURTEEN

I ward off the arm of the one who would
oppose himself against the flame of the desert.
I have set fire to the desert, I have deflected the
path, for I am the protection.
—The Egyptian Book of the Dead, Chapter 151

"YOU HAVE BETRAYED YOUR kind." The accusation, soft voiced and direct, came from the cowled figure on the left. Amunet.

Calliope blinked. She had expected a question or, more accurately, many questions. She had not expected a flat accusation.

"No." She didn't elaborate. She would wait until they asked for more information.

"Your acolyte consorts with the enemy."

So they already knew about Roxy. "She is no longer my acolyte. She mustered out, as was her right at the level she had achieved."

"You let her."

"More than that, I *encouraged* her."

None of the Matriarchs offered an overt display of surprise at her words, but she sensed it nonetheless.

"Explain," Amunet commanded.

"The soul reaper Roxy has taken as her mate is Sutekh's son. To anger him is to anger his father. I could not allow the wrath of Sutekh to descend on the entire Asetian Guard. Had she remained one of us, she would have been required to forsake him. I was convinced he would not allow that."

In fact, she knew with certainty that the reaper would have fought for Roxy with any and all means he possessed. That would have meant significant risk to the entire Asetian Guard.

"You chose to sacrifice one in order to protect us all."

"I did." She sincerely doubted that Roxy saw it as a sacrifice, but from the Matriarch's point of view, and her own, it had been.

"And we allowed it," Beset said. "There is a traitor amongst them. One who works against their kind. It is not unfortunate for one of our kind to know their every move."

Uneasy with this revelation, Calliope chose her words with care. "The traitor, Gahiji, is dead. He was Sutekh's general."

The silence lengthened, and it was in the lack of reply that Calliope read the truth. They spoke not of Gahiji, but of another. Calliope shook her head. "As I understand it, Gahiji was the oldest of their kind. He had been with Sutekh for millennia. The only soul reapers higher in the ranks are Sutekh's sons—"

The energy that crackled in the air ramped up a notch, and the Matriarchs bent their cowled heads toward each other as though communicating without speaking aloud.

Calliope stared at them. Could it be possible? Could the traitor be not only in Sutekh's own ranks, but one of his sons? Which one?

Dagan? If it were, then that put Roxy at risk.

Malthus Krayl? His desire to take Kuznetsov could certainly be explained if he were the traitor. He wouldn't want the High Reverend to reveal that to anyone. On the other hand, he would also want Kuznetsov if he were only seeking information that would allow him to have his revenge.

That left the third brother, Alastor. Roxy had mentioned his name.

"You must now answer a second charge," Beset said. "Do you deny that you fed from a soul reaper? Do you deny that his prana and blood are only now beginning to fade from your body?"

"No, I do not deny it."

On the far right, Hathor edged slightly forward in her seat. "To feed from one such as he is a betrayal."

"It is not specifically forbidden," Calliope said, her tone even and cool. "We are discouraged from feeding from other supernaturals. There is no law against it that I am aware of."

"She speaks truth," Beset observed.

"She *bends* truth. The law is implied."

"Implied is not the same as inscribed," Calliope said.

"A betrayal," Hathor repeated.

"A choice," Calliope replied. "The good of the collective over the preference of the individual."

"Explain," Beset ordered.

"I was sent to retrieve Pyotr Kuznetsov. I was about to lose him to a soul reaper. It was either feed from him and use his strength for the successful completion of my mission, or forfeit my prize. A prize of great value to the Guard and all Daughters. The latter was less acceptable than the former. I fed from him and used his own power against him."

She wondered if they knew what it had cost her to take his blood, if they knew the disgust that had crawled from her belly up her throat in a bitter, stinging wave. At the same time, she had gloried in the taste. In that moment, she had truly hated herself.

It had been decades since she had required blood in order to sip the prana of another.

"You are linked to him now," Amunet intoned.

That was the risk, the reason that members of the Asetian Guard were not to feed from any full-blooded supernatural. A one-way psychic link, with information flowing to the Guard, would be acceptable. But there was no way to guarantee that. The possibility existed that information would flow both ways. The risk of that increased if there were repeated feedings.

She thought of the dream she had had at the base of the mountain. A dream was not a link. It was only the conjuring of her imagination that had brought him to her. If the soul reaper truly had found her and entered her mind, he wouldn't have wanted to kiss her. After the way she'd left him, burning like a torch, his car stolen, his prize stolen, more likely he'd want to kill her.

"At the base of the mountain, I slept briefly before I climbed," Calliope said. "The soul reaper featured in my nightmare." Nothing but the truth. It was a nightmare to imagine engaging in sexual congress with a soul reaper. Doubly so because she'd almost done exactly that at her own instigation the night she had lured him to the basement of the club.

"Understandable, but do you know if it was only a dream and not a true connection?"

"I felt no link," Calliope said. "I feel none now."

"No?" Beset asked, sounding almost amused. "Have you sought it? Reached for it?"

"No." The very thought of crawling into the soul reaper's thoughts was disturbing.

"Do so now."

Calliope blinked. Of course, they would order her to do that. It was exactly the course that made the most sense. They needed to know if she shared thoughts with the soul reaper now that she had shared his life force.

She took a slow breath, knowing that argument was futile. Knowing, too, that this must be done. The choices she had made had all been to protect the Guard; it would be bitter irony were she the one to lead the soul reapers directly to them.

"If you find him, if your thoughts become one with his, we will know," Hathor said. "And your freedom will be permanently forfeited. If you can see through his eyes, we will be forced to consider the likelihood that he can see through yours. We cannot risk that he will discover this place, discover *us*. You understand this?"

Despite the circumstances, Calliope's lips turned in a dark smile. Did it matter if she understood? Would her preferences matter? She preferred to stay alive and free. She would have preferred to have never tasted the soul reaper's cursed blood. But it had been the right choice in the circumstances. Even viewed through the clear glass of hindsight, magnified and clarified, it had been the right choice. Her assignment had been to retrieve Kuznetsov. She'd completed her assignment. Taking the reaper's blood had been a means to an end.

"Understood." Her stomach churned at the thought that he might invade her mind, know her secrets.

As though sensing Calliope's concerns, Amunet explained, "If your efforts do produce a link, be at ease for your privacy. He will not know all. Such a link is more of a dreamlike state. It is not mind reading, but rather a *sense* of the other being. He might share the scene that is before your eyes in that moment, or you may share a view of what is before his eyes. But unless you are thinking about them in that moment, he will not be able to crawl through your memories, or you through his."

Calliope nodded, unsure if Amunet's words comforted or made her all the more concerned. Shared emotion with the soul reaper didn't exactly appeal.

"Seek him," Beset ordered, and with a soft whirring sound, black metal shields descended to surround Calliope's glass cage, leaving her in utter darkness. They were a form of insurance. If there was a link, he would see nothing but darkness.

She focused on finding the vestiges of the reaper's blood and life force in her system. She couldn't feel it now. The sense of power and strength had faded with each hour that passed.

She traced the memory of pulling his blood from his lacerated flesh, swallowing it, the taste indescribable, to its root. She isolated it from the tangle of all her other memories. Separate now, it glowed, alone and clear in the center of her thoughts. She followed the recollection to the cellular level, sifting to the genetic blueprint that marked her for what she was.

In vain.

He was not there.

She summoned him, willed him to link his thoughts to her own, pulled on the threads of connection that she imagined into existence.

But that was just it. They were only imagination. She could find no link to him no matter how hard she searched.

With a gasp, she came to herself, sucking air, her chest screaming against the lack. Her heart thudded against her ribs, the pounding of her blood so loud she felt certain the women across the chamber could hear each beat.

Then she realized she was on her knees on the ground, hands planted flat, head hanging low. Her hair was a black pool that spread past the edge of the silk carpet to the gray stone.

Blinking, she oriented herself. Time had passed. She felt it. A great deal of time. She was weak with hunger, her lips and tongue parched with thirst. They had left her here to find her way there and back, and now that she had, she was subject to their justice.

She lifted her head. The black metal plates had ascended into the ceiling once more. She was surrounded only by glass. The Matriarchs sat upon their thrones, though whether they had been there the entire time or whether they had returned as she came to herself was a question she could not answer.

"You found nothing," Hathor said, her voice low and melodic. Was she pleased by the outcome? Impossible to tell. Perhaps the Matriarchs had hoped that she would have a connection, would find the reaper's lair and offer a way to destroy him. Or perhaps they were glad that the taint of his blood had been only temporary.

Amunet spoke then. "We must wait. Time must pass. We must be certain."

Calliope stared at them, feeling woozy and weak.

Without further explanation, they rose, the cloth of their dark red robes flowing around them like water. As they moved, the light caught a glint of gold. Her gaze flicked from Beset to Hathor to Amunet. Each wore a thick chain and a cartouche outside their robes. Which made her think of the soul reaper threading his necklace through Aset's cartouche.

How had he come to possess it?

Zalika had confirmed her belief that only the Matriarchs and Aset herself wore that symbol.

She opened her mouth to call out, to ask, to reveal this tiny bit of knowledge. And in the end, she said nothing. There was something wrong in all of this, something that smelled like week-old fish.

In a clean, single-file line, the Matriarchs made their way toward the far corner and the shadowed doorway there.

"Wait," Calliope said, pushing to her feet, her head spinning.

They didn't pause. Didn't even appear to hear her.

"How much time must pass?"

The others walked on, but Beset stopped and turned. She waved the guards on, and then they were alone. "Your blood cells remain viable for 120 days," she said, her voice not unkind.

Four months. Trapped here, when she had so much to do. But there was no argument she could offer that would sway them.

"The meeting of allies. I am to be sent—"

"No longer," Beset cut her off. "We cannot take the risk of using you for any task until we know what taint you have acquired. We will choose another."

She thought the Matriarch would leave then, but she did not. Instead, she glided closer, so only half the chamber separated them now.

"Ask your questions, Calliope. I sense them rioting in your thoughts. I have no wish for this to be more difficult for you than it must. We are not monsters. Our choices are for the group rather than the individual, but that does not mean we are without empathy." She folded her arms across her midsection, her hands hidden by the voluminous sleeves. "Much as you had empathy when you released Roxy Tam from service, though her choice of mate repulsed you. You have my leave to ask what you will."

Calliope had no idea how many questions the Matriarch would grant her, so she meant to make each one count, but when she opened her mouth, the words that escaped were not the ones she intended. "Does Kuznetsov know the identity of Lokan Krayl's killer?"

"Yes."

"Is he *aware* that he knows it?"

Beset laughed, a rusty sound, as though it was little used. "No. His memories were locked away, even from him. He knew he witnessed the killing. He knew he was there. He even knew the identity of other mortals who were involved, and he gladly named them for us. But he could not identify the supernaturals who bloodied their hands with the soul reaper's death."

The answers were exactly what she had expected. Which made them suspect. Was Beset telling her the truth, or telling her what she expected to hear?

"Did we kill the soul reaper?" she asked. "Did Kuznetsov ally with the Guard against Sutekh?"

Again Beset laughed, but now the sound had a hard edge. A warning.

"These questions you should ask only if you are certain you are willing to pay the price for the answers, Calliope. You may yet leave this place to serve the Guard in the world of mortals. That is what you wish, is it not?"

The implication was clear. Answers might cost her her freedom. Or her life. Was that an answer in itself? Did it mean that Aset, and perhaps even Osiris, had moved against Sutekh with the murder of his son? And if so, why now? The cease-fire had been in place for nearly 6,000 years.

She couldn't say why the answers mattered. She'd spent most of her life in the Guard, following orders, doing what needed to be done, never questioning the directives that were handed to her. Because losing herself in the hierarchy, giving herself over to something larger than her own hurts, allowed her to rise above those hurts. To be serene. Never again to feel that devastating terror and loss that had once consumed her.

She opened her mouth to question further, intending

to make full use of this rare and unique opportunity. It was unheard of to have a private audience with a Matriarch.

Then she gasped. Beset was no longer halfway across the room. She was directly in front of Calliope with only the shatterproof glass between them.

The cowl obscured the Matriarch's face, and the folds of the robe hid her form. This close, Calliope could see the red velvet was shot with black and edged with black embroidery, the gold chain and cartouche bright against the cloth. Any hope she'd harbored that the cartouche the soul reaper had held had been other than Aset's disappeared. There could be no doubt.

"Let me see your thoughts," Beset said. Only the words did not come from beyond the glass, but rather from inside Calliope's skull, the sound both a booming echo and the softest whisper.

Pain shot through her, from her head down her neck, through her spine. It exploded down her legs through the soles of her feet, anchoring her to the stone. Hot. Cold. The heart of a furnace. The water of a lake beneath a crust of ice. It was the most horrific sensation she had ever known. Like acid eating her from inside.

"I have no wish to cause you discomfort, merely to see what I must. You resist."

A strangled laugh escaped her. "Not on purpose."

"Truly?" Beset paused. "You are strong. I had not expected it. Come. Let me in."

Again, the pain, as though the cap of her skull was

popped open and boiling oil poured through her insides. She sought her center, sought her placid lake, away from the pain, the heat, the burn.

There. Water like glass. Air pure and clean. The pain gone. She stood by a pond in a perfect field. And she was alone.

"The blood of Aset runs true in your veins," Beset said. Then, "We will use a different course."

Though she couldn't see Beset's features or expression, she had the feeling that the Matriarch was looking at her speculatively.

"You do not trust me. Not only do you not invite me in, you bar the door of your thoughts against me. Why is that, Calliope Kane?"

"I don't know," Calliope said in all truthfulness. She knew she feared the power of this nameless, formless woman. She feared her vengeance and her fury. But more than that, she feared what the Matriarch might choose to reveal to her about herself. "I do not consciously make the choice to keep you out." In for a penny, in for a pound. "But I freely admit that the thought of anyone else going through my mind like a filing cabinet is unappealing."

She preferred to maintain her calm and placid mien, to bury all darkness beneath the smooth surface of her own secret lake. Easier that way than to face the horrors of her memories and her terrors. Her hate and pain. Bury something deep enough and even if you couldn't forget it, at least you didn't have to look at it.

Beset nodded, her cowl completely obscuring her features. "You are the first in many centuries to bar my entry. It will be blood, then."

She gestured toward Calliope's feet, the sleeve of her robe long and wide, hiding her hand.

On the floor was a knife. The blade was obsidian, the handle finely carved to shape a snake, or perhaps a dragon. Familiar, but not.

Fatigue made her thoughts sluggish. Calliope wondered how the knife had appeared in her glass cage. Then she wondered why it seemed so painfully familiar. A chill of premonition crawled along her spine.

"Pick up the knife."

She did. Her fingers closed over the handle, and she thought there was some significance to this. To this particular knife. To Beset's demand.

A memory curled up from the deepest recess of her mind, like smoke that carried a whisper. She stared at the knife in her hand. The obsidian blade. The carved handle. A dragon.

Foreign, yet familiar.

"Blood," Beset said, not forcing the word into Calliope's mind, but using her voice in inarguable command.

Raising her head, she stared at Beset. She reached inside herself, found the place of light and simplicity she had trained herself to seek. She held fast to it, her will her own once more.

With deliberate care, she turned the knife and made

a shallow cut on her palm, staining the blade with her blood.

She bent down and placed the knife with care directly against the wall of glass that separated her from Beset. Then she straightened and raised her head.

The Matriarch had the knife in her hand, close to her face. Within the shadows of her cowl, something stirred. Calliope thought it was the tip of her tongue tracing the edge of the knife, tasting blood. But she couldn't swear to it.

"All is as it must be," the Matriarch said.

There was a flash of light, so bright it was blinding, and when Calliope blinked away the dancing stars, she was alone. Beset was gone.

And with her, the knife.

Turning her palm up, Calliope stared at her hand and her brows rose. The skin was marked only by a thin, pink line. There was no blood, and no open wound. Ordinarily, she healed faster than a mortal, but this was accelerated beyond her usual capacity.

Had the remnants of the reaper's life force in her system healed her, or was it something Beset had done?

There were no answers here.

Slowly, she made her way around the glass cage that surrounded her. She didn't bother to beat it with her fists. It was shatterproof. Escape-proof.

There were better uses for her time.

Sinking to the floor once more, she centered herself

on the carpet, crossed her legs and rested the backs of her hands on her bent knees. The best thing she could do was rest. While sleep was out of the question, meditation was not.

She grounded her thoughts and searched for calm, and as she slid into relaxation, the image of the knife burned bright in her mind, the solitary image that refused to be swept out.

A handle carved like a dragon. An obsidian blade.

The knife from the video.

Her eyes popped open and she gasped.

The knife she had seen slicing through the skin on Lokan Krayl's chest.

CHAPTER FIFTEEN

*The roads in the sky and on earth have opened
for me,
And there was none who thwarted me.*
—*The Egyptian Book of the Dead, Chapter 78*

THEY TRANSFERRED CALLIOPE to a cell. A comfortable
one, to be sure, but a cell nonetheless. The door was
steel. There were no windows. A thorough evaluation
of the room revealed no surveillance devices. At least
she'd been afforded a measure of privacy.

There was a bed with Egyptian cotton sheets, a bedside table with a lamp, a desk and chair, and a small
bathroom with a shower, no tub. That was the first place
Calliope headed. She couldn't recall her last shower.

When she came out of the bathroom twenty minutes later, wrapped in a towel, her long hair lying damp
against her skin, she found a tray laden with food resting
on the desk and a pile of clean clothing on the bed.

She pulled on sweatpants and a long-sleeved thermal
shirt, then she managed half the food, and what she did
eat, she didn't taste. The events of the past few days
had turned her world upside down, made it crazy and

frightening in a way it hadn't been for almost a century and a half. She chewed and swallowed only because common sense told her she needed to eat.

Go through the motions. Maintain what control she could.

She rose and dragged the straight-backed chair to the door. There was no lock on the inside, but she'd seen one on the outside as she'd come through earlier. She'd heard the click as her guards locked her in.

Tipping the chair onto two legs, she then anchored the back beneath the door handle. As far as protection went, it wasn't much; it wouldn't keep anything out. But the sound of the chair scraping on the floor would rouse her from sleep if someone tried to come in.

Normally, she would just rely on her gift of prescience, but thanks to her reaper snack, it had deserted her for the moment. She was forced to fall back on more primitive means.

The only thing that would get in here unannounced was a soul reaper.

The second the thought formed, she regretted it. Because it made her think of *him,* and she didn't want to think about him. Didn't want to see his wolf smile in her thoughts or remember the feel of his lips as he'd brushed them across her own in the parking lot before the fire genies had come.

She definitely did not want to think about the dream she'd had where she'd pretty much had her tongue down his throat.

So she cleared her mind and focused only on her immediate need: sleep.

Exhausted, she crawled into the bed, fully clothed in her borrowed sweats. Her eyes drifted shut, and she hung there, in the space between sleep and wakefulness.

The colors were too bright. The sounds too loud.

No. This was not a place she wanted to revisit tonight.

She struggled against the mire of exhaustion, aware that she was tipping over the edge into a dream—a nightmare—yet despite that knowledge, she was sucked in.

They came from the ships. Sailors. Rough and angry, they roved in packs.

Urgency consumed her. She needed to get back to her father's shop. The errand he'd sent her on—

She didn't remember what it was, but she knew it was no longer important.

Hiking up her skirt, she tucked it in at the waist and darted along the streets and through the alleys. The buildings loomed on every side, creating a long, narrow tunnel, the way nearly blocked by the crowd. To her left, two peasant women held a man down while two others beat him with a pitchfork and a broom. To her right, a man in a fancy coat held another by the throat and lifted high a truncheon, ready to strike.

She darted between them, small and fast, her heart pounding, her breath coming in desperate, pained gasps.

The sounds of boots—many, many boots—hitting the street came from behind her. She glanced back and saw them. The Greek sailors from the harbor. They pushed and pummeled and called out jeers, their voices heavy with hate.

She ran, one small girl in a roiling sea of adult bodies. She dipped and ducked and stayed close to the buildings because most of the throng had spilled into the street. Her heart was near to bursting, her lungs screaming. To stop meant they might catch her. To stop meant she might never reach home.

Almost there. Almost there. The shop was before her, just at the end of the street. All around her were screams and cries, but suddenly, she heard her name soaring above the cacophony, a sharp cry. A warning. An order to stay away.

Or perhaps she only imagined the cry as she saw her mother's face, stark with terror, her hair torn from the neat roll she habitually wore at her nape, now a dark snarl tumbling down over her shoulders. Two men dragged her back toward the open door of the shop.

Calliope ducked to the side, clinging to the wall, her chest heaving.

Frantic, she looked all around. Someone was here. Someone was watching her. Panic choked her, and she fought it back, focusing on her father's shop.

The men inside were not like the others running mad through the streets of Odessa, clubbing and kill-

ing. She knew it. She *felt* it deep inside. These men were
something else.

Wrapping her arms around herself, she tried to still
the shudders that racked her body. Her terror swelled and
bulged because she knew what they were. Her grandmother liked to tell her stories of fiends and demons
and flesh-eating monsters that wore human faces. But
the stories terrified her because in her heart, Calliope
had always suspected the monsters were real.

And now she knew they were. They had come for
her family.

These are not men, she thought, and her soul trem-
bled at that certainty.

Her mother had told her about pogroms in the past,
saying that if a mob grew hateful and mean, she must
hide until it was done.

Blinded by tears, she glanced about, frantic. No one
seemed interested in her, one small girl, yet the feeling
she was being watched didn't subside. On every side
was the mob, growing angrier and more reckless by the
second. In her father's shop were the men who held her
parents. There was nowhere for her, nowhere safe.

She fell back and ducked into a clump of bushes.
Hiding in the tangle of branches, huddled into a ball,
she clasped her arms around her knees. Her limbs shook
though she tried to hold herself still, and terror gnawed
at her soul.

Through the open door of the shop she could see
the two men who held her father. One turned his head

toward her and for the briefest instant, she thought he saw her, that he would come for her. A part of her almost wanted that, wanted him to bring her to her parents so they could all be together. But the stronger part knew that they would want her to stay exactly where she was.

Her father struggled against them and once almost tore free of them. A third man backhanded him across the face, and the one who had been looking in her direction turned away.

Choking on her sobs, Calliope scooted back deeper in the shadows.

There were screams and cries coming from all around her, adding to her panic and the feeling of being trapped, cornered. She huddled even smaller, but she could not look away from her father and the men who held him. A part of her was waiting for him—her brave, strong father who carried her on his shoulders even though she was a big girl now, ten years on her next birthday—to tear from their grasp and come for her. Save her.

But the men who held him were bigger. Stronger.

Her eyes widened, and she choked on her horror as the third man drew back his hand and thrust it through her father's chest.

A scream bubbled up, and she bit her lip to keep from crying out, bit it hard enough that her mouth filled with blood. Above the din of the street, she thought she could hear the sharp crack of bone, like a dry twig snapping, and her father's cry, sharp as a crow's.

And then the man tore her father's heart from his chest. Blood sprayed in all directions.

Bile burned her throat. Tears blurred her vision. Her heart pounded so hard she felt it slamming against her ribs like a hammer.

In her stupor of fear and loss and grief, she felt arms close around her, strong and solid, not to confine but to comfort. She didn't dare relax into the embrace, didn't dare trust it. Whatever insidious thing invaded this moment, she knew in some conscious and aware part of her brain that there had been no comfort for her that long-ago day.

Confused, she tried to focus her attention. Then. Now. Time blended and bent and became something other than it was.

Calliope cried out, knowing it was a dream, while at the same time, knowing it was real.

She was a child.

She was a woman grown. She was a blooded Daughter of Aset, one hundred and sixty years old.

The thick, syrupy tendrils of the dream snaked around her limbs and torso, and she struggled against them, almost awake.

She needed to wake up. She didn't want to see this again. Please, never again. She needed—

The man who held her father's heart laughed, wild and uncontrolled. She knew what was coming; she wanted to look away.

He tipped back his head. He lifted his hand. He

squeezed the heart to make the last of the blood trickle out in a rich stream. It poured into his open mouth, like wine from a flask, dribbling over his lips and chin.

He drank her father's blood.

Then, baring his teeth, he brought the heart to his mouth and tore off a hunk. Chewed. Swallowed.

And Calliope watched, unable to tear her gaze away.

Bile burned the back of her tongue. Horror clogged her throat.

Enough. This was the moment it ended. This was always the moment it ended—

Someone else stepped from the shadows, behind her father, behind the monsters who had killed him. She stared as he moved into the light.

Gray eyes looked back at her.

Malthus Krayl.

The sense of being watched earlier. The arms that had held her. It had been him. He had followed her through the streets of Odessa. Rage uncoiled, mixing with the turmoil of horror and fear and confusion that churned within.

Some part of her had accepted his comfort. Some part of her had known all along it was he.

But he had no business in her dreams.

His kind had done this. They were the monsters, the murderers. *He* was a monster. She wanted to leap on him. Stab him. Claw him. But she couldn't because he was only a memory inside her own mind.

He reached out and closed his hand around the arm of the monster who had killed her father, sending the remnants of her father's heart tumbling end over end, taking an eternity as it fell to the floor.

And then Malthus Krayl thrust his fist through the monster's chest.

Calliope jerked upright, panting, sick, tearing free of the nightmare and the emotion it drew.

The dream was always the same. Only tonight it had been different. Tonight, she hadn't huddled in the bushes, sobbing until a gray-eyed stranger pulled her free. Tonight, the timing was off and the gray-eyed man had taken on a new identity, and a name.

One thought slammed her as she sat, gasping a lung-ful of the cold night air.

Malthus Krayl had found her.

MAL STOOD ON A ROAD that was barely a road. A bit of gravel in the wilderness. Step three feet in any direction other than the way he'd come, and the road disappeared, swallowed by the forest. Tipping his head back, he stared up at the mountain that loomed above him. Massive. Eternal.

She was up there somewhere. He only needed to go find her.

His lungs pulled in air, his chest expanding as though he'd run a marathon. In a way, he had. He'd kept pace with Calliope as she ran through the streets, seeing what she saw. Feeling what she felt. Terror. Helplessness. And in the end, horror and grief and despair.

He'd wanted to kill those who had planted the seeds of that grief. He wanted to rip their hearts out and harvest their darksouls. To protect her. To wrap her in his embrace and keep her safe. He didn't like the intensity of those inclinations; they were instincts he'd thought long buried.

Beating his chest over a woman and howling, "Mine," wasn't his thing. But this woman, who didn't need—or want—his protection, brought out the primitive.

Why?

He couldn't say. Didn't want to say.

He'd seen both his brothers, Dagan and Alastor, slam into a wall and fall hard. Fucking love at first sight.

He didn't believe in it. Didn't trust it.

And sure as hell refused to feel it.

He was a one-night kind of guy. And he liked it that way.

But he admired her, the woman who had grown out of that little girl who had had the presence of mind to hide, to stay quiet, to follow the instructions her mother had given her time and again.

That child had saved herself.

And that child had made a mistake, one that had colored every choice since. She'd built her whole life on a lie, and she had no fucking clue.

How was he supposed to tell her that? How was he

supposed to tell her that what she'd seen wasn't actually what she believed?

Yeah, that was going to go over like a car through a guardrail at the edge of a cliff. Crash and burn, baby. Crash and burn.

He reached for the last tendrils of her dream. *His* dream. One and the same. And he saw what he needed to see. A room. A bed. A small table. A chair cocked back on two legs, the back propped under the door.

Not much, but enough.

CALLIOPE SWUNG HER LEGS over the side of the bed. Her heart was pounding as it had in the dream, her breath rasping in the silence. For a second, she thought he watched her still. But there was only darkness, inky and black.

The dream hadn't come to her so vividly for a long while. It had felt so real. The terror her childish self had lived through left her heart pounding even now. She had seen Malthus Krayl there in her dream, and that left her emotions in a tangled knot. Because it was his kind who had murdered her father. And because his eyes made her think of the man who had dragged her— saved her—from the mob hours later. He'd had gray eyes and dark hair. She remembered that he'd seemed old to her then, but she supposed he'd been about thirty. She remembered almost nothing else about him except those eyes and dark lashes and the feel of his hands on her shoulders, steadying her before he left her alone once more.

As far as saviors went, he hadn't exactly been Sir Gallahad. In the end, she'd had to save herself.

She reached for the bedside lamp. Only when light flooded the room did she realize that the enhanced night vision she'd enjoyed since she had taken the reaper's blood had faded now. Before she'd turned on the light, she hadn't been able to see a thing. Perhaps his prana was fading, and with it, the impediment to her pre-science. She missed it, the ability to sense what was coming. She'd had it so long, it was just another sense she accepted as being part of her.

A quick scan told her the chair was still in place under the door handle, and the tray of half-eaten food rested on the table. There was no one else in the room. Only her and the ghosts of her nightmares.

Yet, she felt that there was threat here. Danger.

The air was cold enough that she could see her breath. With a sharp exhalation, she surged to her feet and claimed a pair of socks from the pile of clean clothes her jailors had left her. Then she pulled on a sweatshirt and went to the bathroom to brush her teeth. Her mouth tasted like bile, like tears and desperation.

A child's tears.

She didn't cry anymore. Hadn't for a very long time.

The last vestiges of the dream snaked through her waking thoughts. She didn't want to think about it, didn't want to wonder what Malthus Krayl had been doing in her memories.

There had been only three soul reapers who had taken advantage of the chaos of the pogrom, killing her father under the cloud of mass violence that had descended on Odessa in the form of a group of sailors who had become drunk on the high of killing and dragged others into the frenzy.

Malthus Krayl had not been one of those three reapers.

But somehow, he had been there tonight.

"I am serene. I am a cool, deep well," she whispered, staring at herself in the mirror over the sink in the bathroom. And when the turmoil inside her didn't ease, she gave a short, bitter laugh and said, "I am a fucking placid lake."

That long-ago day, she had been a child, tossed about by the whims of fate. She had huddled in the shadows and had no choice but to let events happen to her.

She had long ago outgrown the skin of that child. And she had buried her childish emotions at the deepest point of the smooth, calm lake that had become her center. Where was that lake now? All she could find were the crashing breakers of a storm-tossed sea.

She finished brushing her teeth, washed her face and then left the bathroom. She had barely crossed the threshold when she froze.

Cold air. Silence. No physical warning, only the faintest tingle at her nape. Her arm came up to block the blow as she spun.

Calliope had a quick view of blue eyes and blond hair pulled back in a ponytail.

And the gleam of a knife arcing toward her throat.

CHAPTER SIXTEEN

O you who come to me in order to disarray,
I will not allow you to disarray me.
You shall not deal harm against me.
I am your protector.
—*The Egyptian Book of the Dead, Chapter 151*

THE HEEL OF THE WOMAN'S palm came at her nose with stunning speed. Calliope arced back, avoiding both the blow and the blade by a hair.

Her attacker was fast, an equal match.

She blocked with her forearm, dipped, blocked again. Her blood raced through her veins, roaring in her ears.

Her opponent went low. Calliope danced beyond reach.

How had someone breached the security of the Guard?

The answer came to her as she landed a blow to her assailant's kidneys, then took one to her own knee. She stumbled and almost went down, and at the last minute managed to pull up.

No one had breached the compound. Her assailant

was a Daughter of Aset. And from the gleaming knife in her hand, Calliope got the message that this visit was meant to be lethal.

An assassination.

With the consent of the Matriarchs? Or was this a product of betrayal of the entire Guard?

If the Matriarchs had wanted her dead, why not simply kill her while she'd been in the glass cage?

The blows rained down on her, and she moved in concert with her attacker, thrust, block. Instinct and an eternity of training guided her every move.

Adrenaline surged through her, hitting her cells, amping up action and reaction.

The knife caught the lamplight as it flashed toward her. She arced, blocked, a fraction of a second too late. The honed edge gashed a long wound in her side.

She stopped thinking about anything but survival. As a blooded Daughter of Aset, she had longevity and the capacity to heal on her side, but she wouldn't survive a stab to her heart or the severing of her carotid artery, and it appeared her attacker was aiming for one of the two.

They circled. The knife slashed toward her. Calliope evaded and blocked. The tip of the blade raked her forearm, slicing through cloth and skin. With a snarl, she struck a blow to the throat and another to the chest.

Suddenly her assailant froze then jerked away like someone had hooked her on a fishing line.

Panting, Calliope jumped back and swiped the sweat

from her eyes with the back of one hand as she pressed the other to the gash in her side.

She was acutely aware of the bathroom fan humming in the background and the light leaking through the partially open bathroom door. Too familiar. She'd been here before.

Lifting her gaze, she gasped.

Malthus Krayl had the woman by the throat, and his free hand was pulled back to strike.

A hand extending toward her. The sliver of light through the partially open door. The faint hum of the bathroom fan.

This was the future she had seen in flashes. Malthus Krayl ready to tear out a heart. Not hers, as she had supposed. The assassin's.

Slowly, his head swung toward her. He stared at her blood-soaked side and then the wound that stretched the length of her forearm, making the light gray sweatshirt flower crimson.

The skin around his eyes tightened.

"Hope you don't mind that I cut short your fun, pretty girl," he said. "Fascinating show. Of course, it would have been even better if the two of you were in a plastic pool filled with Jell-O, wearing only your panties."

He paused, and the smile he offered was feral. "Or better still, nothing at all."

"What are you doing here?" Calliope asked then clamped her lips shut on the slew of questions that threatened to follow.

"Playing the fucking hero, it seems." The soul reaper sent her an enigmatic look and tightened his hold on his struggling captive. But he didn't rip out her heart. Calliope supposed that was a good thing.

Pressing the fingers of his free hand to the side of the blonde's throat, he murmured, "Where's your jugular, sweetheart? Ah, there we go."

He dragged something out of his pocket, and as he pulled the cap off with his teeth, Calliope saw it was a syringe. He jammed the needle deep into the vein in the woman's neck and emptied it then raised his head, snared Calliope in his winter-gray gaze and shrugged.

"Needed to be the jugular," he said. "Intramuscular would take forever to make her drop. Into the vein is far faster."

As if on cue, the woman sagged. He laid her on the floor, patted her cheek and straightened.

Calliope watched him warily, not trusting his motives or his expectations. Instinct screamed for her to call out for the guards. But in this case, she seriously doubted that trusting her guards was the way to go.

The woman lying at the soul reaper's feet was a member of the Asetian Guard, judging from the mark— an ankh with wings and horns—clearly visible on her forearm. Calliope had one like it on her calf, etched in her skin, cut in with precision and care by her own hand then left to heal before she went over the same lines again, carving them deeper still. It had been a painstaking, and painful, process. Every member of the

Guard went through it once they committed to taking first blood.

The soul reaper tucked the empty syringe in his pocket and crossed his arms over his chest.

"How did you get in here?" she asked, forcing an image of serenity despite the emotions slamming against the cage she created.

"A portal."

She glanced around the room and saw no portal. But she should have realized something was off the second she woke up to a temperature that would be perfect for a meat locker.

The chair was still in place under the door handle. She shifted her gaze to her would-be assassin. "How did *she* get in here?"

"Am I a mind reader?" he asked, but turned his head to take in their limited surroundings and then looked up. "There," he said.

The grill over the ceiling duct was askew. The opening was small, maybe a foot square. But there was no other way in that Calliope could see.

"Love to stand here while you ponder all the questions of the universe," the soul reaper said, his tone laced with amusement. "But we're in a bit of a time pinch."

Her gaze shot to his. Yes, he was definitely laughing at her.

Offering a pirate's grin, he stepped closer. "Happy to see me?"

Her breath caught, because the question was

reminiscent of the dream she'd had at the base of the mountain and because a tiny, sick part of her *was* happy to see him. Or, at least, see that he'd escaped the fire genies unharmed. She didn't want even to try to understand the why of that.

"Took a bit of effort to find you, and now that I have, please cooperate." He cocked his head toward the unconscious assassin. "The sleepy-time aid was for you in case you gave me grief, but given the situation, I figured she needed it more."

"Did you kill her?"

"I just told you the drug in the syringe was meant for you. Why would I go through the trouble of coming after you just to kill you?" He held up his right index finger and shot her a look through his lashes. "Scratch that. Why would I come after you just to kill you *quickly?* You fed from me. You left me to burn. You cost me Kuznetsov. I owe you for all of that, darlin'."

The corners of his lips curled in a dark smile. "Or perhaps *you* owe *me*. Especially for the case of the blue balls you left me with the night we first met."

Her pulse leaped at that revelation, and she barely managed to restrain a gasp. He'd strung the bits together. He recognized her as the woman from the club. In the end, she kept her cool facade in place, decades of habit kicking in.

"Yeah, I figured that out," he continued as though she'd actually replied. "Brown contacts. Auburn wig… by the way, I prefer your natural color. I kept wondering why I had the nagging feeling I knew you. It came to me while I was whacking off in the shower."

The image of water pounding on his naked skin, wet and glossy, and his hand sliding—

She stared at him in shock and horror. Had he planted that thought in her mind? Or was it an actual memory? Had she seen it in her dreams? She didn't consciously remember...

But then, that wasn't something she'd want to remember. Was it?

She stared at him, feeling sick. When she'd taken his blood, they'd formed a link as the Matriarchs had suspected. She knew it deep in her gut.

She'd been in his skin, and he'd been in hers.

He rattled her. And the worst thing she could do was let him know it.

Willing herself to betray none of her distress, she offered in a calm voice, "I phoned Roxy and told her about the fire genies so your brother Dagan could get to that parking lot and find you. You owe me for that."

"Oh, I owe you, pretty girl. No doubt about that." When she didn't offer any reaction, he continued. "Yeah. I wondered why you called Roxy, why you'd do that for a soul reaper you hate—"

"I—" She broke off, deciding it was wiser to say nothing because she'd wondered that herself. She told herself it was because she hadn't wanted his injuries on her conscience.

Except, he was her enemy. When she'd sliced him

and drank from him and pinned him to the wall with her sword, she'd been happy to have his injuries on her conscience. What had changed in the short span between then and the attack by the fire genies?

She wanted to pretend it was for Roxy that she'd made that call. That she hadn't wanted her friend to suffer because her mate's brother was burned to ash.

But a spark of honesty in the deepest part of her heart made her admit it was something else. She simply hadn't wanted to see Malthus Krayl's smile, his vitality, snuffed. And she hadn't wanted him to suffer.

Because he hadn't made her suffer.

He could have hurt her a million times over. Could have sacrificed her to the fire genies. And he hadn't. He'd let her get away.

Narrowing his eyes, he studied her, and she had the uncomfortable feeling that he knew much of what was spinning through her thoughts.

"And it's a little hard to be appreciative of a phone call that cost you nothing," he continued, "when it's your fault I needed finding in the first place."

He crossed to the door and leaned close so his ear rested against it. Apparently satisfied with what he did, or didn't, hear, he straightened and said, "You're from Odessa." His tone was casual, but his attempt to glean information was transparent. "With a name like Calliope, I pegged you for Greek, not Russian."

His gaze snared hers, mercury gray, and she just stared for an instant. Because he was handsome, with his dark hair falling across his forehead and the day-old stubble shading his jaw. And because she didn't trust that look. Like he was reading her. Testing her. Seeing far more with a glance than she wanted him to.

Then his comments hit her. He knew about Odessa. Proof that he'd been there in her dream.

Feigning a calm she was far from feeling, she said, "My father was Greek. He was a sailor who came to Odessa, met my mother and stayed. At the time, a chunk of Odessa's population was Greek."

The corner of his mouth quirked. "If your mother was anything like you, I can understand his choice."

"Don't."

"You'll have to acknowledge the attraction at some point, Calli."

"At some point when hell freezes over?" she asked, her voice syrupy sweet.

He laughed softly. "Or at the very least at some point when you dream about wrapping yourself around me and sticking your tongue in my mouth. Or other fun places." He paused. "I was sorely disappointed that you woke up at precisely that moment. Dreams don't quite cut it." His gaze cut to her mouth and lingered. "I'm looking forward to the reality."

She held on to her serenity, showing him nothing of the turmoil that crashed through her.

"How did you find me?"

He shrugged. "I saw what you saw while we were plastered nice and close up against the hood of your

SUV. You narrowed the search parameters nicely when you took a good look at your surroundings."

Sick horror congealed in her gut. She'd led him here. Put a big, red pushpin in the map. She'd effectively betrayed the entire Asetian Guard.

"You were in my head."

"Yeah, I was in your head then and again just now when you were back in your past. I saw what you saw. Felt what you felt."

"Everything?" she asked, amazed that her voice was flat and even.

He stared at her, eyes narrowed. Then he said, "I know I turn you on."

"You—" She closed her mouth, consciously lowered her shoulders and sought serenity. Unfortunately, it was a commodity in short supply at the moment. The best she could manage was gritting her teeth.

Then she kicked into soldier mode and asked the question she should have asked in the first place. "How did you get through the wards?"

His brows drew together. "Don't know. Maybe they only ward off an earthly approach. A portal's a back door, a union and fracture of the energy that surges between Topworld and the Underworld." He shrugged. "Maybe the wards don't take that into account."

"How many other soul reapers have you brought here with you?" she demanded.

"Bossy bit of baggage, aren't you?" He tipped his head a bit. "I came for you, Calliope. I came alone."

Alone. How much danger did a solitary soul reaper pose to the entire Guard? She honestly had no idea. Much of what she knew about his kind was based on rumor and supposition.

Then it hit her, what he'd said.

"What do you mean, you came for me?" The wound in her side gave a sharp twinge, and she pressed her hand against it, feeling a warm rush of blood.

The skin at the corners of his eyes tightened. His lips thinned, and he didn't answer her question. Instead, he moved closer and bent his head, parting the cut edges of her sweatshirt to look at the wound. Then he pulled a knife from his belt—*her* knife, one of the ones he'd taken from her the night they faced the fire genies.

She watched him warily as, with a decisive slash, he cut his own palm, deep. Blood welled in a thick, red line.

He lifted the hand with the knife and curled his fingers around the back of her neck. She tried to jerk away, but he held her still. The hilt of the knife was trapped between his palm and her neck, and she could smell his blood on the blade.

Raising his cut palm, he said, "Take what you need."

That open offer was almost impossible to resist. Blood dripped off the edge of his palm, and she followed a single drop until it splashed to the floor. The drop fragmented into a hundred smaller drops and splashed up before settling back on the floor.

As it had in her dream. Her memory. Her father's blood.

Her gaze flashed up.

She wet her lips and strained back as far as his hand at her nape would let her. "I'll heal."

"Not fast enough." His tone hardened. "Drink. Before the damned cut closes and I have to slice myself again."

Both lured and appalled, she hesitated.

"I get it," he said. "You think I'm a monster. The last thing you want is my blood, but be practical. That's who you are, isn't it, Calliope? The pragmatic, practical soldier in Aset's army. My blood will heal you and give you an edge that would be handy right about now."

His gaze cut to the assassin on the floor in the unspoken implication that there might be others.

When she said nothing, he took the choice from her.

With his eyes locked on hers, glittering and bright, he brought his lacerated palm to his mouth and sealed his lips to the wound. Then he tightened his grasp on her neck and leaned in. She could fight. She could turn her face away.

She did neither.

For reasons she couldn't—didn't want to—explain, she let him press his mouth to hers.

She tasted him. She tasted blood. Her entire body hummed and arched toward him, like she was a parched plant and he was rain.

Pushing his tongue past her lips, he angled his mouth on hers, taking the kiss deeper, letting the blood from his mouth slide into hers.

She jerked back, swallowed. The taste assaulted her senses; the thrum of his life force raced to her cells.

But it was his kiss she craved more than his blood. The weight of him pressed against her felt so damned good. She felt drugged, enticed, and she didn't want to fight against it.

Going up on her toes, she pressed her open mouth to his.

He made a sound low in his throat and met the thrust of her tongue with his own. He teased her, lured her and finally drew his mouth away, and she found herself flush against him. His fingers were tangled in her hair. Her fists crushed the cloth of his shirt.

Her pulse raced, her skin felt sensitized and the sensation of his prana surging through her was like a drug.

Off balance, she reached for the calm of her soul. She wanted the safe shroud of her control.

Because that kiss sliced her open and left her exposed to the bone.

CHAPTER SEVENTEEN

Save me from those who deal wounds,
The slayers whose fingers are sharp.
Who deal out pain,
They shall not have power over me,
And I will not fall into their cauldrons.

—*The Egyptian Book of the Dead, Chapter 17*

PANTING, CALLIOPE JERKED AWAY.

Mal let her go and almost smiled when she wiped the back of her hand across her mouth.

"You trying to make a statement to me or yourself?" he asked, then he went all in and pushed. "Which of us do you think you're fooling?" He lowered his voice. "What you really want to do is fist your hands in my shirt, drag me close and push your tongue back inside my mouth."

She kept her mask in place, but he could see the flush in her cheeks and the way her pulse beat at her throat.

Catching her wrist, he turned her palm up. The slash on her forearm was already starting to close. He tugged her closer, keeping his gaze locked on hers.

"You want to taste me. Feed from me. Sip my life force while you take my dick inside you."

Her expression shuttered. He'd gone too far. Regret bit him and he let her go when she pulled her wrist from his grasp. But he noticed she didn't deny a word of it.

Poor uptight, ramrod-straight Calliope Kane. She was in for a hell of a surprise when he swept aside all her rules and locks and cage doors.

And he meant to do exactly that. Meant to free the wild thing inside her.

That attracted him. The woman beneath the veneer. She had this amazing ability to be both the coldest, and the hottest, woman he'd ever met.

Gently, so gently, he turned her face back toward him and stroked her hair off her cheek. "I think maybe there's a very fine line between love and hate, Calli."

Confusion danced across her features before she locked it down. He figured he pretty much knew what was going through her head. She saw him as a monster. She hated him. And wanted him. That had to have her head spinning.

He knew *his* was spinning. Because he'd already figured out that he'd suffered a broadside hit and he was going down, drowning in the need to have her, mate her, make her his. The feel of her skin beneath his fingers, the smell of her hair, even the way she looked at him, as if she was on the other side of a wall of ice. It made him want to turn up the heat and melt her barriers.

His gaze dipped to her mouth, the shape deceptively

sweet. He knew only too well that those perfectly curved, pink lips concealed a vicious bite.

It struck him then that through their blood connection, he knew more about her than if they'd spent months going on casual dates, more than she likely would have revealed after a year—hell, a decade—of dates. He knew the story of her childhood and her loss. He knew the hate that burned in her heart.

Something primitive stirred inside him. Something possessive. He had no name for it, and he supposed it didn't need one.

"You have no business talking to me about love. Your kind—"

"Loves and cries and bleeds and feels pain." He huffed a sharp exhalation. "I am not a monster, Calli, however much you want to paint me as one. And whether you want to admit it or not, there's something here between us that needs to be addressed—" he glanced around, and his mouth shaped a rueful smile "—just maybe not right now."

For a second, he thought there might be a part of her that wanted to smile back. To let him in. To let a little of her secret self out.

"Since the second I laid eyes on you, everything in my ordered, neat world has been shot to hell," she said flatly.

"Likewise. Fun, isn't it?"

"No."

He watched her gather her emotions and lock them

away. And he gave her the space to do it. He'd been in
her dreams, seen the dark events that had shaped her.
She needed her defenses. He'd leave them to her for now;
he had all the time in the world to break them down.

"I could have sipped your life force without the
blood," she said coldly. "You only needed to let me."

He grunted, unimpressed. "Right. Lower my defenses
and trust you to take only a little." He laughed. "Besides,
I needed to kiss you. And you like taking my blood.
Admit it. There's a bit of forbidden pleasure in it."

For a long second, he held her gaze, waiting for even
a hint of agreement.

She offered nothing.

Good thing patience was one of his very few
virtues.

"Where's Kuznetsov?" he asked, giving her the
out.

"I don't know."

"Where is the most likely place they'd keep him?"

"Anywhere. Could be down here in a neighboring
cell. Aboveground in one of the mansion's bedrooms."
Her tone was flat and cool, but something made him
think that she was edgy, focused. That something was
nagging at her. He wanted to know what that something
might be.

"Maybe he isn't even here anymore. They could have
taken him to another location."

"Which location?" he clipped.

Again, she shook her head. "I don't even know of all

the compounds the Guard has scattered over the world. At this point, your guess is as good as mine."

"I'd still like to hear your guess, darlin'."

She brought her hands up and let them drop. "I think he might be dead. No, actually, I'm fairly certain he's dead. My superior referred to him only in the past tense."

"As far as proof goes, Calli—"

"Don't call me that."

He ignored the interruption. "That's pretty slim."

"Yes, it is."

He blew out a breath, and then he said softly, "My brothers think they can bring Lokan back. They think that if they find all the parts, Ren, Ba, Ka, Sheut, Ib, they can unite them all and reanimate him."

"With the help of a few sacrificed innocent souls and a dollop of vile magic." A touch of venom crept into her tone.

"And the help of some demons." He gave a tight, close-lipped smile. "Your point?"

"You said that your brothers think they can bring him back. You don't include yourself in that select group?"

"No. I just want to make the bastards who killed him bleed. We're not on opposite sides, Calli. The Guard doesn't want Lokan coming back. I don't believe he *can* come back."

"Not the same."

"*Almost* the same."

"Almost isn't good enough." She shook her head. "An Underworld war cannot be allowed to spill Top-world. The casualties and destruction would be beyond measure."

"There were other ways to find out who killed my brother. Interrogating Kuznetsov among them. The end result would be the same. Sutekh's vengeance. Yet, the Guard's willing to risk it. Seems a bit contradictory, doesn't it?"

Her expression was cool and serene, her body relaxed. He couldn't see even a hint of tension in her frame, but he knew it was there. He unnerved her, unsettled her. And a part of him liked that.

"We'd do better working together," he said.

"Are you asking for my help? What possible use can I be to you? I am outcast by my own kind—" she spread her hands and gestured at the cell walls "—and have no access to any sensitive information."

"I'm not looking for your help," he said. "Truth is, I'm here to play Prince Valiant and rescue you from the tower—" he glanced around "—or the dungeon, as circumstances would have it."

"Rescue me?" That startled a laugh out of her. "Why?"

"Because I can—" he held up a hand to still her pro-test "—even though you don't need me to." He dipped his chin toward the blonde on the floor. "I know that if I didn't show up, she'd still be lying on the floor regard-less, only you'd have been the one putting her there. It's one of the things I like about you—" he let his gaze drift to her lips, her breasts, then back to her eyes "—among others."

"Silly—"

"Little. Boy," he finished for her. "Yeah. Silly for you." He waggled his brows. "But not so little."

She looked as if she was going to react, and he found himself anticipating it, only to be disappointed when she schooled her features and made no reply.

Catching her hand, he drew her a step closer as he summoned a portal. He made a circling gesture, as though he was turning a doorknob. A great, gaping black hole appeared in the corner. It seemed to pull in on itself then bulge out toward them, tendrils of dark smoke reaching out like fingers. Incredible cold radiated through the room.

"You don't need to trust me," he said softly. "But you can't trust the Guard, either." Again, he dipped his chin toward the unconscious woman on the floor.

Her nostrils flared as she drew a sharp breath.

"And one small thing, Calli," he continued, his tone growing softer still, his hold on her tightening because he had a feeling that what he was about to tell her just might be the thing that made her bolt. "Those men who killed your father? The ones you thought were like demons from your grandmother's Russian folktales?"

She wet her lips, then rolled them in and pressed them together.

"They were."

"What are you talking about?" she asked, serene, calm, betraying none of the unease that he was certain coiled just beneath the surface, a breath away from erupting. "Were what?"

"Demons. My guess would be incorporeal. They slid into those bodies and wore them like suits."

Beneath his fingers where they circled her wrist, he felt her pulse ramp up.

She cocked a brow. "Reapers can do that? Take over human bodies?"

"No."

"Then what are you talking about, soul reaper?" The question came out on a whisper.

"I think you might use my name. Mal. Soul reaper seems so...impersonal."

Her jaw clenched, but she said nothing.

The moment of truth had arrived, and he was going to offer it to her. The question was, would she be glad to hear it?

"Don't shoot the messenger," he muttered. Then, "You watched your father get his heart ripped out. Soul reapers do that, no question. The hearts we take are a peace offering for Osiris to keep the cease-fire intact. The darksouls we harvest go to Sutekh."

"I saw them—"

"Yeah, you did. And thanks to you stealing my blood, I saw them right along with you." He stepped toward her until he was close enough to smell the scent of her skin, see each individual dark lash that framed her amazing eyes. "Soul reapers don't drink human blood. We don't eat human hearts. Your father's killers did both."

She stared at him, her breath coming in short pants, her lips parted.

He pulled her to him as he dipped his head and spoke against her ear.

"It wasn't a soul reaper that killed your father, Calli. You've spent your life sporting a hate-on for the wrong fucking monsters."

He knew she heard him. He knew she understood. But she didn't give a damned thing away. Seconds ticked past, agonizingly slow, and she offered no reaction. She didn't gasp. Didn't flinch. Nothing at all.

Finally he leaned back in a languid arc. Those incredible eyes were fixed on his, and then slowly, slowly, her gaze slid to his mouth.

An invitation.

One he wasn't inclined to refuse, even though on some level, he knew it made no sense.

Lowering his head, he kissed her.

She didn't just let him, she *met* him, coming up on her toes and angling her head so he had better access to feed off her mouth. She was lush and warm and so damned sexy, her lips opening under his, her tongue twining, thrusting and parrying with his own.

A swell of satisfaction surged. He was back on familiar turf. He knew nothing of emotional connection. But this surge of lust, the blood rushing to his dick and a woman pliant and willing in his arms...*this* he knew.

And he didn't want to examine too closely the part of him that threw back its head and howled. Because she was in his arms. Because she was turning to him for comfort. Because she was his.

Skimming his palm along her back, the indent of her waist, the swell of her hip, he learned the feel of her, kissing her deeper.

In the part of his brain that could actually think, he was aware that this was a piss-poor idea. They were in a cell in the bowels of a compound of hostile supernaturals. The timing couldn't be worse.

And he kissed her anyway.

His dick was hard, his pulse slamming like a jackhammer, his breath coming too fast. He wanted her in his bed. He wanted her naked.

Her palms slid to his chest. She gave a little push. It took him a second to clear his head enough to let her go.

As she drew back and stared up at him, he saw that she was cool as a mint julep. The rock tumbler of emotional and physical upheaval inside him wasn't matched in her. She didn't appear to feel a damned thing.

"What the fuck?" he muttered. He knew he'd turned her world upside down, laying bare the fact that the soul reapers who'd killed her father hadn't been soul reapers at all. And *he* was the one feeling confused to his core? How did that work?

Incredulous, he stared at her. She hadn't felt what he'd felt. The connection. The attraction. The feeling that he'd been hit over the head by a three-hundred-pound sledgehammer.

He'd meant to kiss her as a way to connect, to offer comfort, to touch the part of her that was iced colder than a glacier. In the end, it looked as if he was the only one affected. He was as hot for her as a teenager, and she hadn't felt a damned thing.

He mastered his emotions and looked deeper, and then he saw the telltale signs. Dilated pupils. Flushed cheeks. Her lips plump and swollen. Her hand shaking just the tiniest bit as she drew the length of her silky, dark hair over her shoulder.

In that second, it hit him: she had set this up on purpose. She wanted him to think she hadn't felt a thing. It was all about distance with her, all about the mask.

Damn, she was good. But not quite good enough. He'd affected her. Physically. Emotionally.

She knew damned well there was something between them. She just wasn't ready to admit it yet.

Very gently, he reached out and ran the pad of his thumb over her lower lip. One dark brow lifted a fraction of an inch, and her lips parted ever so slightly, just enough to tell him he was right.

He had to restrain the urge to slide his thumb into her mouth, into the moist heat, to feel her teeth and her tongue close on him. Damn.

He let his hand fall away.

"Nice try, Calli, but you're not that good an actress."

She sucked in a sharp breath and her gaze flashed to his.

"I think it's time we took this somewhere we can finish it," he murmured, and lacing his fingers tight with hers, he dragged her into the icy black hole.

The portal swallowed them, the cold absolute and bone-numbingly cruel. There was no ground beneath their feet, no sky overhead, nothing but disorientation and frigid air.

As they came out the other side, Mal tightened his grip, angling his body to take Calliope's weight, expecting her to stumble, perhaps even puke. He'd come damned close to that himself the first time he'd come through a portal. He'd been with Dagan, who'd laughed his ass off as Mal had turned green.

Aiming to offer her more compassion than his brother had offered him, Mal schooled his features into an expression of sympathy. Calliope pulled from his grasp. But instead of weak and unsteady, her movements were decisive. He studied her, surprised that she showed no ill effects from having come through a frigid tunnel that would send most to their knees.

"You traveled through a portal before?" he asked.

"No."

Either she was uncommonly adept at masking the effects on her equilibrium, or she had suffered no ill effects.

"How'd you like it?"

She shrugged. "Quick. Efficient. An excellent means of transport."

"No nausea? No dizziness?"

She raised one hand in a negligent wave and lifted those amazing cat-green eyes to his for a long moment. "Small price for efficiency," she said at last.

"Right," he said.

"Right," she said.

And they each took a step back.

Mal turned his attention to their surroundings. A long driveway, little more than short grass grooved by deep lines where a vehicle had passed, curved through the woods behind them. Turning, he faced the two-story farmhouse that stood against the backdrop of trees like something in a magazine for the perfect country life. The porch was creamy yellow, the wood siding pale gray.

"You're hidden from the road," he said.

"That's the point." She was back to serene and distant, her voice like water flowing over stones. Beautiful. Soothing. But a faint frown marked her brow.

In front of the house was a patch of lawn and a garden that was groomed and tended, but at the edges, the forest lurked, threatening to reclaim what had been hewn out in the name of civilized living.

"Would you mind telling me how we got here?" she asked.

"Through a portal," he said slowly, wondering if she'd lost it and how he'd missed the signs.

She shot him a look so cold it made his balls shrivel. "How did we get *here?*"

"Dagan was here the night Gahiji went after Roxy."

"Is that how a portal works? One of you goes to a place and then any of you can find it?" There was a faint edge to her tone.

Which made Mal watch her carefully as he replied, "No. I asked him for the location. I figured you might want to gather a few of your things for the trip."

He expected her to ask what trip. Instead, she snared him with a cool, crystal green glance and asked, "Can you return to the mountain any time you want?"

"You mean to the Asetian Guard's compound?"

"I do." Her expression was blank, her features smooth, and that had unease crawling all the way up Mal's spine.

"I can. Is there a particular reason we need to go back? 'Cuz I'm thinking that isn't a great plan."

She turned, strode toward her front door, pushed it open and stepped inside. She didn't invite him to follow. Didn't look back to see what he did. But she left the door open behind her.

He figured that from Calliope, that amounted to an invitation so warm it'd bake cookies.

CHAPTER EIGHTEEN

Be gracious to me,
and remove all anger
which is in your heart against me.
—The Egyptian Book of the Dead, Chapter 14

CALLIOPE WENT TO HER secure landline and lifted the receiver, ready to dial. At the last second, she froze. Sarita had been her superior in the Guard for twenty years. She was reliable, efficient, and up until the past couple of days, Calliope would have said she would trust her with her life.

But at this moment, Calliope wasn't sure about trusting anyone.

So she went with her best bet: Zalika.

When her mentor answered, Calliope kept it brief.

"The Guard has been breached. I have been compromised. And I am no longer on premises."

"We are aware," Zalika said. "The soul reaper allows you to make this call?"

So they knew he had come for her. She wasn't surprised. For an instant, she wondered if the Matriarchs had known it all along. She had a vivid recollection of

Beset saying that all was as it should be after she tasted Calliope's blood, and she thought that the three knew a great deal they chose not to share.

Wily and clever political plotting seemed to go hand in hand with power.

The air crackled and sparked, and Calliope turned to see the soul reaper in question standing in the open archway of her kitchen, leaning one shoulder against the wall, watching her.

"It would be fascinating to see the outcome were he to try to stop me," Calliope said.

Malthus Krayl's lips twitched in response.

"We already knew of the breach," Zalika said. "There are three fire genies here, each marked with Aset's symbol. They infiltrated the lowest ranks. I am presently investigating exactly how that happened. We found one unconscious in your cell." She paused. "I feared for you."

That admission touched Calliope's heart, but she knew that to acknowledge it would only make Zalika uncomfortable. Instead, she said, "Fire genies. I hadn't even considered that my would-be assassin was other than she appeared."

Mal straightened off the wall at the mention of fire genies.

"You believed it was one of your sisters in the Guard who had been sent to kill you," Zalika said.

"Yes." A thousand questions spiraled through Calliope's thoughts. How had Xaphan's concubines infiltrated the Guard? Why had they disguised themselves as Daughters of Aset? And why come after her?

Through the phone, Calliope could hear voices and the sounds of people moving around. She knew there was an emergency protocol to clear the compound of all valuables and antique treasures before its destruction. From the noise, she deduced that all was going as planned.

"I must go," Zalika said. "I will tell the Matriarchs that you chose to offer a warning. It will reflect well on you."

"That isn't why I did it."

"I know. Be safe, Calliope."

"And you, Zalika."

The line went dead.

"What happens to you now?" Mal asked.

Until this moment, she'd thought of him as *the soul reaper* or *Malthus Krayl*. That had allowed her a measure of distance from him. But he'd asked her to call him Mal, and oddly, she wanted to. The question was, why? Why did it feel right and comfortable?

Because she believed his assertion that it wasn't soul reapers who had killed her father?

Maybe.

She wasn't sure.

"What happens to me now?" she asked, her lips curving in a faint smile. She had no answer. For a century and a half, her life had not been her own. Now, suddenly it was.

She had no idea what to do with that.

It would not have been her choice to leave the Guard. But she was a grain of sand among many. She could only be the best grain of sand she could be.

Turning her head, she stared at the window over the kitchen sink as the first patter of rain hit the panes. All that was familiar to her was gone now, in a matter of days. She had known ever since she made the choice to feed from Mal's life force, to take his blood, that she had tossed everything away.

Had it been worth it?

That depended on what the Matriarchs had learned from Kuznetsov. The irony was, she would never know.

She turned to face Mal. He hadn't moved. The dimness of the kitchen contrasted with the light in the hallway behind him. He was cast as a silhouette, tall, broad shouldered. His face was in shadow.

"You ask questions to which you have no right to know the answers," she said.

He moved toward her, sinew and grace. Everything about him was shadow and pewter and ash. His hair. His clothing. Even the gray of his eyes had darkened in this light.

"Tell me anyway."

She shrugged, not because the answer was of little import, but because there was nothing she could do to change it. She could only plan and prepare the best defense she could. "They will call a council. They will banish me at the very least. More likely, they will send a termination party."

His lips tightened. "By termination, I assume you don't mean that they'll offer you a package with a gold watch and a 'thank you kindly' for your years with the company."

"No."

"I won't let them hurt you."

Both the declaration and tone were so outlandish that she couldn't help but laugh. "How is my fate any of your concern?" She paused. "And what will you do, Mal? Stand guard over me every second of every day?"

"Nice. You called me Mal." He slanted her a glance through his lashes, and his mouth took on a mulish slant. "Yeah, I'll stand guard over you." He raked his fingers back through his hair. As soon as he dropped his hand, the straight, sleek strands fell over his forehead once more. "You plan to just sit down and wait for them? Let them take you when they come?"

She blew out a heavy breath and pressed her fingers to her temples. "No. Of course not. I am not without skill. I will know when they come. I will stay a step ahead of them as long as I can." She shrugged. "But eventually they will find me. I will fight. I will win—" she cut him a sidelong glance "—because I am good at what I do. At some point, they will send one I cannot escape, and then I will no longer be free. Perhaps, I will no longer be alive."

"You say that like you don't care." He stepped toward her, his expression fierce.

She stared at him, stunned by his intensity, and whispered, "You say that like you *do*."

"Of course I do." He prowled closer still, until he was there right next to her, the heat of his body crossing the thin span of air between them. "Did you think I chased you to some fucking mountaintop dungeon because I had nothing better to do?"

"I think you chased after Kuznetsov."

"Then why did I come after you first?"

She'd thought about that and come up with the obvious answer. From all he'd said, she understood that he had to know where to open a portal. That he had to have seen the place, or been there, or been told about it by another. He had seen the base of the mountain, and likely her prison room, through her dreams. He had no way to see where they held Kuznetsov.

So he'd come after her, likely hoping she could take him to his prey.

"You don't know me. How can you possibly care what happens to me?" She shot him a look of pure ice. She knew exactly the image she projected. She had practiced it for decades, perfecting the facade of frigid calm, a mirage, an illusion. Inside, she was anything but calm.

"Silly." He lifted his hand and brushed his thumb along her brow. Her pulse kicked up. "Little." He traced the line of her nose. Her skin warmed. "Girl." He rubbed her lower lip.

She was breathing too fast, shallow pants that made her chest rise and fall and gave her away. She knew he noticed because his gaze dipped then rose.

"What do you want?" she whispered.

"You." His lips shaped the barest hint of a smile.

"Why?"

"I have no fucking clue." He shook his head. "Call it the thunderbolt."

"I don't know what you're talking about."

"I know." He paused. "Why did you come on to me at the club?"

"I didn't know you were a supernatural. You masked your power."

He nodded. "But why me?"

Truth? Lie? "Because you are beautiful. Because the way you moved made me think that you would—" She broke off. She'd already given more than she should.

He huffed a low laugh. "Yeah. I would." He paused. "Why did you run away?"

"You know why."

"Because I let my shields slip and you figured out I was a supernatural."

"Yes."

"And that's too complicated."

"Yes."

"You prefer the no-strings approach."

"Yes."

He laughed then, a gorgeous rich sound that twined around her and through her and made her want to lean close against him and feel it rumble through his chest.

"Funny, I wouldn't have thought we were anything alike, but I'm a no-strings sort of guy myself." His eyes glittered. "Until now. I want you, Calliope. And not for an hour. I want something more, and I have no idea how or why that happened."

And she had no idea what she wanted. Because everything was upside down. The certainties she had lived with for decades had evaporated. The Asetian Guard was her job, her allegiance, her life. She'd spent a hundred and fifty years believing that soul reapers had murdered her family and stolen her childhood.

In her reality, soul reapers were the enemy.

Suddenly, she had to get used to a new truth. She was on her own. Several weeks ago, a soul reaper, Dagan Krayl, had *saved* her life. And now Mal had done so again. Two debts she owed to those she had long imagined to be the enemy of her kind. Her personal enemy.

"We don't have to plan the whole future, Calli. We can just live one moment at a time. They'll add together into an hour and then a day, and slowly we'll build months and years. Building blocks."

"*Why?*"

The smile he offered was so taut, she thought it might split like an overwound guitar string. "This is going to sound majorly fucked—" he held up his hand palm forward "—but hear me out. I was in love once. A long time ago. Her name was Elena. It was before I knew that I was Sutekh's spawn. Back then, I just thought I was one dumb-lucky mortal. I went away. She disappeared. I didn't know she was dead and I looked for her for ten years before I found out she'd been raped and murdered within a week of my leaving."

The look on her face said it all.

He accepted her sympathy and continued. "I mourned her. I missed her. But I wasn't eternally scarred by her loss. I didn't play the melodrama card. But her death shaped me." He paused and stared hard at her. "I couldn't protect her. And she couldn't protect herself."

A band tightened around her chest and she felt as if she couldn't breathe and her heart couldn't beat. He couldn't possibly mean—

"I can protect myself," she said, the words sliding free though she ought to have held them back.

"Yeah." One corner of his mouth twitched. "That's exactly my point."

He held her gaze for what felt like an eternity, then he went on. "I was one hell of a slut after that. Hard-core. One woman. Two. Hell, I'd bed five at once. They had fun. I had fun. They didn't care about me. I didn't care about them."

Something inside her unfurled at his words and tone.

"You didn't think less of your partners." She let nothing of her emotions leach into her tone.

"And they didn't think less of me."

Seconds ticked past, and then she said, "I thought less of myself. I had no choice if I wanted to survive. It was blood or sex."

"And with the memory of the demon drinking your father's blood guiding your choices, you went for nameless, emotionless sex."

"Yes."

He stroked her cheek with the backs of his fingers, watching her intently. "With me, Calli, you never have to choose again. Blood and sex. With me, you can have both."

His words and his tone seduced her. He made it sound so easy.

She looked directly into his eyes, pewter and ash. She drank in his features. Firm lips, Straight nose. The thin, white scar that cut through the dark stubble that shadowed his jaw.

He was incredibly beautiful.

After all she had lost, she supposed she owed herself that. His incredible beauty.

Perhaps in a different time she would have made her excuses. *I'm not really this sort of girl. I don't usually do this.*

But, really, what was the point?

At this precise, perfect moment in time, she had no one to answer to but herself. And there was no question but that she wanted him.

Her gaze slid down his body. His shirt clung to his leanly muscled torso. His pants fit to perfection. She was left with no doubt as to his inclination. There was a solid ridge outlined beneath the cloth.

"You're mad. We—" she made a gesture to encompass both of them "—*this* isn't anything. It's your male pride. Because I walked away from you that first night. Because I left you disappointed. You want payback."

"You think?" He bared his teeth in a smile that was positively savage. "Then let's get that out of the way and prove your theory, because I disagree. This has nothing to do with my bruised ego and everything to do with you." He gestured back and forth between the two of them. "Us."

"There is no us."

He laughed. "Yeah. There is."

In a blink, he had her backed up against the wall, his fingers curling around her hips. He dipped his face to her neck and breathed in against her skin, and her whole body clenched in response.

"Push me away," he said. "Tell me no. This is the one chance you get." He drew back enough that she could see his eyes, the pupils dilated and dark, leaving the irises a thin gray rim. "After this, I'm in charge."

She knew all the things she should do. Say no. Push him away. Get as far from him as she could.

Instead, she reached up and tangled her fingers in his hair. His mouth came down on hers in a kiss that was hard and deep and hungry.

She went up on her toes, molding her body to his. The solid ridge of his erection pressed against her mound, and she almost whimpered at the harsh tide of desire that slammed her.

There was nothing gentle in the way he touched her, his fingers biting into her hips, his kiss rough and wild, lips and tongue and teeth. Lust kicked her, low in the gut.

She felt hot and swollen and wet, and she wanted him inside her. Wanted to finish what they'd started that night in the club. It felt as if it was a million years ago. It felt as if it was only a moment ago.

She only knew that she wanted him to stretch her and fill her.

He twined his fingers through her long hair and pulled her head back until it touched the wall and her neck was exposed. His lips traced her pulse. His teeth nipped her skin. Shivers chased up her spine and along her limbs, leaving them weak and heavy.

This was passion. This was lust. But it was nothing she had ever felt before. Gone was her mask. Gone was the icy control she maintained always. He swept it away.

This was a wave of tidal proportions that took over her body, took over her thoughts. This would not be a coupling that allowed her to keep her checks and balances in place. This would be all-consuming.

A whisper in her thoughts warned that she ought to be afraid, ought not give him this power.

Then it coiled away and vanished like smoke.

She had made her choice.

From the corner of her eye, she saw the knife in his hand, and she gasped as he slit the sweatshirt from neck to waist then did the same to the thermal shirt she wore underneath.

He tossed the blade away and it clattered to the floor, discordant in the quiet that was punctuated only by the harsh rasp of their breathing.

For a long second, he only looked at her, his eyes glittering, his mouth hard.

He traced the tip of his finger along the wound on her forearm. It was a thin pink line now, healing, thanks to his blood. Then he moved his hand to her side, his touch gentle. The shiny scar over the wound there was darker, wider, but healing as well.

Then he raised his gaze to hers, open, unshuttered, and he let her see the naked longing and the heat.

"I've never wanted anyone as I want you," he rasped.

And she believed him.

CHAPTER NINETEEN

Someone stands behind you,
And you have power.
You shall neither perish nor be destroyed.
—*The Egyptian Book of the Dead, Chapter 177*

MAL TRACED HIS LIPS ALONG the lovely warmth behind Calli's ear, urgent, driven. He moved to her neck, nipping his teeth against her smooth, pale skin. She tasted like heaven. She tasted like heat and strength and passion.

He drew his fingers over her skin, smooth and warm, up along the delicate bumps of her spine, and buried them in her hair. The long, sleek strands poured through his hands in a fall of silk.

The sweatpants rode low on her hips, and he saw that she was lean and muscled, yet curved everywhere a man could want her to be. Flared hips. Round, soft breasts. She was created to tempt him, and he was happy to be lured.

Moving his lips along the arch of her throat, he kissed her and tasted her skin, the tip of his tongue leaving a wet trail.

With a gasp, she pressed against the back of his head,

drawing him closer. He turned his head, letting his ear rest against her heartbeat.

Her chest rose and fell, rapid, uneven.

He licked the curve of her breast to her nipple, his hand searching out the other breast. His fingers closed on her, teasing, stroking, and then his mouth. He sucked her gently, then harder, grazing her tender flesh with his teeth.

A wordless cry escaped her, low, ragged, and he felt it in his gut, in his groin.

Sinking down onto his knees, the backs of his thighs resting on his calves, he fisted his free hand in the cloth of her sweatpants, dragging them down with him.

"What—"

"Shh." Lifting her foot, he pulled off her sock and tugged the sweatpants free, then did the same with the other. She was left naked before him. Long legs. Curved hips.

The urge to taste her drove him. He closed both hands around her hips and steadied her against the wall as he leaned forward to trail kisses along the arc of her hipbone and then the indent of her navel.

She was gorgeous, responsive. Her breath hitched with each feathered touch of his lips.

But he wanted more than that. He wanted her to scream his name as she came.

"Mal, no." She tangled her fingers in his hair but didn't quite pull him away. "I—"

"Shh," he repeated. He knew what she meant to say,

the protests she meant to make. He didn't want to hear them. She was his. For this shining, glorious moment, she was his, and he would taste her and take her and mark her. He would give in to every primitive instinct that rode him.

This wasn't just about sex. This was…something more, though he couldn't—wouldn't—put a name to it right now.

Leaning back, he tipped his head and looked up at her. Her pupils were dilated, her irises darkened to jade. She wet her lips, swollen from his kisses. Her nipples were full and pink and so pretty that he couldn't help himself. He leaned forward and sucked first one then the other, leaving them wet.

Panting, she watched him. He leaned back and held her gaze as he ran his palms up the insides of her thighs, pushing her legs wider, and finally sliding his palms up to cup her buttocks.

"My way," he reminded her as she made a half-hearted gesture, as though she meant to deny him.

Without waiting for a reply, he leaned forward and pressed his mouth to her mound, let his tongue trace her sweet, wet folds. She jerked. Cried out. And he only tightened his hold on her buttocks and angled her hips a little forward so he could kiss her and lick her.

Her scent, hot and ready, drove him wild. And his tongue drove her wild as he stroked her again and again; he read her response in the thrust of her hips and the gasps of pleasure that came low and breathy. Whatever protests she might have made drifted away.

Beneath his hands, he felt her muscles twitch and tremble. He shifted his hand and slid a finger inside her hot, tight sheath. She bucked against him, and he felt it in his dick, so hard and ready he was crazy for her.

"You're so wet. So ready. Fuck," he muttered. "Fuck."

He ran his tongue along her one last time as he flicked open the button of his jeans and dragged down the zipper. Then he was free and she was so sweet and hot.

Letting his weight fall back on his heels, he pulled her toward him, guiding her thighs down on both sides of his. He surged up as her weight came down, and her soft, pliant sex opened against his shaft.

Her lips parted. Her breath came out on the softest exhale.

Blood pounded through his veins.

Reaching between them, he fisted himself and shifted the angle as he lifted her.

He squeezed her buttocks and thrust up as she came down. The head of his dick slid inside.

She gave a low, sexy hum of approval.

When she tried to take control, to take him fully inside her, he closed his hands on her ass—fuck, her ass drove him wild—and held her where she was. He teased her, letting her take just a little, then a little more, until she was panting and writhing and digging her nails into his shoulders.

Head thrown back, body arched, she was pagan and gorgeous.

He gave her what she wanted, surging up to fully sheath himself inside her to the music of her throaty moan.

CALLIOPE CLUNG TO MAL'S shoulders. He had one hand under her buttocks and the other looped around the small of her back as he brought her up, then down. She rode him, the width of his penis stretching her, filling her. The sensation was lush, wonderful, a gorgeous invasion that made her want to move faster, push harder.

He didn't let her. He guided the rate and the depth, making her feel wild and out of control.

Waves of pleasure poured through her.

Dipping his head, Mal drew on her nipple, teasing her, making her arch to offer him more. He used his tongue, his lips, then his teeth, taking his time as he moved from one breast to the other, pushing deep inside her, making her burn.

She tangled her fingers in his hair and yanked back, giving her access to his mouth. She kissed him, her tongue sliding into his mouth, keeping time to the thrust of his penis.

Drawing back, she looked at him, his face hard and savage, teeth bared, eyes slitted. He was glorious in his passion. Wild. Feral.

Tension coiled, a knot at her core. Her breasts ached. Her sex ached. She was strung so tight, so close to the edge—

With a growl, he surged forward, tumbling her onto her back on the floor, her hips and thighs bent so she was spread wide for his pleasure. And he took that pleasure, and gave back in equal degree, pumping deep and sure.

She felt as though she was flying and unraveling. As if she was someone else. Her reactions were far beyond her control, and that coiled yearning was about to burst. She had never experienced anything like this. She'd never allowed herself the freedom to let go.

She'd never before been with anyone who'd made her want to let go.

Her power surged, as did his. She felt it inside her. She felt hers move into him, blending and sparking like a live wire.

She was open to him, in his thrall, the pressure and need growing and surging.

Reaching between their bodies with fingers sure and slick, he pressed against her clitoris as he moved deep and hard, in, out, the rhythm set to his pace.

She couldn't breathe. Couldn't think. It was so close and she was so—

He moved his fingers in a slick, smooth glide. He closed his lips around her nipple and gave a hard, suctioning pull as he surged into her.

With a scream, she shattered. Her insides clenched

tight, holding him inside her, clutching him as he throbbed and came with her on a last deep thrust. He shuddered, his body a long, tense line, his head arched back as he pulsed his release.

She wrapped her arms around his shoulders and her legs around his hips, and she held him to her in a way she had never held another, her face dropped into the curve of his shoulder, his body a perfect shield over hers.

And she thought, *This is what it was supposed to be. All along, this is what it was supposed to be.*

The Underworld, the Territory of Osiris

FEAR UNFURLED LIKE A white curl off the top of an incense stick, rising inside Pyotr Kuznetsov. He walked through a swamp, the air heavy, his feet sinking into sludge. The water was dark with the mud that dredged up from the riverbed.

All around him were trees. Tall. Thick trunked. Limbs reaching to a sky he could not see.

He shivered.

The air was cold.

No…hot.

He wasn't able to differentiate, and on some level he thought that was a terrible thing. But uppermost in his mind was the urgent need to press on, so he did, forcing his feet through the sucking bog.

Sweat trickled from under his arms, down along the

swell of his ribs and down his back, along his spine to the base. Cold sweat. He shivered even as he labored.

He stopped to drag his forearm across his brow, then he closed his eyes and wiped the sweat from there as well.

And when he opened them once more, he was somewhere else entirely.

A church. The pews were polished to a high gleam, the scent of orange peel heavy in the air. Before him rose the glorious colors of massive stained-glass windows. A giant yellow sun surrounded by glass of variegated shades of blue and in front of that a—

He fell to his knees with a gasp, his reality shifting with vertigo-inducing speed. The church of his childhood disappeared in a blink. He was left in utter blackness with only lines of small red lights breaking the gloom on either side.

No. Not lights.

Eyes. Dozens of sets of eyes. They glowed like hot coals. Like the fires of hell.

Surging to his feet, he looked to each side then behind him and in front, terror rising up to fill his throat and sit bitter on his tongue. Which way to go? The eyes to his left appeared to multiply and move closer.

He didn't wait to be certain. He ran.

Panting, ill, he kept moving, not daring to stop, not daring to look over his shoulder to see how close they came. He didn't know what they were. He didn't *want* to know what they were.

They stalked him as he had stalked others.

Images flashed through his thoughts. The men he had killed, members of his own temple, men who had threatened to leave the group and take what limited knowledge they had of Abasi Abubakar's plan with them. Fools. They had not known enough to make that a worthwhile threat, but he had killed them anyway. Because betrayal could never be allowed.

He had killed women. Weak-blooded descendants of Daughters of Aset who had failed to claim their heritage and let their power grow thinner and thinner with each generation.

Their blood had mattered. The blood of Aset. He had bags of it, flash frozen and stored away safe.

Too, he had been part of the murder of Lokan Krayl. The blood of Sutekh had flowed from Sutekh's son.

Of all the murders, only the last could not be laid solely on his head. He had not killed Lokan Krayl alone because he did not possess such power.

But no matter how hard he tried, he could not recall *who* had stolen the soul reaper's life. When he struggled to remember, a smooth, obsidian wall slipped into place in his thoughts and stopped him from going further.

And he needed to remember. Despite the terror that clawed at him, he was lucid enough to understand that his very life depended on his remembering the identity of the killer...betraying the identity of the killer when he was asked.

He *would* be asked. He knew it as he knew his own name.

Stumbling, he fell, his hands coming forward to save himself, slamming into what he quickly realized were stairs. Lifting his head, he saw that he was at the foot of a wide stone staircase. And at the top—

"What do you see?" The voice, wonderful and terrible, was inside his mind, and he was helpless to do anything but answer.

"I see a massive stone pillar…"

"Go on." Not a request. An order.

"There are hieroglyphics etched in the stone, and near the top, an ankh. On each side are stone arms and suspended from the ends are—" Chains. Three chains holding up massive gold plates.

"What do you see?"

"I see a scale." Cold terror slithered down Pyotr's spine.

His breath hitched and for a long moment, he thought he would never breathe again. And then he did, each inhalation rasping down his throat, each exhalation almost more effort than he could bear, as though his airways were closing, clogged by his fear.

"Why—" He swallowed. Tried again. "Why do you ask me what I see?"

"I am always curious about the way that mortal minds work, the things they choose to see when they come to me." A pause, then, "Come to me, Pyotr Kuznetsov,

High Reverend of the Cult of Setnakht, loyal follower of Sutekh. Come to me, now."

Pyotr tried to push to his feet, but he collapsed against the stairs once more, his chest banging the sharp stone edge.

"Come to me."

With a whimper, he crawled forward, up the stairs, his vision expanding the higher he went until he saw the full tableau. Horror iced his veins. He had hoped—prayed—that he had been brought to his master, to Sutekh. He saw now that prayer was in vain.

At the top of the stairs, beside the central stone pillar of the massive scale, was a man. His body was broad and heavily muscled, and his head was that of a jackal. *Anubis.* Beside him was an enormous statue of a beast, carved with forelegs thrust forward. It had the head of a crocodile, the body of a leopard—

"Ammut, the Devourer," Pyotr whispered.

Not a statue, but the Eater of Hearts herself. She would wait as Anubis judged the heart of a man against the feather of Ma'at—truth. If the heart was heavy, she would eat it, eat the soul, devour and destroy any hope of rebirth.

The trembling that took him then made his arms collapse out from beneath his weight, and he lay on the cold stone, a wriggling worm.

"I—" Panting, he struggled to master his emotions. Again he tried to rise. Again, he failed. He lay there on the stone, his legs trailing down the stairs, his body on the landing. His muscles were jelly. His bones were limp. "I am sworn to Sutekh. I am under his protection," he managed at last.

Anubis stared at him with eyes like black marbles. Expressionless. Pitiless.

"You are sworn to him," Anubis agreed, but then his next words squashed the hope that unfurled in Pyotr's breast. "But *he* is not sworn to protect *you*."

"Am I dead?" The words erupted, laced with terror. Even as he asked the question, he thought himself foolish to waste his words looking for confirmation of what he already knew. But it was human nature to hope, to imagine that against all odds, he might prevail.

"You are."

"Will I be reborn?" he croaked.

Anubis stared at him, saying nothing.

A shadow moved behind the pillar, and then a woman stepped forward. She was dressed in a flowing, white, diaphanous gown that left her arms bare and stood in contrast to the obsidian curtain of her hair. The cloth undulated as she moved. She was incredibly beautiful, her features delicate, her expression strong. Her eyes were black, lined in kohl, fixed on him with malice.

"Aset," he breathed, somehow knowing it was she, the enemy of his master, the mother of his enemies.

He had murdered those of her blood. From the way she looked at him, he was convinced that she knew his every crime.

"With your own hand you cut them and bled them,"

she said, confirming his fear. "By your orders, others did so. The flesh of my flesh, the blood of my blood. I heard their cries. I heard their sighs and lamentations. Now you will do me the courtesy of telling me why."

"The prophecy." The words tore free of his lips, though he didn't consciously form the thoughts. She summoned them from the depths of his heart and soul and somehow forced him to speak. "The blood of Aset. The blood of Sutekh."

"Go on." Aset glided closer, her expression composed and serene, her movement like water flowing smooth and tranquilly. He could not make himself look away, and he could not do other than she bid.

"And the God will pass the Twelve Gates and walk the Earth once more."

She stared at him for a fleeting second, an eternity, it seemed. And then she turned and walked away, her white gown swallowed by the darkness beyond the scale.

"You will be judged," Anubis said in a voice devoid of inflection. "Rise."

Pyotr tried. He put all his will into getting up on his knees, but he failed, collapsing against the cold stone with a piteous whimper.

He never saw Anubis move, but the jackal stood before him now, his sandaled feet inches from his face. With a quick movement, he caught the back of Pyotr's hair and dragged him up until his torso was off the ground. His other hand streaked forward and a blade gleamed.

Pain exploded in Pyotr's chest, such pain as he had never imagined, so vast and encompassing that it stole his breath, stole his voice. He could not even cry out.

Anubis let go of him and tossed Pyotr's dripping heart on the scale.

For an instant, the two sides were even, his heart a match to the feather of truth.

And then slowly, slowly, it sank, the feather rising, his heart falling until the gold plate that held it scraped the stone floor.

Anubis turned his head and held Pyotr's gaze, and then he raised his hand to Ammut and beckoned her near.

CHAPTER TWENTY

...the male and female fiery serpents, to whom was given a head after it had been cut off. Your head shall not be taken from you afterward, Your head shall not be taken from you forever.

—*The Egyptian Book of the Dead, Chapter 166*

CALLIOPE OPENED HER EYES. Her back was pressed against hard wood, the little bumps of her spine squawking in protest. She noted the familiar—the scent of the pine cleaner she used on her floors—and the unfamiliar—a man's weight full and heavy on her chest. Mal's weight.

She could barely breathe, but she tightened her arms around his back. She didn't want him to move. The warmth of his skin, the lush, heavy sensation of his body on hers and the puff of his breath against the curve of her neck, were wonderful. And terrifying.

Had she ever been in this position? Had she ever held a man in her arms, and been held in his, after she had taken what she needed from him?

If she had, she couldn't pull up the memory.

She lay there, feeling filled and empty, buoyant and bereft, and she couldn't explain why her emotions were bouncing around like a silver ball in an arcade game, sinking into a hole then popping up again, ready to roll.

Lifting up on his elbows, Mal shifted his weight, and again she tightened her arms around his back.

"Don't go," she whispered.

"I'm not going anywhere, Calli." He kissed the tip of her nose. "I just figured you might need to breathe." He paused then smiled at her.

"It's been a while." She didn't know why she told him that. It wasn't important.

Or, maybe it was.

"Define a while," he said, stroking her hair back from her face, his eyes locked on hers.

"I don't know." But she did. She knew down to the day. And the truth was, being with a man had *never* been like this. "Two years. Maybe two and a half."

He opened his mouth. Closed it. Then drew her against him and pressed his lips to hers in a kiss so tender it made her senses sway.

"Been a while for me, too," he murmured.

"Define a while."

"Two weeks? Maybe two and a half?" He didn't sound too certain, and there was a tinge of humor in his tone. His answer didn't surprise her. She'd had no illusions about who he was.

Besides, who was she to judge him when she'd spent

decades using men for sex to circumvent the necessity for blood?

Taking his weight on one arm, he drew back and stared down at her, his palm resting against her cheek.

"Calliope," he said, her name honeyed and rich on his tongue. "Calli…I haven't wanted anyone else since the second I saw you get out of the cab in front of Kuznetsov's."

She shook her head. "That's ridiculous. You couldn't have even seen my face clearly."

"I saw your face when you pinned me to the wall like a bug. And I felt the connection when I kissed you before Xaphan's concubines so rudely interrupted us, and when you let me into your dream and kissed me at the base of the mountain."

"I didn't let you in. You arrived uninvited."

He laughed. "Semantics." He rolled to his side and drew her against him, pressing his lips to her crown. "I just need you to know…I'm not rushing to anyone else's bed."

"Apparently, you aren't rushing to mine, either," she said with an arch look at the floor beneath them.

"You want me to say it. Fine. I think we might have something here. You and me."

Actually, she hadn't wanted him to say it. She didn't believe him. Didn't know why he even made such an outlandish statement. "You're crazy."

"No doubt about it." He paused. "I'm no prize. I lie. I cheat. I steal. Hell, I'd love to pretend I'm charming, to let you skim only the surface, because if you go even an inch deep, you might decide that what's inside isn't worth seeing, or knowing."

"You don't believe that."

"What? That I'm not worth knowing?" He offered her that pirate smile. "Nah. I like myself just fine."

His fingers splayed across her lower back subtly urged her closer.

"And I'm planning to hang around and see if *you* like me just fine."

"Fair warning?"

"Something like that." His hand rounded the curve of her buttock and squeezed. "Except I'm not a play-fair kind of guy."

Flattening her palm against his chest, she held him off with only that flimsy pressure. "This is absurd. How can you say any of this? You don't know me. I don't know you."

"You're wrong, Calli. If I'd taken you to dinner a dozen times, would you have told me about that day in Odessa? Would you have told me about your father's murder."

"What? No, of course not."

"How about two dozen dinners? Three? I could have dated you for a year and still not known you at all. You'd have shown me only your smooth, tranquil mask and nothing more."

She had nothing to say to that because it was only the truth. He had learned a great deal about her in a very short time. But what had she learned of him? She hadn't had the same access to his thoughts and deepest emotions, to the shaping events of his life.

Did she want to have access to them? Did she want to know him on that level?

"This is about sex, Mal. Nothing more." But even as she said it, she didn't quite believe it. She took a deep breath and forced the words out in a rush. "This is about me feeling tense and a little out of control and wanting to blow off steam, no questions, no strings."

"No connection other than the physical, right? No commitment."

"Yes." She exhaled in relief as she saw he understood. "Exactly."

His eyes glittered. His teeth flashed. "Calli, you're a lousy liar."

His stomach rumbled, and he changed the subject, just like that, offering her no chance to argue. "I need food."

Of course he did.

Never breaking the contact of his body with hers, he rose and lifted her against his chest. With a laughing gasp, she clamped her legs around his waist and her arms around his neck. He slid his hands under her naked buttocks, balancing her as he walked toward the kitchen.

"Nice position," he said. "Has possibilities."

With one hand supporting her weight, he used the other to open the first cupboard he came to then close it with a soft grunt when all he found were dishes. He opened a second cupboard and said, "Perfect."

To her astonishment, he uncapped and upended the squeeze bottle of honey, tipped his head back and squirted a mouthful.

"That's gross."

He swallowed, licked his lips then pressed them against hers for a kiss. He was sticky and sweet, and she opened her mouth to taste him.

Maybe not so gross after all.

"Two birds with one stone," he murmured and tipped her back onto the kitchen counter as he poured a stream of honey down her chest, across her breasts then down to her belly. "I need sugar. And I want you." His brows rose and fell. "This works."

Dipping his head, he licked honey off her chest, the rasp of his tongue both ticklish and erotic.

"Mmm… You are absolutely delicious," he said against her skin.

Again, her emotions surged in an unpredictable wave. She pulled back and locked down, making the silent assumption that he wouldn't notice.

Wrong assumption. His expression grew serious.

"Don't like honey? We can play a different game."

"A different—" Words failed her. She just pressed her lips together and shook her head quickly from side to side.

"What?" he asked, looking genuinely alarmed. "Did I hurt you? Are you sore?"

"No. No." She reached up to splay her fingers across his chest. Only in that moment did she realize that he was still fully clothed. His shirt was on. His jeans were on. Only the button and fly were undone, the waistband hanging low on his hips to bare his erection.

And she was naked, spread out on the kitchen counter like a banquet.

"I've just never—" She met his gaze, silver and bright and so focused on her it was as if she was the only thing in the world that mattered to him in that moment. "I've never done this just for fun." Or because she cared about someone and wanted to share herself with them.

"Never..." His eyes widened as he caught her meaning, that she'd used sex as a means to control the power of the prana she took when she fed. "You've never made love just for pleasure."

Her breath caught at his choice of words. "I've never *made love*," she corrected softly. She'd had clinical, emotionless sex out of necessity.

Until now. Until him.

He leaned in and kissed her, soft and tender and sweet. "You have now," he whispered. "And you're about to again."

He licked the honey from her breasts, taking his time, making her gasp and clutch at his hair to hold him close. He pulled off his shirt and his jeans and poured more honey, this time on his own skin. And she tasted him, his chest, his taut belly, his erect penis, thick and full.

Then he was the one leaning back against the kitchen

counter as she went to her knees and teased him, taking him into her mouth and reveling in the sounds he made, low in his throat. She raked the length of him with her teeth, loving the way he groaned and pumped his hips.

She took him deeper than she had before and sucked hard.

With a growl, he dragged her up and sat her on the cold granite. He pushed her legs apart and thrust deep inside her, his fingers clever and slick on her clitoris, until she threw her head back and screamed her release.

His hips jerked, and he made a raw, dark sound of unfettered pleasure, his body shaking with his climax.

And then he kissed her, his mouth soft on hers.

She had the crazy thought that it wasn't just a kiss, but a promise.

"*Kuso*. I WILL NOT TALK about this again," Naphré Kurata said coolly, holding on to her temper. She had one foot resting on the twisted, rusted-out bumper of the nearest car, and she leaned forward, her forearm across her thigh. Behind her was an endless sea of old clunkers. "Alastor, I was a Topworld enforcer for years before I met you, and I'm not going to take up baking cupcakes now just because you have control issues."

Her statement was met with dead silence on the other end of the line.

She sighed. "I fed from you not an hour past. With

your blood and life force ramping me up, there's very little that could hurt me."

More silence, then a grudging, "You bloody well better be in one piece when I get back."

"Love you, too," Naphré said and ended the call.

She'd taken this job for three reasons. One: because she needed Alastor to get used to her doing her thing. He had the personality of a battering ram at times, and she needed to take a stand. Two: because with Butcher gone, she needed to cement her name as a lone enforcer and make certain the jobs kept coming. She was used to a certain lifestyle, and she wasn't about to sacrifice that, or let Alastor pay the shot, though he'd hinted at that possibility more than once. Three: because there was a possibility that this job might have the added benefit of information about Lokan, at least indirectly. She hadn't mentioned it to Alastor, knowing that if she did, he'd want to tag along.

From behind her came the clank of a chain and a piteous whimper. Naphré ignored it, turning instead to do a perimeter check. It was dark. Not a lot to see. Nothing jumped out at her—literally or figuratively—which suited her just fine.

Again came the clank of the chain behind her.

She turned toward the worthless piece of trash she'd brought here for a nice private chat. Jeffy Prince.

Funny, he bore absolutely no resemblance to royalty.

He looked like a skinny, lanky kid with his long,

greasy hair and baggy jeans. But when he lifted his chin to glare at her from beneath his brows, the play of shadow and weak light cast by the security lamp on the shack in the corner showed his age. Closer to forty than twenty. No kid.

She eased her knife from its sheath and let it catch the light. A promise.

If the way he jerked and squealed was any indication, Jeffy Prince wasn't fond of that promise. He gave a garbled moan. "I don't know nothing. I don't. I swear it. I don't."

And she hadn't even asked a single question yet.

His breath came in ragged gasps as he lurched and tugged at the restraints Naphré had looped around his wrists then anchored to the bumper of a mangled minivan. He yanked on the chains, testing them even though he had to know they wouldn't be any looser now than they'd been ten seconds ago. There was no give in the way she'd bound his wrists, and just enough length ran from wrists to bumper to let him shove back a lank hunk of hair.

His fingernails were dirty, crusted black.

With a tight, close-lipped smile, she stalked closer, circling, circling, knowing that each ticking second she was behind him and out of his line of vision ratcheted up his terror.

"I swear it. I don't know nothing."

"Swear it on what? Your mother's grave? Your life?"

Naphré asked, leaning in close from behind to speak softly near his ear.

He squirmed and twisted, trying to keep her in sight, his head swiveling to one side then the other.

Naphré rounded the van and hunkered down before him, knees splayed, hands hanging loose. He jerked back as far as the chain would go and dug his heels into the gravel, pushing and straining to get as far from her as he could.

Their eyes were level. Pressing himself against the bumper, he cringed as shudders racked his frame.

"What exactly are you swearing on?" she asked again, whisper soft.

His eyes rolled white with fear.

"Don't kill me." The words came out in a garbled rush. "Please, sweet Jesus, don't kill me." The more Jeffy yanked on the chains, the tighter they got. Naphré figured his hands had to be growing numb by now.

"You know...you really are in sore need of a manicure." She tapped her index finger against the back of his wrist and he jerked and cried out as though she'd stabbed him.

"Don't move," she ordered. With careful attention, she reached over and grabbed his thumb, slid the tip of the knife under his grime-blackened nail and ran it in a smooth arc. "You move and I might inadvertently take the whole thumb."

He bleated in terror but didn't move. Didn't jerk away. Because the chains were quite tight. And because he had enough intellect to realize her words were no empty threat.

"Now, I have a simple question for you before we discuss the two girls you sold to Big Ralph." Turned out the two girls were from Izanami's line, and she didn't want them working as psy-whores for Asmodeus. So the *Shikome* had hired Naphré to look into things.

"Anything. Anything," Jeffy said.

"You were involved in an altercation a couple of months ago. In an alley. It involved a man, a woman and a box."

The only reason she knew about the box at all was because she'd noticed it when she picked up a chai latte in the little coffee shop around the corner from Tesso's Bar and Grill. The box was old, small, made of what appeared to be lead, with a cartouche and Aset's name on the top, along with a number of hieroglyphs that were far beyond her ability to read. The owner of the coffee shop kept it on the shelf above the cash register.

And then Jeffy had gone and stolen it, and that's when things got strange.

"I don't know nothing."

"We're back to that, are we?" She let the knife catch the light.

The chains clanked as the guy shivered and moaned. "Don't kill me. Don't kill me. Don't kill me."

"I'm not going to kill you." She made an all-encompassing gesture toward the rows of wrecked cars and trucks. "See, this junkyard is old as fuck. And the guy who owns it? He does things just the way he did thirty years ago." She laughed. "Not a fan of newfangled ideas. He's one mean bastard. Doesn't bother with a security service—" she glanced at the chain-link fence "—or barbed wire."

Lowering her lashes, she brought the knife up and slid it under the nail of Jeffy's index finger, tracing another smooth arc. Then she lifted her lids and pinned him with a hard look. "But he has dogs. Loves those dogs. Feeds them the occasional treat."

She held his gaze for a long moment before she said, "Live treats. They like to play with their food. And they like their meat raw and fresh—"

She caught his wrist and made a shallow cut on his forearm. He yelped and jerked, but the chains held.

"And bloody," she continued. "Only reason they're not here now is because the old man doesn't let them out till eleven." She made a show of looking at her watch. "Almost eleven now."

"I don't have the fucking box. I don't."

"Who does?"

"How the fuck should I know?"

"Wrong answer. Tell me enough to make me happy, and we leave here together. All nice and friendly. Tell me anything less and you spend the night with Old Man Kerouik's pets."

"The guy. I saw the guy pick it up. He took it. The guy."

Naphré stared at him, judging the truth of his words.

True or not, he definitely believed what he was saying. Which made no sense. It had been a soul reaper in that alley. And if a soul reaper had that box, shouldn't Alastor know that?

When he'd told her about the casket in Sutekh's territory, the one that held Lokan's partial remains, his description of it had triggered her memory of that box. She couldn't help but note the similarities between the carvings he described and the ones she'd seen. But he hadn't mentioned a smaller casket.

If Jeffy was right and a soul reaper had the box, Alastor should know about it. The fact that he didn't meant…what?

"It was the guy," he said, dragging out every word in a desperate whine.

Satisfied with the answer, she turned and walked away with Jeffy screaming frantically behind her. She paused, turned.

"I think you did a nasty thing selling those girls to Big Ralph. So I'll do a nasty thing in return. Hope you like dogs," she said and walked away.

She was almost at the gates when the air crackled and sparked. Feeding from Alastor had given her a definite edge as far as detecting supernatural energy signatures went. This one was off the charts.

Whatever was out there was immensely powerful.

She turned, saw nothing and turned again, her knife still in her hand, her every sense on alert.

And as she completed the circle she stopped dead. A

woman stood before her. Or maybe *stood* wasn't quite the right word. Naphré had the distinct impression that the woman's feet didn't touch the ground.

She was garbed in red velvet shot with black, her face hidden by a deep hood that was drawn up over her head. A gold chain hung about her neck, and on it hung a cartouche of Aset.

A chill chased up Naphré's spine. She stared at the woman in shock, fairly certain that she was in the presence of a Matriarch. Except, the Matriarchs never left the compound. Yet, here one was.

That couldn't be good.

"Naphré Kurata," the woman said, her voice resonating in Naphré's mind.

"I'm afraid you have me at a disadvantage," Naphré said.

"I am Hathor. I have come for you."

"So I see."

Hathor made a sweeping gesture, indicating that Naphré should precede her, and though Naphré didn't will herself to take a step, she did just that. Glancing down, she found that her feet were a good three inches off the ground and she was gliding forward as though she was standing on a conveyor belt.

The gates swung open before them, the chains curling away like serpents, though no hand touched them.

And Naphré thought, *Kuso. Alastor is going to be pissed.*

CHAPTER TWENTY-ONE

Get back! Retreat! Get back, you dangerous one.
Do not come against me, do not live by my magic.
—*The Egyptian Book of the Dead, Chapter 31*

THEY DOZED ON THE COUCH, and when Calliope made a soft little sound of complaint and burrowed against his warmth, Mal lifted her and carried her up the stairs to her bed.

She protested. He persisted. And won.

Then he lay on his side and watched her sleep and wondered exactly what the hell he was feeling.

He couldn't explain it. He just knew he couldn't get her out of his head and that he wanted *something* with her, something more than just a single night. He had absolutely no intention of letting her go.

All he needed to do was convince her that they were on the same page.

They slept.

Then he woke her with slow, deep strokes, entering her from behind, her round buttocks pressed against him, his hands on her breasts.

They cooked pasta that they ate from a single plate,

sitting on the couch, wrapped in a quilt, sipping red wine from a shared glass.

"I'm thinking we should leave," he said. "I actually only meant to stop here for you to get some things together before we went somewhere else."

"Somewhere else? Where?"

He raked his hand back through his hair. "Somewhere where you'll be harder to find. Safer."

She shot him a veiled look and said, "If the Matriarchs want me, they will find me no matter where I go. There's only false security in running."

He couldn't argue her point. "Can't run from what's meant to find you."

"No." She sipped the wine, turning the glass to drink from the spot he'd put his mouth to. He wondered if she even realized she was doing that. "Did you find them?" she asked. "The ones who tried to run? The ones who killed the woman you told me about. Elena."

He almost chose not to answer. Then he thought of the way he'd learned things about her from her dreams, and he realized there'd been no reciprocity. She knew almost nothing about him. If he had any hope in hell of figuring out what this was between them, he'd have to give, at least a little.

It wasn't a place he was used to being in. Generally, all he gave to a woman was sexual satisfaction. But this was different. Calliope was different.

"Not all of them," he said. "Some were dead already before I managed to find them."

Tipping her head, she studied his expression. "You're no longer angry about that."

"Angry isn't a productive place to be," he said.

"Angry is better than afraid. Cunning is better than angry."

He gave a short laugh. "Great minds think alike."

"Tell me about her." She set the wineglass down, but she didn't ask anything more, didn't push. She just sat there watching him. Waiting.

"I was young. I didn't know yet that I wasn't human. My life had been a series of near misses, always staying one step ahead of the hangman's noose. I'd had one hell of a near miss when I met her. I'd been locked in the brig when the ship went down. It was burning from above. Filling with water from below. I barely made it out. Had nightmares for years."

He figured she knew a thing or two about nightmares herself.

"Then I met Elena. For me, she was serenity. Peace. Constancy and consistency. All the shit I'd lacked in my life to that point. She was lovely and sweet. Uncomplicated."

Calliope shot him a look and he winced. Maybe not the best word choice, given that he was sharing a couch with the queen of complicated. But he wasn't going to make excuses, so he explained it the best way he could.

"I loved her with my little boy's heart, not really understanding anything at all."

She nodded, clearly understanding what it was he was trying to say. Or maybe just pretending to.

"I went back to the sea, to seek my fortune—" he shot her a grin "—by less than legal means."

The corners of her mouth quirked up. "That I believe."

"I had dreams of being a pirate king. Of setting Elena up in a castle with jewels in her hair." He wove his fingers through Calliope's hair, the dark strands pouring across his palm like silk. "Nine, maybe ten months later, I got back and she was gone. People in her village gave me a shitload of conflicting stories. No one seemed to really know what happened to her. I searched for ten years."

"You never found her."

"Not alive. But in the end, I managed to find her bones. Made a marker for her grave." He shook his head. "A statue of an angel. She'd been dead the entire time, dragged off by a group of men who raped her and murdered her."

Calliope linked her fingers with his and held tight.

He kept going, figuring this was the part that mattered most, the part that would really tell her something about him. "I searched for them. In the end, all I got were the cold ashes of weak vengeance. There were seven men. Four of them fucking died before I ever found them."

"And the other three?"

"I killed them. Took my time. Made it hurt. Two of

them didn't even remember her. I only learned the truth of her fate from the last man I found, and he remembered her only because she managed to scratch his face. The wounds got infected and healed with a scar."

"When you were with Elena, were you a soul reaper already?"

"No. I thought I was human."

"And when you found the men who killed her?"

"By then Sutekh had come for me. I ripped out their fucking hearts. Took their darksouls to my father." He realized then what he'd said, and how it might affect her, but when he looked into her eyes, he saw no hint of revulsion. "It's what I do," he said, just to be sure. No sense dancing around what he was. What he would always be.

"I know."

And he couldn't tell a damned thing about what she was thinking or feeling from that.

"Do you still feel guilty?" she asked.

"Cut straight to the heart of it, don't you?"

"Yes."

"I don't dwell on her death. I don't wallow in self-flagellation." He didn't even really blame himself anymore, but there was no doubt that the choices he'd made ever since had been colored by her loss. He never spent more than one night with a woman. He never cared about them on a personal level, other than making sure he saw to his partner's sexual satisfaction.

That was key. He always saw to his partner before he saw to himself. What fun was it otherwise?

But Calliope was different. He didn't have a name for what he felt for her. He didn't want to have a name for it. Not yet.

He drew back and looked down at her, studying her face. "Speaking of feeling guilty…any residual remorse for the havoc you've wreaked on my life since the second I laid eyes on you in that club?"

Again, that barely there smile. "You mean from the second *I* laid eyes on *you*."

"Mayhem. You've done nothing but steal from me. Stab me. Feed from me. Leave me to burn. You're my own personal disaster zone." He huffed a breath through his nose. "Maybe that's what I like about you. Maybe I'm just one sick fuck."

"Elena couldn't protect herself. But I can."

"Yeah, you definitely can."

"Maybe that's the attraction," she said, her brows drawing down in a frown.

"No 'maybe' about it. If you can best me, pretty girl, I figure you can best just about anyone."

"And you find that appealing?"

He nuzzled her temple, breathing in the scent of her skin. He slid his hand over her naked hip, down her belly, between her legs. She gasped as he eased his finger inside her. "Sexy as hell."

HOURS LATER, MAL SAT bolt upright in Calliope's bed, images dancing at the edges of his thoughts. Cool fingers splayed over the cap of his shoulder.

"What is it?"

He rolled toward her. She was on her side, the weight of her torso raised up on her arm. The sheet draped the curve of her hip and flowed over the edge of the bed to the floor.

"I had a dream," he said.

Her gaze was clear and direct. Of course, she didn't understand the significance of that. How could she?

"I dreamed of a hawk being torn to bits by demons, the blood flowing across a wooden floor." He raked his fingers back through his hair. "There were women there, cavorting with the demons, bathing in the blood. Laughing."

He could see them still, as though the picture was captured on film, playing again and again in his mind's eye, infinitely disturbing.

"The demons turned to soul reapers, men I know well, and others, whose faces I've seen. The hawk became Lokan, his body cut into fourteen parts, neatly severed at the joints.

"Then there were only two soul reapers left, standing knee-deep in blood, the level rising like a river in a storm." He paused then finished. "Their faces. I saw them. Alastor and Dae."

Something flickered in Calliope's eyes. Recognition. Acknowledgment. It made him wary.

"I felt terror, only I couldn't say if it was *for* them or *because* of them." He shrugged. "And then I woke up."

Calliope stroked her hand along his arm to his

forearm and, finally, to his hand, where she laced her fingers with his and just let them rest there. Her hand in his.

"An unpleasant scenario," she murmured.

He stared at her, wondering what to say, how much to tell. How much to trust her with.

"More than unpleasant. Fucking unlikely. Soul reapers don't dream."

Her sharp intake of breath told him she got it. She understood the ramifications of what he was telling her.

"Only time I ever dreamed was when I saw what you saw, Calli, felt what you felt. And that was more of a psychic connection with you than my own dream. This was different." He huffed out a sharp exhalation. "This was something entirely different."

She studied him, her expression contemplative. She knew something. He could feel it.

"I figure the hawk symbolism is Horus, Aset's son with Osiris. He turns into Lokan, Sutekh's son. Then gets cut into fourteen parts just like Sutekh cut up Osiris. But the rest of it…I got nothing."

"The women in your dream," she said. "The night we went after Kuznetsov. There were Topworld grunts there, sent by Big Ralph—"

"Who works for Asmodeus, demon of lust."

"Yes. So that could explain the women's presence in your dream."

"And?"

Calliope met his gaze, her expression shuttered.

"You know something. What? Tell me."

"You said that you only dreamed when you saw what I saw. Perhaps this dream too was colored by my thoughts."

She paused, and he had the feeling that he wasn't going to like what she was about to say.

"The two soul reapers left standing in your dream. Your brothers. You said you felt afraid." Her expression smoothed, and that ramped up his unease because the cool, remote Calliope mask meant she was hiding her emotions. Which meant that whatever she was about to say, it was not going to be good.

"The Matriarchs said that there is a traitor among your kind."

"There is. *Was*. Gahiji. Sutekh's former second-in-command. He's been dealt with. He's dead."

She shook her head. "Not Gahiji. Another."

"You have my full attention now." He meant it. Every nerve in his body was humming on high alert.

"The Matriarchs believe the traitor is one of Sutekh's sons."

For a second, Mal didn't even process what she'd said. Her words made no sense, and he turned them over and over in his thoughts trying to see some hidden meaning. But there was none. She was actually saying that her Matriarchs thought Dae or Alastor had killed Lokan.

"What the fuck?" The question just exploded out of him and he stared at her, feeling as if he'd been kicked in the head by a horse. "Seriously. What the fuck?"

She shook her head, opened her mouth—

His phone rang. His gut churned. He almost ignored it, but in the end he snatched it up.

"Yeah," he snarled.

"Bad timing?" Dae asked.

THE SUN WAS A GIANT BALL of flame in a yellow sky. A sheet of sand, white and smooth, reflected the light, sending off a piercing glare. Mal tipped his head back. The single sun shivered and danced until the shapes separated and became three suns.

He turned, shading his eyes as he studied the steep rise that erupted out of the sand. It was improbably covered by a thick tangle of high grass and creeping vines, and Dagan was already halfway up and climbing, catching hold of the greenery as he went.

The heat and the blistering suns should have fried it all brown. But in this place, "should have" didn't apply.

Following Dae's path, Mal climbed.

The higher they went, the denser the vegetation grew. They topped the rise, panting, sweating.

Nothing stirred. The air was still and heavy and damp. Again, that made no sense. He'd have thought desert air would be dry.

Mal shot a scathing look at the suns and scraped his forearm across his forehead, wiping away sweat.

"I don't fucking get it. Who set the weather control in this place? The humidity's like a rain forest and the sun's blistering like the desert. And the damned grass is growing out of sand. The place is creepy."

Dagan shot him a look over his shoulder. "Creepy?" Amusement laced his tone. "It's the Underworld. No one said it has to make sense."

Pulling his drenched T-shirt off over his head, Mal used it to wipe his face then strung it through the belt loop of his jeans and let it hang.

"Not exactly the Underworld," he muttered. They were actually in what was effectively a null zone, a realm that wasn't quite part of the Underworld, or Topworld, but a pocket somewhere in between.

"True enough," Dagan said. "Funny, but if Naphré and Alastor hadn't made that unexpected trip to Jigoku—" a sort of purgatory associated with Izanami's realm "—none of us would have thought to search for Lokan's remains in these little patches of unclaimed territory."

"You tell Sutekh about this place?" Mal asked.

"Don't want to get the old man's hopes up."

"You think he has hopes?" Mal asked, incredulous. "I don't think he has any capacity for emotion."

Dagan shrugged. "Whatever. If we find something, we'll tell him. If we don't…" He shrugged again.

Mal grunted a reply. Alastor and Naphré had found the lead casket with Lokan's partial remains that now sat in Sutekh's greeting chamber, but he wasn't counting on having similar luck. He didn't feel Lokan here, didn't sense him.

But then, Alastor said that when he'd found Lokan's

remains, the energy signature had only become stronger the closer Alastor had come to the box.

Dagan seemed to think they might hit the jackpot here.

The fact that his two brothers were so hopeful made Mal edgy. He didn't get why they couldn't see what he saw. He was the least pragmatic of the three of them. He was more of an optimist than Alastor and Dae put together. Yet he seemed to be the only one who could see that Lokan wasn't coming back.

No matter how many body parts they managed to find, too much time had passed. By now, their brother would have partaken of the food of the dead. His soul was lost to them.

But the sweet taste of revenge was still on the menu.

Mal wanted those who'd killed his brother to pay in blood and pain. And no matter what Calliope's Matriarchs implied, he fucking well knew that the list of suspects didn't include either Dae or Alastor.

"Fuck," he snarled as his foot sank into a pocket of sand buried beneath the greenery.

Dae paused and turned. "Who pissed in your cornflakes?"

"Calli."

"Calli, huh?" Dae's expression grew speculative. "She's okay with the variation of her name?"

"It's growing on her."

"I'll bet. Like a fungus."

Mal kicked at the vegetation and waited to see if it would kick back. You never knew. Maybe it was something other than it seemed.

But the vines did nothing more threatening than lie there, snaking along the ground and up the sides of the squat, single-story gray brick building that sat about fifteen yards away. They twined up the walls and over the flat roof. A quick circle of the perimeter revealed that three of the four walls were obscured by vines as thick as Mal's wrist.

Dagan took the hint and let the subject drop. He gestured at the one wall that was nearly bare. "Of course, that one couldn't be the one with the door."

"You looking for a free ride?" Mal grabbed hold of a vine, testing its strength. Damned strong. He put his back into it and started tearing away at the vines. No easy task. When he peeled one back and yanked it off, there were more tangled underneath.

Kind of like Calliope.

Peel away one layer, and there were dozens more.

He figured it was going to take a hell of a long time to work his way through all of them, and oddly, he was looking forward to that.

"So…you and Calliope Kane," Dae said, his voice too casual, tinged with discomfort. Guess he hadn't taken the hint after all.

Mal snorted. "Roxy put you up to asking me about this?" He knew Calliope had spoken to her, mentioned that she and Mal were together. It was no stretch to imagine that Roxy had started connecting the dots.

"Yeah."

Mal got hold of another vine and pulled. It was stubborn and intractable and it took several tries to get the insidious little tendrils that wove into the other vines free.

"So what'd she do?"

"She did more than piss in my cornflakes. She dropped a bag of dog shit on my head right before you called," Mal said. Which was the perfect way to describe Calliope's untimely revelation.

"Care to explain?"

"No." What was he supposed to say? That her Matriarchs believed one of his brothers had killed Lokan? Which one? Dagan? Alastor?

Osiris had made a similar accusation weeks ago, couched in terms of condolence in the missive he had sent to each of them when Lokan died. The messages had been identical, written on papyrus with shiny gold leaf. *So sorry for your loss. I understand your pain. I, too, was murdered and dismembered. By my own brother.*

That message had as many layers as a bean dip, and the possible interpretation that Osiris thought one of Lokan's own brothers had killed him.

Mal thought the same thing now that he had then: No fucking way.

"You called before I could clear the air with her," Mal finished at last.

"I actually kind of like her," Dae said, pausing to shoot Mal a look over his shoulder. "Even though she can barely look at me without hauling out a knife."

"She has something of a hate-on for reapers," Mal said. "Or *had*. I think she's working on it."

"She's not the only one who doesn't exactly warm to our kind. I have a feeling that her superiors in the Asetian Guard would have preferred she had killed Roxy rather than let her muster out to be with me."

"I have a feeling you're right."

"But she doesn't hate *you*…" Dae shot him a speculative glance that went on just a shade too long.

"She has her reasons." Mal offered no more than that. Those were Calliope's secrets and he'd hack off his own arm before he'd betray them, even to his brother.

The thought jarred him. He was loyal to Dagan and Alastor and Lokan, and to his father, after a fashion. When the hell had he become loyal to Calliope Kane?

Dae shifted a few feet to the left and kept tearing vines, and Mal figured that was that.

But his brother must have made one hell of a promise to Roxy, because he wouldn't leave well enough alone. "You, uh…you think you've been hit by the thunderbolt?"

Straightening, Mal felt his lips shape a rueful smile. When Dagan had been slapped upside the head by his feelings for Roxy, he'd been on such unfamiliar ground that he'd actually asked Mal for advice, in a convoluted sort of way: he'd asked Mal if he'd ever read *The God-father*, and if he'd ever been hit with the thunderbolt that had struck Michael Corleone when he saw the girl for the first time and couldn't get her out of his head. Michael Corleone hadn't had a reason. It just was. He couldn't stop thinking about her. He had to have her.

That's exactly what had happened to Dae. Then Alastor.

"You asked me that before," Mal hedged, not certain he wanted to go there, to admit out loud how far Calli'd got under his skin. "Remember what my answer was?"

"Yeah. That you got hit like that every time you saw a nice rack or a sweet ass."

Mal exhaled a sharp laugh. "That's what I said."

Then. But now he thought he might have been hit by that same fucking thunderbolt that had felled Dae the first time he saw Roxy Tam. Or Alastor the first time he saw Naphré Kurata. The thought was both disturbing and oddly appealing.

Problem was, Michael Corleone's story hadn't had such a great ending. He hadn't been able to protect her—

Mal veered away from that thought. He couldn't think about that. Part of Calliope's lure was the fact that she could damn well take care of herself. She'd done so for a hell of a long time before he ever came along, and he was going to have to trust that she could continue to do so now.

It was his faith in her abilities that had allowed him to leave her alone while he joined Dae on this little jaunt into a null zone.

"Here," Dagan said as he finally tore away the last of the vines and uncovered the door. Then he turned his hands palms up and asked, "You feeling something?"

Mal glanced at his hands. The skin appeared unmarked, but he felt as if the flesh of his palms and fingers were blistered to the bone. "I think the vines were warded."

"Then how'd we manage to get through?"

"They were warded against supernatural power, not against good old sweat and labor," Mal said.

One side of Dae's mouth quirked in a half smile. "Well, wasn't that our dumb luck?"

"Depends on what we find inside. I don't know about you, but my hands feel as though I dipped them in acid. I wouldn't call that luck unless we get some sort of reward."

"True enough." Dae gestured at the locked door. "Do your thing?"

Mal never went anywhere without at least a couple of picks. He pulled them out now and played around with the lock for what felt like hours. Hard to tell for sure, though. Time was relative. It did one thing Topworld. Something entirely different in each of the different territories of the Underworld. And who the hell knew how time was measured here in what amounted to a null zone.

The burn in his fingers made him clumsy. He shifted the pick on the right, and the lock gave.

Inside they found a cavernous space far bigger than it appeared from the outside. The walls were lined with shelves that seemed to go on forever, and the shelves were lined with jars. Canopic jars. They were used to store the organs of the dead. Some were limestone. Some were clay.

Dagan moved deeper into the building, while Mal studied the area near the door. Etched in the bricks and painted in bright colors was a depiction of the twelve gates of Osiris; they acted as a road map for resurrection of the dead. Some texts had as few as seven gates, some as many as twenty-one. But the end point was the same: the passage from the Underworld back to the world of man. The dead would live again.

After a few moments, Dagan called, "The jars back here have plain lids." He walked toward Mal, paused to examine some jars, and said, "These are more recent. They all have carvings of human heads."

Mal looked at the shelf to his left. The lids of these jars bore carvings of the heads of the four sons of Horus. Hapi—the baboon. Duamutef—the jackal. Qebehsenue—the falcon. Imseti—the human-headed god. The lungs, stomach, intestines and liver of the deceased were each held in a separate jar.

He reported his find to Dagan and said, "Looks like these are the most recent of the bunch."

"So, if this is a null zone, not claimed as part of the territory of any Underworlder, why are these here?" he asked as Dagan stepped up beside him.

"Good question."

"This is a storage facility." Which made no sense. The organs were supposed to remain with the mummy, otherwise there could be no reanimation. Why separate the organs from the body and store them here? "Who would bother to set all this up?"

"Another good question." Dagan lifted one of the jars and studied it for a moment then put it back on the shelf and turned to look the length of the room. "Definitely an Egyptian deity." He shrugged as he turned back to face Mal. "Could be Aset. Osiris. Horus. Anubis. Apophis. Thoth. Shit, there are so many it'd take us a day to list all the possibilities." He spread his hands, palms up. "Hell, for all we know, the place could belong to the old man."

"Yeah," Mal said slowly, "but if Sutekh knew about this place, wouldn't he have sent us searching for Lo-kan's remains in similar null zones a long time ago? You'd think that if he knew about one, he'd at least suspect there were others."

"True enough," Dagan said. "So we cross the old man off the list."

Mal scraped his hand along his jaw as he looked again at the wall painting. His gaze slid to the last depicted gate, the final obstacle to living, the final barrier to walking in the sun.

Walking free of the Underworld.

A chill chased across his skin.

"The blood of Aset. The blood of Sutekh," he murmured, the prophecy Kai had recited for them echoing in his thoughts. "And the God will pass the Twelve Gates and walk the Earth once more."

Dae shot him a look then followed his gaze to the far wall. "Damn," he breathed.

"Damn," Mal echoed.

CHAPTER TWENTY-TWO

May you give me a path that I may pass in peace,
for I am straightforward and true;
I have not willingly told lies,
I have not committed a second fault.

—*The Egyptian Book of the Dead, Chapter 15*

ROXY TAM PERCHED ON the rail of the bell tower that rose from the north end of the deconsecrated church she called home. Calliope and Mal. She didn't know what to think about that. And from the odd tone in Calliope's voice when they'd talked on the phone, Roxy thought that maybe Calliope didn't know what to think about it, either.

She adjusted her weight on the rail and stared out at the dark line of the horizon. She liked to come here to think. To be alone. She liked the cool air and the stars and the view of the bare branches of the trees reaching up toward the night sky.

This was her place, and Dagan left her to it. Though they now shared the home that had once been hers alone, he respected her need for moments, and spaces, where he didn't follow.

Not that he was here to follow now. He'd gone off with Mal after he'd managed to find the location of yet another null zone between the Underworld and Top-world. It was in such a place that Alastor and Naphré had found the lead casket with some of Lokan's remains. Dae was convinced that he'd find the rest in another one like it.

Roxy wasn't convinced. There was something off about all of this. Before she'd ever met Dae, she'd been hunting information about the dead soul reaper, Lokan Krayl. Everything she'd found pointed to a reenactment of Osiris's murder by Sutekh millennia past, with the body hacked to bits and the parts scattered.

So who'd been collecting Lokan's parts all neat and tidy in a lead casket with Aset's name carved on the lid?

A question without an answer.

Restlessness crawled through her. She felt as if some-thing was out there, watching her, stalking her. But when she closed her eyes and let the charge in her blood seek a supernatural's energy signature, she found nothing. No one.

She'd been in this exact position before, not too long ago. That night, it had been Dagan out there watching her, masking his energy signature.

Tonight, she wasn't too sure. Not a soul reaper. None would dare hunt Dagan Krayl's mate. But her gut was telling her that *someone* was on her turf.

Time to roll out the welcome mat.

She swung off the rail and shimmied down the metal ladder set into the inside wall of the tower. At the base was a scarred wooden door. Pushing it open, she stepped out of the tower into her living room.

And stopped dead. At the far end of the room was a woman. She was garbed in a red velvet gown, shot with black, and a cowl was drawn up to hide her face and head. Around her neck, outside her gown, was a thick gold chain with a gold cartouche hanging between her breasts.

Instinct had Roxy pulling her knife from the sheath at the small of her back.

"I offer no threat," a female voice said. "For the moment."

As if jerked on a string, the knife flew out of Roxy's hand. Incredibly fast, the woman snatched the hilt from the air. Roxy never even saw her hand. Her movements were too quick and the voluminous sleeve of her gown extended well past her fingertips.

"No threat, huh?" Roxy straightened and cocked one hip. "Nice to know."

"Roxy Tam." The voice reverberated inside her skull. "You look a great deal like your mother."

Roxy's heart gave a little twist.

"And you wear her pendant."

"What do you know about my mother?"

"That she was lost to us. A tragedy. Your grief is ours."

Roxy said nothing, not trusting a word of it.

"Your mother was beloved, though she had not completed her transition. She was marked but not blooded. She had not yet chosen to take first blood."

"I remember she had a mark on her forearm, an ankh. It's how I knew where to put mine." Roxy dragged up her sleeve and bared her own dark mark, etched in her skin, an ankh with wings and horns. "Who are you?"

"I am Amunet. I am your progenitor. Your sister among Aset's Daughters. I am the keeper of the archives that document our line. And I join you in mourning the loss of Kelley Tam."

"Do you? Then why didn't you save her?" *Why didn't you come for me? Find me? Save me?* She didn't ask those questions out loud, but she got an answer nonetheless.

"The Matriarchs regret the years you were alone and unaware of your gifts. Though powerful, we are not omniscient. We did not come because we did not know we were needed."

"The Matriarchs." Roxy's breath caught. This woman with her velvet gown and speed and power. She was one of the Matriarchs. And she'd left the compound. Why?

"I have come for you now, Roxy Tam."

CALLIOPE STEPPED OUT of the shower, feeling off. Having taken Mal's blood to heal the wound in her side, she'd again forfeited her ability to sense events before they happened. She felt naked without it. Uncomfortable. As if she was missing a limb.

She combed her wet hair and drew it back in a covered elastic then pulled on clothes.

Pure instinct told her something wasn't quite right. She closed her eyes for a second and listened.

Silently, she made her way to the spare bedroom at the front of the house. She didn't shift the blind. Instead, she positioned herself so she could peer through the half-inch crack between the roller shade and the window frame. At the same time she reached for any hint of a supernatural energy signature.

Nothing out there.

But the fine hairs on her forearms prickled and rose, and she wondered if feeding from Mal had dulled her other senses rather than heightened them. His prana was like high-voltage electricity cranking her system, but there was a price for everything, and her prescience was definitely part of that payment. What else had she lost in the process?

The other option was no better: that whatever was out there was powerful enough to mask any hint of its presence.

She crept to the next bedroom and repeated her movements then went to the back of the house and did the same.

No car was visible, other than her own. There were no shadows that moved when they shouldn't.

She stole silently down the stairs, not bothering with a light, careful to avoid the creaking fifth step.

When she reached the bottom of the staircase, she froze, trying to catch some hint of what was out there.

Or in here.

On a sharp inhalation, she leaped back, brought her knee to the groin at the same time as she jabbed for the larynx.

Her knee missed. Her jab connected, but barely, not nearly hard enough to do real damage.

There was a strangled grunt.

Then, "You think we'll ever get to a point where you stop attacking me?"

The breath left her in a rush as she fell back. Stood down.

Mal stood there, one hand rubbing his throat, and she realized that feeding from him had enhanced her night vision. That's why she'd been able to see outside so clearly on a nearly moonless night. She'd been so focused on finding the intruder, she hadn't even thought about that until now.

"Must you sneak up on me?" she asked, liquid cool.

"I was trying to be considerate," he said, sounding wounded and a little hoarse. "In case you were asleep."

She cut him a look through her lashes, suspecting he lied. "Were you? Or were you testing me? Trying to make certain I didn't just lie there asleep while someone broke in?"

He made a noncommittal sound.

Stepping toward him, she laid her hand on his cheek and he turned his head and pressed his lips to her palm. But his eyes tracked hers, glittering mercury-gray and bright, and in his gaze she saw turmoil. Something was wrong.

"What is it?" she asked softly.

"I have something for you," he said. Without waiting for a reply, he handed her her sword, hilt first, the one she'd lost to him that night at Kuznetsov's condo.

She took it, the heft familiar in her hand, the weight of it like an extension of her arm. He had to have brought it to her for a reason.

Lifting her head, she studied his expression, and the glint of gold caught her eye. Aset's cartouche. He was wearing it around his neck now. He hadn't been when he left. That, combined with her sword, made her uneasy.

"What is it?" she asked again.

"Someone came for Roxy while Dae and I were gone. And someone got Naphré, too."

"What? Killed them?" Her usual calm deserted her, and all she seemed to be able to do was parrot useless questions at him as horror surged.

"No. *Took* them. Kidnapped. We don't know who or why."

"So that's the real reason you were slinking through

my house. Because you weren't sure if there was a threat hiding somewhere."

"No. I would have sensed a threat. And I could sense your energy signature." He offered a half smile. "I really was trying to be considerate in case you were asleep."

"Why would someone take Naphré and Roxy?" She felt sluggish and slow, as if her brain was chugging up a steep hill. Roxy was in trouble. Calliope couldn't help the protective urge that made her want to wield the sword Mal had just returned to her and cut down any who threatened her charge.

For years, Calliope had been Roxy's mentor, responsible for guiding and teaching her. Then their relationship had evolved and Roxy had found her feet, become a formidable force in her own right. But Calliope could never quite shake the feeling that she needed to watch out for her, as though Roxy was her kid sister.

"Dagan…" She couldn't imagine what he was feeling. She knew he loved Roxy. Truly loved her. She remembered the look on his face when he'd had the choice to go after Gahiji and possibly find information about his dead brother or stay with Roxy because she needed him. He'd chosen Roxy, and he'd saved Calliope's life for her, though she had been his enemy.

"Dae's ready to kill someone. As is Alastor." Mal stared at her for a long moment. "I'd feel the same way."

She heard what he didn't say. That if he'd returned to find her gone, he would have been after blood.

"They've gone ahead. We're to meet them."

Calliope shook her head. "But why? Why take Roxy and Naphré? And why take me with you? You'll move faster without me, and I can help here. I could contact the Guard. I could—"

"No." He caught her wrist and drew her close against him, his gaze locked on hers. "I'll answer the last question first. I'm taking you with me because where I go, you go. Until we fucking figure out what the hell is going on, we're joined at the hip. I'm not letting you out of my sight. Because if I come back and you're gone—"

The skin around his eyes tightened and there were lines etched on both sides of his mouth. His lips drew a hard line. "You stay with me, pretty girl. We stay together."

She swallowed. Nodded. Hearing all he said and all he didn't say. That he cared about her. Maybe too much. That he wouldn't risk her. And that there was a real danger here that neither of them would be coming back.

He looked down at his fingers where they braceleted her wrist, and he let her go. She could feel a bit of tension leave him when she made no move to draw away.

"Now tell me about Roxy and Naphré," she said. "Who took them? What do they want?"

"You ever hear a prophecy about a god rising? The blood of Aset. The blood of Sutekh. And the God will pass the Twelve Gates and walk the Earth once more."

A shiver chased up her spine. She'd didn't recall ever hearing those words, yet she felt as though she had. Or as though she should have. "What does it mean?"

He raked his fingers back through his hair. "Fucked if I know. Dae and I think it's something about Sutekh. About using Aset's blood and Sutekh's blood to raise him. To allow him Topworld."

"That breaches the agreement," Calliope said. "All the Underworld gods are confined to their own territories. It's the only way to keep peace." It had been keeping peace for 6,000 years.

"Yeah. But if someone's using that prophecy as a blueprint, then it explains everything. The Daughters of Aset who were murdered in the past quarter century, right back to Roxy's mother. The involvement of the Setnakhts. Of course they'd want Sutekh to rise. Can you imagine what they believe their reward would be if they managed that?"

"But this raises more questions than it answers. Why kill your brother? And why take Roxy and Naphré now? Tonight?"

"Actually, it explains everything. If they needed the blood of Sutekh to make him rise, what better way to accomplish it than taking the blood of one of his sons? Lokan's blood, or mine or Dae's or Alastor's, is the purest source outside of Sutekh himself."

"Why Lokan? Why not—" She broke off, unwilling to say it. *Why not you?*

"Lokan had a weakness none of the rest of us had, an

Achilles' heel. Hell, she's an impossibility. She shouldn't even exist to be Lokan's weakness. They used her to draw him out, make him weak. Make him go along with whatever they had planned."

"She?" Calliope shook her head. "I don't understand."

Mal stared at her for so long, she thought he wasn't going to say another word. Then something in his expression shifted, as though he'd silently been warring with himself and finally come to a decision.

"Soul reapers can't reproduce. Not even Sutekh's sons. But somehow, Lokan did. I have a niece. Lokan had a daughter."

She tipped her head to the side, running through scenarios, trying to pin down exactly what he was saying. Then everything clicked.

The girl Roxy had saved from Frank Marin. The one she'd been so hell-bent to make disappear in plain sight.

"Dana Carr," she said.

"Dana Krayl," he corrected softly. *Lokan sacrificed himself to save his daughter,* he didn't say. He didn't need to. Calliope got it.

"The Setnakhts were involved in Dana's kidnapping," she said. "Do they believe Sutekh will forgive them for that, that he will forgive the murder of his son if they manage to bring him Topworld once more?"

"Yeah. I guess they do." Mal exhaled sharply and met her gaze.

"And Roxy and Naphré?"

"Whoever is behind this has gathered the blood of Aset. But I suspect the blood is too weak, too thin. They've only killed women who never took first blood. The strongest by far was years ago, when they killed Roxy's mother. She'd carved the dark mark in her skin, but she wasn't blooded. She held off because she wanted a kid."

Calliope felt dizzy. Sick. "Whoever took Roxy wants to sacrifice her. And Naphré."

"I believe so."

"And me."

The look he turned to her was stark. "Yes."

She felt as though she stood at the edge of a cliff, and if she took a single step forward she would fall. A wise woman would step back.

But she couldn't. She needed to know.

"Because we are not merely Daughters of Aset. We are marked. We are blooded."

"And more than that, each one of you has fed from one of Sutekh's sons. You've mixed the blood. It's never happened before."

Her thoughts spun a dizzying spiral, coming out the end with a point of blinding clarity. "If our blood could allow Sutekh mortal incarnation, could it bring Lokan back?"

When he said nothing she asked again. "Could it?"

"I don't know."

There was a lump in her throat and she could barely

breathe around it, barely speak. Her voice came out thin and stretched. "If it comes to a choice, Mal. If killing me, taking my blood…if my blood will bring Lokan back—"

What would he do? If he had the chance to bring his brother back, what would he do?

"We need to go," he said, his tone tight.

"Where?"

"The meeting of allies."

That was not what she had been expecting him to say. "It's in the Underworld."

"Yeah."

"I can't go there."

He offered a dark smile, and it was then she noted the tension in his frame. As if he was ready to fight. To kill. Energy hummed off him like a generator. "You can now. You have a free pass, courtesy of Sutekh."

Her stomach sank, and genuine fear touched her. A trip to the Underworld was generally one way. Except in rare cases where an Underworld god gave a guarantee of a safe return. Izanami had done that once for Naphré Kurata.

Somehow, Calliope doubted that Sutekh had offered that for her. And even if he had, she wasn't inclined to trust his word.

"Does that free pass include a return trip?" She kept her tone peaceful, her muscles relaxed. But it was an effort.

"Yes." His gaze never wavered. "You have my word on that."

Logic over emotion. Fear had no place in this equation. The meeting of allies was an opportunity to get information about where Roxy was, and if she was safe. It might even be an opportunity to get her back. And who knew what secrets she could glean to share with the Guard. Old habits died hard. If she could find out anything of value, she would pass it on to Zalika.

So logic told her to go. Be wary. But go.

And the look in Mal's eyes was telling her to trust him. She wanted to. She did. But did she dare?

"Then we go."

But Calliope was well aware that Mal was a soul reaper. His loyalty was to his kind. His father. His brothers. He'd never made any secret of that.

Trusting him might be the stupidest thing she ever did. And the most deadly.

CHAPTER TWENTY-THREE

*In the presence of the great tribunal which is in
the Two Banks on that night when Aset mourned
for her brother Osiris... In the presence of the
great tribunal which is on the Road of the Dead
on that night of making inquiry into him who is
nothing.*

—The Egyptian Book of the Dead, Chapter 20

"WHERE ARE WE?" CALLIOPE asked as they stepped from the portal.

Mal studied her, noting the tension in her shoulders and the pull at the corners of her mouth. She stood perfectly still for a second. He figured she was letting the vertigo pass. Or just getting the lay of the land. Hard to tell.

"Egypt," he said.

"Between the sand and the pyramid, I might have guessed." She raised one delicate, dark brow. "Care to be more precise?"

"We're about five kilometers north of Edfu, near the village of Naga el-Goneima."

She glanced around. "Why here?"

"Because this is one of seven small step pyramids scattered along the Nile between Seila and Elephantine Island. They're commonly disregarded because of their size and lack of internal chambers or underground labyrinths." He shrugged. "A fallacy. Those things are here. You just need to know where to look."

"And you know where to look."

"I do. Alastor is the research king. He can find almost anything."

"We are near the Temple of Horus?" she asked.

"Yeah." He took her hand and headed for the pyramid straight ahead. "Near the place where Horus faced off with Sutekh."

"Why did you not simply open a portal into the Underworld?"

"No can do. The far side of the River Styx isn't reachable that way. Only one way to get there. Boat. We need to get to a pickup point."

"And the pickup point is here."

"Close enough."

"Close enough" turned out to be a half-hour's walk, but Mal couldn't open a portal any closer to the pyramids. No one could. He led her up the side of the pyramid that ran parallel to the Nile. Halfway up, he touched a series of stones in what appeared to be a haphazard manner.

It wasn't. The pattern was specific. Then he ran his fingers along the massive stones, looking for the faint unleveling that would tell him which one to work on.

"Here," Calliope said, and he glanced over to see her mirroring his actions.

The stone slid in when he pushed on it.

"In here?" Calliope asked dubiously.

They stood at the opening of a very narrow, very dark tunnel.

"In here," Mal answered, his tone gruff.

Again, she peered into the darkness. "Do you have a flashlight?"

"Don't need one. I can see well enough in the dark."

He turned to her then. Her eyes were cat green, bright against dark lashes. There were things he wanted to say to her. And things he didn't want to say. In the end, he only reached for her and drew her close.

"Calli."

Pulling his knife from the sheath at his thigh he cut his hand and held it out to her, hoping she understood his intent. He would protect her any way he could, starting right here, right now, with another dose of his blood. It would make her stronger and faster. Make her heal if she got hurt. It was the best he could offer.

She held his gaze as she took his hand and cradled it in hers. Then she lowered her mouth and sealed her lips to his skin. The suction as she pulled from him was erotic.

"When this is over," he said, "I want you to feed from me while I'm inside you."

She was close against him, and he felt the faint tremor of her response to his words.

Then she let go of his hand and lifted her head. Her lips were dark and wet with his blood.

He reached for her and lowered his mouth to hers. He kissed her, tasting the copper salt of his blood, letting her taste everything he wouldn't put words to. Because she wasn't ready to hear it. Not yet.

And then he drew back and let her go.

"Now you can see in the dark, too." He grinned, a flash of white teeth against day-old dark stubble. The effect was unsettling. Sexy. Calliope wanted to kiss him again. To feel that stubble rub against her skin. To feel the smoothness of his lips both hard and soft against her own.

A dangerous inclination. She shoved it into a closet in her mind and slammed the door shut. She had no idea why Malthus Krayl made her *feel* things. And something told her she was better off not knowing. She only hoped it would pass.

But she had a feeling that wasn't going to be the case.

Turning her attention back to the tunnel, she asked, "Where does it lead?"

"We'll find out." He held his hand out toward her. Despite the seriousness of the situation, there was a hint of teasing in his tone.

She made an effort to answer in kind. "Am I to

understand that you expect me to cling to your hand and follow you into the darkness?"

He paused, shot her a glance over his shoulder, eyes smoldering. "Tight squeeze. No light. More than a little danger. What I like to call fun."

He meant it. Anticipation hummed around him like an aura. He wanted to go into this cramped little tunnel, in the pitch-dark, descending hundreds of feet into the bowels of the earth.

"You *do* consider it fun," she said.

He shrugged. "Despite my claustrophobia."

"What?"

"Not fond of tight spaces. Especially elevators. I really dislike elevators. They remind me of cells. Or the hold of a ship. But tunnels are okay. There's a way forward and a way back. It's just the sides that are tight."

"Right." Crossing her arms over her chest, she asked, "How long is the tunnel?"

"About four hundred feet. Then there's a link tunnel to another tunnel and then a tributary of the River Styx. A boat will be waiting."

THEY WERE FERRIED ACROSS the river in a massive boat. The wood was ancient, stained black with age and rubbed shiny in places. There was nowhere to sit, only stand, and this they did with a nameless, faceless peon in the stern, steering the course with a long wooden pole.

As they neared the midpoint of the river, the water

surged up in great plumes and then settled back, water no more. Instead, it undulated and danced, a vast expanse of flame and heat.

Mal glanced back to see the fire receding behind them. Before them was only flame.

This was a crossroads, a place where the Underworld Territories came together, the only place where all the gods and demigods and demons could meet and talk face-to-face. They weren't allowed in each other's territories. They weren't allowed Topworld. Only here, this small window, allowed them to pass.

The boat glided soundlessly up the far bank.

Beside him were Dagan and Alastor, equally grim, equally tense.

They didn't know where their mates were. Didn't have a clue how to find them. But they figured that keeping to the plan and showing up at the meeting was the best chance they had of finding information. None of them had any doubt that an Underworlder was responsible for Roxy's and Naphré's disappearances. With all the Underworld powers collected in one place, there was no better chance for them to find out what the hell was going on.

Both Alastor and Dae said that nothing had been disturbed. There were no signs of struggle. And there were no supernatural power residues left behind that they could detect.

It was as if both women had disappeared willingly. And that made no fucking sense.

If patience was one of Mal's few virtues, punctuality was Sutekh's. He was already there. As the host, that was both his obligation and right. Mal could see his father's tent set off a bit apart from all the others that he'd arranged for the comfort of those who were soon to arrive.

The boat beached on the far side of the River Styx at the precise second the flames of the river died and became clear, turquoise water once more.

Mal got out. Calliope followed.

Alastor and Dae had disembarked before them. He was a little surprised to see Dae take Calli's hand and give a brief squeeze. And then he'd thought that maybe it wasn't so surprising. They both cared about Roxy Tam, and worry united them as nothing else could.

"Stay close enough that I can hear your heartbeat," he said.

"Count on it."

Mal knew her reasons for such easy acquiescence. While she might find an ally or two here, she was more likely to find enemies among the attendees. Many here would have the protection of a hostage exchange. She wouldn't. The Guard had cut her loose. Other than him, she was on her own. And she knew it.

"The hostages won't be brought here," she said, and Mal figured she was thinking of Roxy and Naphré.

"No." He offered a dark smile. "That would be too easy, wouldn't it?"

The hostage exchange was a complicated dance. With

every powerful territorial ruler of the Underworld scheduled to attend, a simple exchange of hostages between two players wasn't a guarantee of peace.

Instead, they created an intricate promise and counterpromise scenario with each god or demigod sending a hostage to another, who in turn sent a hostage to a third. If any hostage was harmed, it automatically dragged two players into the war.

Of course, being cruel and murderous creatures, the rulers whose hostages were killed would then kill the one in his possession, even though there was no connection to the one who had done the killing in the first place.

Domino effect.

That would then drag a third leader into the melee. Hostages who were themselves too powerful to be killed—and those were few and far between—would be consigned to a hell of endless torture. In the end, everyone would have a dead or tortured hostage. Everyone would be pissed.

And the 6,000-year-old cease-fire would be over.

Better to keep all the hostages safe. At least, that's what every participant who had sent a hostage as a show of good faith was hoping the others believed as well.

Mal glanced at Calliope, who stood as close to his side as he could get her to without absorbing her into his skin.

"Look," she said softly, and he turned to see two soul reapers carrying out the lead casket that had been in Sutekh's greeting chamber. They opened the lid and carefully removed each body part, aligning them in their proper place on a stone table in the center of the area where tents and seats had been erected for the comfort of the participants.

Sutekh had arranged all. He was the one who had initiated this meeting. He was the host. That in itself put him in a position of power.

A second casket was carried forth and opened, and the contents were removed with reverent care.

"Where did that come from?" Mal asked Alastor.

"No bloody clue."

Thirteen body parts lay on the stone. Head, hands, feet, arms, thighs, lower legs, torso, pelvis. The only thing missing was Lokan's heart.

Sutekh emerged from the tent that had been set a little apart from the others.

"Is that your father?" Calliope asked.

"Yeah," Mal said. "Wearing Lokan's face. He does that. Wears whatever appearance strikes his fancy that day. None of us know what he truly looks like."

But it wasn't merely fancy that had guided Sutekh's choice today. His father had chosen to wear Lokan's face to this meeting. A reminder to all those present that his son had been murdered. A statement that his memory lived on, burning in the hearts of Sutekh and his remaining sons.

Calliope turned and looked out at the wide expanse of crimson river. "The others are coming," she said.

The boats drew nearer, carrying the other Under-worlders to a meeting that would decide the fate of all.

A woman with night-black hair and a face that made a man sit up and take notice was in the first boat. She was dressed in a flowing, diaphanous white gown that clung to her curves.

"Aset," Dagan said.

Calliope stared, and Mal could feel the tension and awe pulsing through her. Aset was her progenitor. In effect, her mother. She was the root of Calliope's line. The first blood drinker. The first pranic feeder. She was the goddess, the mother, the giver of life. And Calliope had never seen her before.

Mal got it. He remembered the first time he'd met Sutekh.

Aset lifted her head and turned her face to Calliope, her expression shuttered. Then her gaze slid to Mal for a split second before she looked away. In that second, Mal felt as if the goddess had looked into his soul.

Damned unsettling.

Directly behind Aset was a muscled man with the head of a falcon. Horus. Aset's son, conceived when she brought her husband/brother Osiris back from the dead long enough to give her a child.

"She didn't bring a guard," Mal pointed out.

"Which means she's either foolish, brave or knows something the rest of us don't," Alastor said.

"Like where our mates are?" Dagan asked, his voice hard, his fists clenched at his sides.

"It would make sense," Mal said. "If Aset sent for Roxy and Naphré, that would explain the lack of any evidence of a fight. If their goddess called them, they would go."

But none of them was in the boat.

"I want to bloody well kill someone," Alastor said, his voice cold and brutal.

"Don't we all," Dae snarled.

Mal cut a glance at Calliope and marveled at his brothers' control. He thought he'd be taking heads if she were the one who was missing.

Asmodeus came next, with a phalanx of female warriors in his wake. He didn't even glance toward Aset, instead going straight to Sutekh and embracing him before leaning back to study his face. Lokan's face.

"The loss of a son is a pain none should bear." With those words, Asmodeus sealed his alliance to Sutekh.

"That explains what his grunts were doing at Kuznetsov's condo," Mal said softly, wanting only his brothers and Calliope to hear. "He probably wanted to make a gift of the High Reverend to Sutekh."

"Either that, or his failure to secure Kuznetsov and figure out what the hell is going on made him decide better the devil he knew," Dae replied. "A new alliance with Osiris would be risky for him."

"And what that boils down to is that he'd switch allegiance in a blink," Alastor said.

"Wouldn't they all?" Calliope asked, her tone cool and even, betraying none of the turmoil that Mal knew she had to be feeling at being here, in the Underworld and seeing all these deities up close and personal.

Another boat arrived. Eight women stepped down, each garbed in robes of gray. As they moved forward, it was clear that their raiment was not cloth at all, but a writhing, living drape of all manner of spiders and centipedes, insects and maggots that moved and shifted. Their faces and bodies were completely obscured, as were their hands and feet.

"The *Shikome*," Alastor murmured and inclined his head in greeting as one paused briefly to nod first at him, then at Mal.

Another woman stepped down. She was perhaps five feet tall, very delicate, draped entirely in white. No part of her body was visible through the layers of cloth.

She moved with regal elegance and as she drew near, she dipped her head to Alastor, who made a courtly bow in return. When she came to Mal, she stopped and said, "They do indeed bloom at night, soul reaper."

Her voice was gorgeous. A song. The sound of it made him smile, as it had the last time they'd met.

Then she turned her head toward Calliope, and when she spoke, the smile in her voice was unmistakable. "And I see you have found your own *Ipomoea alba*, Malthus Krayl."

Then she walked on and joined the eight *Shikome* standing apart from all others who had arrived. She offered only the barest nod to Sutekh, and no greeting at all to Aset.

"Who is she?" Calliope asked.

"Izanami-no-mikoto. Naphré Kurata's progenitor."

Calliope turned to him then, not bothering to mask her surprise. "Naphré is a Daughter of Aset."

"On her mother's side," Alastor interjected. "She's Izanami's daughter on her father's side. And I am the holder of the sins of her soul, which puts her under Sutekh's protection, as well."

"So whoever has taken her risks pissing off three of the most powerful Underworld deities," Dagan said.

Mal glanced around at each of the three Alastor had named. "Unless one of them has her. Which means they also have Roxy."

For some reason, his gaze slid to Sutekh, who was sitting on what amounted to a stone throne, accepting the embraces and condolences of each Underworld deity that approached as their boat arrived. Like Asmodeus had, Xaphan went directly to Sutekh, embraced him and offered words of condolence, making a clear statement of alliance.

Mal tried to figure the angles, and came up empty.

Why would Sutekh kidnap his sons' mates? It made no sense.

At length, Sutekh rose and went to the broad stone table that sat in the center of the gathering. It was the elephant in the room. The remains of Lokan Krayl. The reason for this gathering.

"I extend a hand in peace," Sutekh said. He spoke as though Lokan's hacked-up body was not lying on the stone behind him, as though his son were not dead, murdered. Likely by someone here. "I thank each of you for answering my invitation in kind. I am not here to seek vengeance. I must preface all conversation with that assurance. Those of you who have had dealings with me in the past know that I would not make such a statement without every intent of abiding to my word."

Mal tamped down the rage that surged in his gut. With those statements, Sutekh cut all of them off at the knees. If he said he would not seek vengeance, he was effectively promising that none of his line, neither sons nor servants, would go after Lokan's killers.

He felt Calliope stiffen at his side. She leaned against him, ever so slightly, not enough to draw attention, but just enough to offer silent support. She got it. She understood. She'd spent most of her life living with a burning, tearing hate. She knew it wasn't so easy to put it aside.

"I am here to offer peace. And to offer a chance to bear witness." Sutekh raised his hand and beckoned Kai Warin forward.

It was then that Mal saw the box in his hand. Small. Made of lead. Carvings on the lid and sides. A memory flashed at him. He'd seen that box for a split second once before. That's why the casket that Alastor and Naphré had found had seemed so familiar.

He remembered standing in Sutekh's greeting chamber weeks past, talking with his father about being sent to Osiris as a hostage. The door had opened. Kai Warin had stood there for a brief instant. He had not yet been elevated to Sutekh's second-in-command. That role had still been held by Gahiji.

Kai had said nothing. Sutekh had waved him away. And Mal had forgotten the entire incident until now.

Alastor and Dae had both gone stiff, and Mal felt it then. His gaze locked on that box, his every sense humming. And he knew even before Kai opened it what it contained.

Lokan's heart.

They had all Lokan's parts.

That was why they were here. It truly was a meeting of allies, an opportunity for peace.

"I have my son's parts. His body awaits only a soul. I will make his body walk once more. And I make this vow. We will talk about other matters. We will solidify alliances. All will leave here unencumbered by my hate. There will be no vengeance for what was done to my son, to Lokan, the one who sat at my right hand."

Mal's heart slammed against his ribs as Sutekh laid Lokan's heart inside his chest. This was it. This was what Alastor and Dae had been fighting for, believing in, all along. He'd given up. He'd lost hope. He'd wanted only revenge, believing dead was dead, that he couldn't get Lokan back. Not ever.

But here he was.

His gaze shot to Dae then to Alastor. They both looked stunned. Jubilant. Awed and disbelieving.

Then he looked at Calliope.

Her brows were drawn in a frown, and her lips were moving though she made no sound. He had the bizarre thought that she was sorting through the possibilities, seeing things he was missing.

Around them, the other Underworld deities were buzzing, talking amongst themselves, discussing the ramifications of Sutekh's revelations.

Mal thought he ought to be dancing a jig. But something, some kernel of unease, nagged at him.

Because Sutekh wasn't the type to want peace.

Especially not with his son's mangled remains lying on the stone before him.

CHAPTER TWENTY-FOUR

The blood of Aset. The blood of Sutekh.
And the God will pass the Twelve Gates
and walk the Earth once more.

"I ASK THAT YOU CONSIDER and make your decision as I make my preparations," Sutekh said.

And Calliope didn't trust him for a second, though there was nothing concrete that made her think he was putting up a smokescreen. All she had to go by was instinct, and it was screaming like a fire alarm. The words of the prophecy kept spinning through her thoughts, and she felt like she was missing something so obvious that a child should have seen it. Beside her, Mal was stiff and tense, and she wondered if his thoughts were running along the same lines.

"A question," Aset spoke up, stepping forward. Her eyes were no longer black as onyx but completely white, as though she saw not what was before her, but something deeper. "This ceremony requires blood. And death to bring life. What is your intent in that regard?"

Sutekh turned to her, his expression arranged in a

sorrowful mask, so out of place on his face, so truly inhuman that it made Calliope flinch.

"Sadly, the deaths have already taken place. Without my knowledge or consent. The Setnakhts took it upon themselves to collect blood from the Daughters of Aset. And to kill them in an effort to cement my reanimation and my ability to walk in the world of man.

"But they miscalculated. I can be corporeal only in the Underworld. Without a human body, their efforts were misplaced. Those who carried out the killings and masterminded them, as well, have been dealt with."

"Yes," Aset said. "I recently *dealt* with one myself."

"She speaks of Kuznetsov," Calliope whispered.

Mal glanced at her but said nothing.

Sutekh inclined his head to Aset, as though acknowledging more than her spoken words.

Around them, the discourse grew louder. Neighbors debated the pros and cons. And all the while, Sutekh remained apart.

"Mal," Calliope said, grabbing hold of his arm. "Something isn't right. I don't know what, but I'm telling you. Something doesn't add up."

He studied her with narrowed eyes, but she had no idea if he believed her. Then their attention was diverted.

"The blood of innocents," Sutekh said, and three soul reapers exited his tent, carrying pitchers.

Calliope felt sick. She knew whose blood was in

there. Women—Daughters of Aset—whose lives had been stolen because mortal worshippers of Sutekh had wanted to make him corporeal. All for nothing. By his own admission, he could not return Topworld. He could be corporeal only in the Underworld, regardless of the prophecy.

"Those women are dead," Mal said softly. "Nothing can bring them back. But their blood can bring my brother back."

She shook her head, torn and appalled. She understood what he wanted and why he wanted it. She understood that these women had been murdered, but out of their deaths someone else could live. Lokan. Mal's brother.

"Wait," Dagan said, stepping forward. He turned slowly and looked at all those assembled, each in turn. "Two Daughters of Aset are missing. Taken from their homes. Before any peace is cemented here, before any decisions are finalized, I want whoever took them to return them."

He shot a glance at Sutekh, who watched him impassively. Alastor stepped up to stand beside his brother, and Mal followed.

Tears pricked Calliope's eyes. They were risking everything for their mates. And in Mal's case, not even his own mate, but his brothers'. She remembered him telling her that soul reapers bled and felt pain. And love. She believed that, seeing the three of them standing together, demanding Roxy and Naphré's safe return.

But a part of her couldn't help but wonder, if it came to a choice, to their mates versus their brother, who would they choose?

Who would Mal choose?

"They were taken to safeguard their lives," Aset said, sending a long look toward Izanami, making it clear that the two goddesses were complicit in the agreement. "We were made aware of the desire for the blood of Daughters of Aset when Pyotr Kuznetsov died while in the care of the Asetian Guard. He revealed much when he came to the Hall of Two Truths. It was agreed that Roxy Tam and Naphré Kurata would be brought to sanctuary for their safety."

Izanami spoke then, in her beautiful lyrical voice. "We attempted to offer the same to your mate, Malthus Krayl. But you had already taken her by the time my *Shikome* arrived to offer her safety."

Calliope shifted her gaze to Mal, wondering how he felt about the goddess referring to her as his mate. Wondering how *she* felt.

She didn't know, and this was not the moment to sort through the confused tangle of her emotions.

"Neither Roxy nor Naphré will be harmed," Aset said. "They will each be returned to you when this is over."

Dae opened his mouth, looking as if he wanted to say more, but Alastor rested his hand on his brother's arm.

"Thank you, Aset, O Isis, goddess of motherhood and

fertility and magic," he said in clipped, tight tones, his accent more pronounced because of strain. He made a courtly bow and then he turned to Izanami, bowed to her, and said, "Thank you, Izanami-no-mikoto, grandmother of my mate, and so, my grandmother."

Izanami laughed softly, the sound incredibly beautiful. "You have gained a small thimble of wisdom in your dealings, Alastor Krayl. You are slightly less brash than when last we met—" she paused "—my grandson." With those words, she clearly stated that whatever side she chose in her alliance or nonalliance with Sutekh, she would ensure that Alastor and Naphré were reunited.

"Begin," Sutekh said, and all eyes turned to him. He stood next to the stone table and the body of his dead son. "With the reanimation of Lokan's remains, my promise of peace will be sealed."

He brought his hands up before him and blue fire danced along his skin, bright, blinding.

"Now," he ordered, and the three soul reapers poured blood from the pitchers all along Lokan's body parts.

Sutekh raised his head, the blue flame growing brighter still, and he pinned his sons with his gaze, each in turn.

Calliope felt her stomach turn over, horror and fear congealing in her gut. There *was* something wrong. She stared at the body and the blood that dripped down the severed limbs and over the edges of the stone to the ground.

"The blood of Aset," Sutekh said. "The blood of Sutekh."

Kai Warin stepped forward with a fourth pitcher and poured that over the body. Calliope thought it must be Lokan's blood, gathered in the black oblong bowl in the video, reclaimed along with the blood of the murdered Daughters of Aset from wherever the Setnakhts had stored it.

The flame in Sutekh's hands grew brighter. It swelled until not only Sutekh but the body of his son and the entire stone table were enveloped in blindingly bright light.

Calliope's pulse raced and bile crawled up the back of her throat. Was she the only one who saw that there was something not right in this? She didn't begrudge any of them the return of Lokan, but she felt as though something else was going on here, something darker.

Before her eyes, the parts began to knit together, writhing along the stone until severed edges approximated and tissues began to coalesce.

"The blood of Sutekh," Sutekh boomed and pinned each of his sons with his gaze.

One by one, they went forward.

One by one, they took the blade handed to them by a soul reaper who stood to one side.

Dae slit his palm, cutting deep, and his blood splashed on Lokan's body. He cut himself again and used his lacerated palm to stroke his blood along his brother's limbs. Then Alastor did the same.

Stepping up beside his brothers, Mal took the knife. He turned it in his hand, and Calliope saw it had an obsidian blade and carved handle. She gasped, her gaze flicking to Aset. It was the knife she had cut herself with when Beset ordered her to. It was the same knife that had been used to skin Lokan Krayl.

With a gasp, she stepped forward. But she *didn't*. Couldn't. Something held her in place. She couldn't move. Couldn't speak.

Her heart slammed against her ribs.

The blue flame grew brighter still, a bubble around Lokan's body and his father, Sutekh.

Panting, Calliope watched. Waited. As did they all.

But nothing happened.

Sutekh's head swiveled, and he pinned her with his flat, soulless gaze.

"The blood of Aset," he whispered, only Calliope heard it in her head as a roar.

And she found herself moving forward, reaching her hand toward the knife. Not of free will. By compulsion.

Whose?

Terror such as she had never known crashed through her. If she did this, if she gave her blood with theirs, something terrible would come of this. She felt it with every fiber of her being and she couldn't understand how the other Underworld deities could just stand there and let it happen.

She looked around, frantic. She felt as though she

was invisible. As if they couldn't see her. Or wouldn't. All around her was light. She was inside the light that Sutekh had built into a glowing blue-white ball.

Of its own volition, her hand clasped the knife. Of its own volition, her free hand came up, her fist unclenching to bare her palm.

And all the while, her heart pounded in time to the litany that sang in her thoughts. *This is wrong. This is wrong.* But she couldn't say why, couldn't pinpoint what was missing.

Some key ingredient.

Suddenly, Mal's hand shot out, his fingers closing on her wrist, preventing the slash of the knife against her skin.

His pupils were dilated, leaving a thin rim of gray around an endless dark lake.

And then she knew that he felt it, too. The wrongness.

Dae's hand closed over Mal's and Alastor's over Dae's.

"Tell me," Mal ordered, and as she focused only on his eyes, she found she could speak.

"He isn't trying to bring Lokan back," she said in a rush. "He's trying to use Lokan's body as a vessel. He wants to put himself inside it and wear it as a suit. Mal, you had it right. Not an incorporeal demon, this time, though. An incorporeal god.

"Don't you see? In order to reanimate your brother,

his soul needs to enter his body. Where is it? Where is his soul?"

"Fuck me raw," Dagan snarled, rounding on his father. "This was it all along, wasn't it? Your plan. You planned this back when Gahiji took Roxy's mother to Frank Marin. You planned this for decades. You knew all along you would sacrifice Lokan."

"I knew it would be one of my sons. It was not until your brother revealed his growing power, the threat of it, that I knew it would be Lokan who must be sacrificed."

Each of the three brothers recoiled in shock, and Calliope felt as though Mal's pain was her own. His own father had betrayed him. Betrayed them all. He had sacrificed his own son and had, by his own admission, been willing to sacrifice any one of them.

"Growing power?" Mal asked. "What are you—" He broke off. His eyes widened and he whispered, "Dana. His ability to sire a child. You saw it as a threat."

"No soul reaper can beget progeny. Only a human or a supremely powerful god."

"So you killed him." The horror and pain in Mal's expression tore at Calliope like jagged blades. She wanted to help him, to heal him, to ease his torment.

"It is the prophecy," Sutekh said simply, and he reached for Calliope.

"No," Mal snarled and pushed her behind him, placing himself between her and his father. Then he said,

"Call him. Dae. Alastor. Reach for Lokan. Reach now. This is our chance. Our one chance."

They did. Calliope felt the massive surge of energy that emanated from the three of them, and she felt the power of Sutekh's wrath as he built the blue flame higher still, trying to take his son's body before Lokan's brothers could find his soul.

Beyond the bubble of light, the Underworld deities stood watching the tableau unfold, and Calliope realized they were in a separate place, isolated from what was going on here, within the microcosm Sutekh had created.

"There," Mal yelled. "I feel him. Lokan!"

The power was so intense that Calliope couldn't breathe. She felt as if the weight of it was swirling around her and through her, and for what little it was worth, she added her will to theirs, willing them to find Lokan's soul and draw it back.

And then she felt it, a flash of prescience bright and clear. The blood of Aset. Her blood. The blood of Sutekh. Mal's blood. Together. Inside her.

She felt the thread of Mal's connection to his brother's soul, and she lunged forward, slashing her palm deep as she moved.

She slammed her hand down on Lokan's body. She smeared her blood across his chest to the wound that had allowed his heart to be torn out, then down over the inverted ankh that had been tattooed in his skin. She saw it now for what it was. An insult to Aset. And a red herring to throw Lokan's brothers off the trail.

She heard Mal screaming her name. Screaming at her to come back. Calling to her that he didn't want to live without her. And she realized that she was spinning through nothing, through a black hole cold and vast and before her was an endless zigzagging staircase and a night-black sky dotted with stars.

"Mal." She screamed his name and reached for him with her blood-streaked hand.

Lokan's body spun away and she didn't try to catch it. She let it go. She had done what she could. She had given him the blood of Sutekh and the blood of Aset.

She reached with all she was as the hole grew smaller and smaller behind her. She could no longer see Mal. She could see only the tips of his fingers as she reached hers toward him, and she thought, *I love him. And he'll never know that. He'll never know.*

Love.

There was no logic in that.

But there was great power.

She surged forward and caught his hand and she felt a terrible pressure, as though she was being crushed beneath an unbearable weight. Her skull. Her chest. The bones of her pelvis being compressed until they felt as if they would shatter. Then she pushed through, into the vast blue light, into Mal's arms.

"I thought I lost you, Calli. I thought I lost you."

His face was pale. Drawn. His eyes so dark they looked black.

Behind him was the table, empty now of his brother's remains. They had been sucked into the hole as she had been sucked into the hole. And she realized in that second that he had been forced to choose only one, and he had chosen her.

"I'm sorry," she whispered. "He's gone. I'm sorry."

He kissed her, his mouth hard on hers. "I'm not. I'm not sorry. We gave him a chance. There's a chance his body was called to his soul. He has a chance."

"I'm sorry you had to choose."

"It was my choice and I made it."

His embrace was so tight she could hardly breathe.

"I love you, Calli. Prophecy or not. Fate or not. I love you and I'm not going to give you up."

He said it as though it was a challenge, as if he thought she would argue.

"I love you, Malthus Krayl," she said, uncaring of the audience, uncaring that the future loomed before them dark and confused. Sutekh had murdered his own son.

Where did that leave Mal? And Alastor and Dagan?

There would be ramifications. There would be up-heaval. And as she pulled Mal's mouth to hers and kissed him, a kiss of life, a kiss of hope, she thought that as long as they were together, they'd figure it out.

AT FIRST THERE WAS ONLY a sliver of light, but he'd been in the dark so long, he'd forgotten what light was like, and it hurt his eyes. The pain bored into his skull, sharp and bright, and then spread to his hands, his feet, his forearms, his calves.

He swayed but refused to fall. The world spun around him and through him, a vortex of pain and incredible suction, as though a giant vacuum pump was pulling on his limbs, anchored there by barbed talons.

For balance he shot his arms out to the sides and felt rough stone beneath his fingers.

His heart twisted in his chest, a sharp jab of hope and fear. Because the stone was real. He could *feel* it. He wasn't imagining it, and he knew that was important.

"My name is Lokan Krayl." He whispered the words aloud, and as he did, he knew he had forgotten them a dozen, a hundred, a thousand times before.

Panic surged, but he choked it back and looked down to see a bizarre staircase twisting through a black void, the stairs gleaming, polished gray, the world all around him dotted with stars.

Down. Or up.

There were only two choices open to him. Three, if he considered standing exactly where he was. The latter seemed the poorest choice, so he went up, taking the stairs two at a time, his legs shaking as he forced them to move by sheer will alone. His lungs filled and emptied too fast, his heart beat too hard. He was weak and faded. He was not the creature he had once been.

Up he went, and then he stopped, his back bowed, head hanging, palms flat on his thighs as he gasped for air. He felt as if he had not used these muscles in a horrifically long time. How long?

He had no idea.

When he lifted his head, he saw that he was on a landing and on the polished stone was a pile of apples. Red. Shiny. His belly cramped, so empty that it felt like a hole at his core. He was starving, right down to the cells that formed his organs.

His mouth watered and he reached for an apple. So tempting. The weight of it in his hand was lovely; the scent of it filled his nostrils. He brought the fruit to his nose and inhaled then opened his mouth, ready to taste.

The food of the dead.

Was he dead?

He couldn't be. He was Lokan Krayl. He was a soul reaper. Soul reapers didn't die. But he had.

Horror sank its claws into him. With a cry, he let the apple roll off his fingers, watched it tumble toward the ground.

But he never saw it hit.

The world around him spun at a dizzying pace, and he saw things, so many things, that he was sure he had seen before.

He stood on concrete slabs, a crimson river stretched before him, the color of blood, the color of wine. There was a boat. There was a ferryman. There were thousands of souls—

He reached out and it all disappeared.

In its place was a scale with plates of hammered gold and a stone staircase. A knife. A white feather. The Hall of Two Truths.

He was Lokan Krayl, son of Sutekh. He was his father's ambassador. His right hand.

Anubis stood beside the scale. He turned his jackal's head and handed him a knife. It was the only way in. The only way to see Osiris.

Stretching out his hand to accept the blade, he gasped as all fell away and he was falling, falling.

A river.

A blood-red moon.

A feeling that he was being pulled limb from limb, the pain more than he could ever have imagined.

The sun was so hot it burned his skin. And then the breeze came and cooled him and he turned his face toward it and opened his eyes. Before him was a swing set and a little girl. Her face turned to his, her eyes denim blue, her mouth opening as she laughed.

He knew her. She was his daughter.

Memories came at him in a dizzying rush. His death.

His father had murdered him, carved his skin from his body using the knife that the goddess Izanami had sent 6,000 years ago as a gift to each and every Underworld deity to mark the start of the cease-fire.

His father had murdered him to take his body. And to put an end to his growing power.

He looked down at his hand and clenched his fist and felt the sting of his nails digging into his palm.

He was alive. His name was Lokan Krayl, and he was alive.

* * * * *

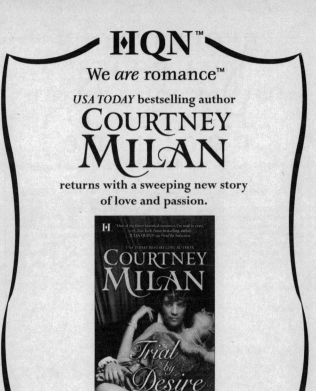

REQUEST YOUR
FREE BOOKS!
2 FREE NOVELS PLUS 2 FREE GIFTS!

HARLEQUIN®

nocturne™

Dramatic and Sensual Tales of Paranormal Romance.

YES! Please send me 2 FREE Harlequin® Nocturne™ novels and my 2 FREE gifts (gifts are worth about $10). After receiving them, if I don't wish to receive any more books, I can return the shipping statement marked "cancel." If I don't cancel, I will receive 4 brand-new novels every other month and be billed just $4.47 per book in the U.S. or $4.99 per book in Canada. That's a saving of at least 15% off the cover price! It's quite a bargain! Shipping and handling is just 50¢ per book.* I understand that accepting the 2 free books and gifts places me under no obligation to buy anything. I can always return a shipment and cancel at any time. Even if I never buy another book from Harlequin, the two free books and gifts are mine to keep forever.

238/338 HDN E9M2

Name _____ (PLEASE PRINT) _____

Address _____ Apt. # _____

City _____ State/Prov. _____ Zip/Postal Code _____

Signature (if under 18, a parent or guardian must sign) _____

Mail to the **Reader Service:**
IN U.S.A.: P.O. Box 1867, Buffalo, NY 14240-1867
IN CANADA: P.O. Box 609, Fort Erie, Ontario L2A 5X3

Not valid for current subscribers to Harlequin Nocturne books.

Want to try two free books from another line?
Call 1-800-873-8635 or visit www.ReaderService.com.

* Terms and prices subject to change without notice. Prices do not include applicable taxes. N.Y. residents add applicable sales tax. Canadian residents will be charged applicable provincial taxes and GST. Offer not valid in Quebec. This offer is limited to one order per household. All orders subject to approval. Credit or debit balances in a customer's account(s) may be offset by any other outstanding balance owed by or to the customer. Please allow 4 to 6 weeks for delivery. Offer available while quantities last.

Your Privacy: Harlequin Books is committed to protecting your privacy. Our Privacy Policy is available online at www.ReaderService.com or upon request from the Reader Service. From time to time we make our lists of customers available to reputable third parties who may have a product or service of interest to you. If you would prefer we not share your name and address, please check here. ☐

Help us get it right—We strive for accurate, respectful and relevant communications. To clarify or modify your communication preferences, visit us at www.ReaderService.com/consumerschoice.

HN10

EVE SILVER

DEC 2010

77483 SINS OF THE SOUL	___ $7.99 U.S.	___ $9.99 CAN.
77482 SINS OF THE HEART	___ $7.99 U.S.	___ $9.99 CAN.

(limited quantities available)

TOTAL AMOUNT	$ _____
POSTAGE & HANDLING	$ _____
($1.00 FOR 1 BOOK, 50¢ for each additional)	
APPLICABLE TAXES*	$ _____
TOTAL PAYABLE	$ _____

(check or money order—please do not send cash)

To order, complete this form and send it, along with a check or money order for the total above, payable to HQN Books, to: **In the U.S.:** 3010 Walden Avenue, P.O. Box 9077, Buffalo, NY 14269-9077; **In Canada:** P.O. Box 636, Fort Erie, Ontario, L2A 5X3.

Name: _____

Address: _____ City: _____

State/Prov.: _____ Zip/Postal Code: _____

Account Number (if applicable): _____

075 CSAS

*New York residents remit applicable sales taxes.
*Canadian residents remit applicable GST and provincial taxes.

HQN™

We *are* romance™

www.HQNBooks.com

PHES1010BL